I0582198

BOURBON SUNSET

A Bourbon Canyon Novel

WALKER ROSE

LE Publishing

Teller Bailey is the last single son in a Montana bourbon empire. He's also arrogant, infuriating, and unfairly handsome with his beard and flannel.

Everyone in town loves him. Everyone in town detests me.

I'm "Mad Maddy" Townsend, the only surviving daughter of Bourbon Canyon's most reviled family. I'm also mouthy, broke, and spectacularly alone.

I've wanted nothing more than to get away from this small town and the opinions of me since birth, yet I'm stuck here with nothing but a trashed dive bar and a shoestring budget to get it back in business—or my mom will be evicted from her nursing home.

But there isn't a contractor in the county who'll return my calls, at least without including a few four-letter words in their messages. My only hope for competent help is the annual bachelor auction featuring the town's most eligible Bailey. The prize? One project completed for the highest bidder.

I must be every bit as crazy as this town thinks to bid on Teller. The man I can't stand will be mine until I'm ready to serve my first drink. All I have to do is not fall for his charming smile, his unyielding support, or the way his name opens all the doors slammed in my face. I've never been treated so well, but I know how this goes. When this job is finished, he'll ride off into the bourbon sunset —without me, just like everyone else in my life.

CHAPTER ONE

Madison

I was here for one thing and one thing only, and a big, bearded prick of a man was standing in my way. I'd had a crap morning, one in a long line of crap weeks, months —years—and I craved my jelly beans. The red apple ones, to be exact. And some root beer flavor, just to balance it out.

But *he* needed to move first.

Teller Bailey was carved from stone and moving just as fast. What was he doing in the candy aisle anyway? Did he even know what sugar was with that big, chiseled body of his?

But then he was talking to Cassie Horner, in her short little shorts with her shirt tied at the waist. It was a pleasant June day, but didn't she get chilly? I was in a black T-shirt with a red plaid flannel over it, worn jeans, and cowboy boots that doubled as work boots for the new line of work I was now in.

Technically, the bar was my second job. Flatlanders Prohibited was also my biggest priority, yet somehow not my biggest stressor.

I tapped my foot.

Teller smiled wider at Cassie.

Ass.

Cassie tore her insipid gaze off Teller. "Oh, hey, Madison." Sympathy filled her eyes, and I steeled myself for what was coming next. "I'm really sorry about Scooter."

Scott "Scooter" Townsend wouldn't be missed by many, but he was missed by me. Grief tore at my heart, but I gave her a quick smile. The months had dulled the pain since my brother's death, yet I'd rather be run out of town naked than cry in public. "Thanks."

Teller's dark gaze bored into me, and I could only imagine what he was thinking. Good riddance to Scott? Did I start a new hobby chopping wood with my attire? How dull my skin was compared to glowing Cassie's? I didn't know the man well, but I knew him well enough. I had gotten to see a side to him not many others had, and it wasn't his nice guy persona. Everyone loved Teller Bailey.

The Baileys were as beloved as the Townsends were disdained. The biggest difference was that there were a ton of Baileys, and they were all charming and gorgeous, Teller included. He didn't waste his charisma on me though, not after the one real conversation we'd had.

His words reared up in my head. *Was this fun for you? You gonna go laugh about it with your brother?*

I doggedly ignored his inspection of me.

Awareness filled Cassie's face. "Oh! Am I in your way?"

"Not you, no." I finally slid my gaze to Teller's, wishing away the sizzling of awareness that happened around him. His eyes really were a deep, rich brown, much darker than any of the bourbon produced by his family's distillery. A girl could get lost in them, but not me.

His eyes narrowed, but he didn't move.

I was one of the few women immune to Teller's charm. More like I was one of the few who had never experienced his charm. I never gave Teller heart eyes, and I wasn't a customer of his family's distillery, Copper Summit. Therefore, he usually acted like I didn't exist.

The longer his attention was on me, the warmer I got. Had the AC quit working in the grocery store?

He took his gaze off me and casually studied the shelves over his shoulder. "Tootsie Rolls?"

I pressed my lips together and gestured for him to move to the side. "No. Excuse me."

He didn't move. "The Blow Pops?"

"I don't blow."

One of his brows arched. Cassie made a choking sound.

"A no to the Blow Pops," he drawled, "or all candy that takes sucking?"

Cassie made another strangled noise. "Teller, just move for the poor woman."

He didn't.

Nothing I wanted was on the shelves anyway. The stand-alone rack of Jelly Bellys was right behind him. The two packs with the flavors I wanted the most were behind his broad back.

I had no vices. I didn't drink too much my brother. Drugs were a no. I didn't gamble like my mom had, and I didn't thrive off anger like my dad when he was alive. But I had a sweet tooth, and it raged.

"I'll grab it for you," he offered, "so I can keep chatting with an old friend."

Cassie's smile widened.

A bite of envy clamped around my neck. Because I wasn't getting Teller's attention? God, no. Because I wasn't anyone's old friend? Possibly.

Teller was waiting, challenge in his eyes. This was the story of my life. I butted up against six foot something bearded walls in cowboy boots while other girls got to giggle with them.

"Or you could move, and I can get what I came for and go," I said tightly.

Cassie grimaced. She squeezed Teller's biceps, and no, I did not want to know if they were as big as they looked through his green flannel. The irony that I was dressed more like him than her wasn't lost on me.

"I've gotta get going," she said to him. "See you around." She turned her hazel gaze on me. "I sure do miss Flatlanders. I can't wait until you get it reopened."

It was my turn to flinch. That damn bar was becoming my life. *Thanks, Scott. For all the backbreaking work. For the giant damn money drain. For leaving me with a mess.*

"It's a work in progress," was all I said. I didn't mind Cassie. She'd been a steady customer when Flatlanders had been open, and she'd never been catty like many of the other girls I'd gone to school with.

She sauntered off. Surprisingly, Teller kept his gaze on me instead of her rolling ass. Even I wanted to stare at her butt. I'd always admired Cassie's body and her style. If I dressed like her, I'd look like a lumberjack trying on skimpy lingerie, only I didn't have a beard.

Teller kept his beard trimmed close to his chin, never letting it get shaggy. It was nice. From what I could tell anyway.

"Excuse me," I said in another attempt to get at my candy.

"How's the cleanup going?" he asked, his tone neutral.

Cleaning up the trashed bar was about all I could do. Repairing it was a different story. But why would he care? "Worried about the competition?"

He scoffed and the flash of a grin made my belly flip. *No.* I could not be attracted to Teller. I was *not* like every other girl in town. Growing up in Bourbon Canyon had shown me that.

"You can't compare apples to oranges," he said. "People come to Copper Summit for quality bourbon. They go to Flatlanders for cheap booze."

"It worked for Scott for years."

"Did it?"

His simple question poked at the troubling facts I'd learned since getting access to Flatlanders' books. "Seems like that's none of your business."

"Nope, it's yours now."

My jaw tightened. The thought of renovating the bar and running it piled heavy on my shoulders until my knees wobbled. Flatlanders was the best chance I had at making a decent living, the only way I wouldn't ruin my body working as a certified nursing assistant for the rest of my life. I already had tendonitis in both elbows, my knees ached after every shift, and the spot I'd tweaked in my back years ago was acting up. I wasn't even thirty-five yet.

"Yeah. It's mine now." I gave the candy on the shelving next to him a pointed look, hoping he'd get the hint and move.

"How bad is it?" he asked softly.

I stiffened. It was none of his concern, and pretending to care wouldn't get the information out of me. "Why?"

His mouth flattened. "I'm just asking. Flatlanders is a local business and everyone heard that Scooter destroyed the place and you got stuck with it. People care."

An indelicate snort sneaked out of me. "Sure. They care so much they peer through the windows instead of asking and whisper behind my back."

"You aren't exactly approachable."

"I'm approachable as fuck."

He leveled a flat look on me.

My hair would stand on end, but there was a tingling along my skin that liked his attention. "Maybe not to you because what was it you said? 'How can I believe what comes out of a Townsend's mouth?'"

He blanched and cleared his throat. "That was different."

He continued to be in my way. "Is this payback for chasing off your girlfriend?"

"What girlfriend?"

I rolled my eyes. "The one who was just giggling at you?"

Incredulity filled his dark gaze. "Cassie? We're just friends. You do know what those are, right?"

I heard the teasing in his voice but it didn't stop the

chafing at my neck. No, I didn't know what friends were. "I don't win popularity contests like you."

He tapped his fingers on his cart. I didn't trust the glint in his eyes. Then he said, "You might if you smile once in a while." My mouth dropped open and I sputtered. He laughed, a deep, pleasing sound that made me wish I was in on the joke for once instead of the butt of one. Guys like Teller didn't joke around with me. "I'm kidding. I'm not that big of a dick."

I begged to differ. "Can you move please?"

He cocked an ear. "Did Mad Maddy say please?"

A gasp burst out of me. I *hated* that name. I hated that I earned it in my teen years when my temper was as explosive as my parents'.

I had to get away from it and away from the man who made me want to regress and shout at him to MOVE THE HELL OUT OF THE WAY. His brawny shoulders were blocking my jelly beans.

I could've really used something sweet to face the day, but this giant ass wasn't moving. I'd think of something else or go without, like I always did. I spun on my heel and stormed past him.

"Madison."

I continued, grateful I hadn't grabbed a cart or even a handbasket. I nearly ran into an older lady. Mrs. Henderson, my high school Algebra teacher.

She pursed her lips and shook her head. "Still not watching where you're going?"

I had plenty of new grudges to deal with, I didn't need old ones. I curved around her, earning the rude reputation behind my family name.

"Mads," Teller said.

Tension bunched behind my shoulders. "Mads" was too close to "Mad Maddy."

"Maddy!"

His bootsteps hit the floor behind me. A wheel on his cart squeaked, and I put the afterburners on, power walking my way through the store. The nickname. My brother. The goddamn bar. I couldn't stay. I couldn't fall apart in public, and I wasn't going to give anyone the satisfaction of seeing me lose my temper.

I sped to my old pickup, cringing when I noticed Teller's big fancy truck a few spots down. My ride had rust over the fenders, a dent in the driver's door, thanks to my ex, and a crooked bumper. Teller's pickup gleamed shiny silver and blue. He had a nice box cover in the back, and while the vehicle looked well used, it still screamed *money*.

Cassie would look really good reclining on the tailgate, watching him ride in on horseback from moving cattle. I could picture it in my head. Only the image forming didn't include Cassie, and the twinkle in his eye definitely wasn't aimed at her.

I shook off the thought of a wide-shouldered rider in sync with his horse, his cowboy hat tipped low, crushing those loose curls of his that popped out when he went a few weeks without a trim. I erased myself from any part of that nonsense.

Quit thinking about him!

I hopped in my beater and drove the few minutes to the bar. I parked in the alley, right by the rear exit. Flatlanders Prohibited was in an old brick building in downtown Bourbon Canyon. The place was three times longer than it was wide, and there was a pervasive, musty smell I hoped would disappear when I replaced the sinks and toilets.

I slipped inside and locked the door behind me. Slumping against it, I blew out a breath. Tears gathered in my eyes and I let them fall. I gave myself a few moments to miss Scott. Another moment to wonder what it would've been like if I hadn't interfered in Teller's love life all those years ago. Maybe I'd have my jelly beans. Infuriating man. Then I wiped my cheeks dry. I opened my eyes and took in the place. A long sigh eked out of me.

The damage Scott had done bore the proof of his state of mind. At least he hadn't been drunk when he'd crashed. That was one thing people couldn't pin on him. Nor had he hit anyone else when his pickup had gone off a curve and hit a tree.

I brushed aside a strand of hair that had escaped my braid as I walked past the empty storeroom that Scott had used to crash after a long night and was now my temporary residence. Then the office, the bathrooms, and a larger storeroom. Brightly colored balls littered the floor beneath the pool tables, along with busted pool cues. I hadn't picked those up yet.

I could've been so much further ahead, but probate had been a bitch, along with Scott's ex-wife.

I blew out another hard breath. So much damage. Scott had taken a pool cue to the mirror and bottles behind the bar. The booze had all evaporated, but the caramel scent of whiskey grew stronger the closer I got.

At least there wasn't Copper Summit bourbon in the mix. Scott had disliked Teller, just like our parents had hated all the Baileys, and since the Baileys owned and operated the rustic and wildly successful bourbon distillery outside of town, that meant Flatlanders didn't carry the stuff.

I could change that and send my mom into a rage. My dad might even come back to haunt me. I didn't want more trouble. I had enough of a mess here. Scott had taken a sledgehammer to the bar and countertop. Tables were destroyed, their parts littered around the main area. Booths had been shredded, and splintered wood was everywhere. Broken glass from the light fixtures and glassware mingled with the wood shards.

"The bones of the place are good," I muttered to myself. A new mantra to keep an anxiety attack at bay.

I scratched the side of my head. I knew where to start, but the whole thing was overwhelming. I needed money, and this would require a financial sink first, a lot of work, and a ton of energy.

I was also on the night shift at the nursing home.

Dread pushed into my throat, closing off my air supply. So much work. I didn't know the first thing about remodeling a bar, but when it had been open, this place had paid for Mom's stay at Cliffside Nursing Home. My wages working there certainly wouldn't.

There was a knock on the door. A large shadow blocked the window. Another nosy lookie-loo? I threaded through the debris and stopped at the window.

I barked out a yelp just as Teller squinted in. His eyes widened when he saw me.

"Jesus, Teller!" My heart was racing for a completely different reason now. He couldn't be here. Scott would roll over in his grave if he knew a Bailey was rubber-necking the remains of his precious baby.

Teller grinned and held up a grocery bag.

"What is that?" I called. Why would I want whatever he had?

He put a hand to his ear. He couldn't hear me through the glass. I hesitated and glanced at the door. I'd have to open it, and then he'd see clearly. But he was already shading his eyes and trying to look in.

Wasn't I used to being a sideshow in this town?

Resigned, I flipped the deadbolts and cracked it open. "What are—"

"I got candy." He brandished the bag again.

"Candy?"

"Don't worry, no Tootsie Rolls or Blow Pops."

My stomach woke up at the thought of candy. "I don't need it." Not from him.

"No one needs candy."

I bristled as my mom's words tracked through my head. *Don't eat that shit. You're a big girl already.* "Are you judging me?"

His lips formed a troubled line. "For what?" He seemed sincerely confused. Before I could speak, he lifted his gaze over my shoulder and his eyes widened. "Shit. Scooter really did a number on the place."

I crossed my arms and tried to block his view, but he was half a head taller than me. "You can take the candy with you."

His brow was furrowed as he scanned the mess at my back. "Structural damage even?"

"Just to the bar counter and shelving." I hadn't meant to answer him.

His gaze dropped back to me and warmth infused my veins. I tried to stay cool toward him, but I'd been out in the cold for so long.

"The bar counter is pretty important for a bar."

"Oh my god, I would've never known without your wisdom. Thanks for stopping by, but it's unnecessary." I tried to shut the door.

He put a big hand on the surface. "Will you quit getting upset at everything that comes out of my mouth?"

"Will you quit saying shit to upset me?"

He frowned. "I don't do that." At my hard look, he shrugged. "All the time."

"This time I'm the one who doesn't believe you." I hip-checked the door, but it didn't budge against his hold. Why did he have to be strong in addition to everything else?

He handed the bag over. "Look, I'm not going to eat it. I prefer my sugar in the form of baked goods."

My stomach growled. A long time ago, I'd had some of his mom's desserts. She'd made a giant platter of Christmas cookies for the school program. Since Mom would've had no way of knowing if I ate any, I'd had five. The most delicious chocolate chip cookie I'd ever had on my tongue. I'd been trying to figure out the recipe ever since.

He jiggled the plastic bag, and I leaned back like it was full of venomous snakes.

"Christ, Madison. Do you think I'm that bad of a guy?"

"You haven't shown me otherwise. I give you some bad news thinking I'm doing you a favor, and you make comments about how cheap I am."

"I never said that!"

"'I only let my tongue taste quality.'" My face burned from the memory of running into him last year in the coffee shop downtown.

He grimaced. "I was literally talking about the quality of the bourbon I make compared to what was sold here. As for the other thing." He sighed. "I'm sorry. You gave me the shit news that my girlfriend was cheating on me with your brother, and I shot the messenger."

Oh. I hadn't prepared for an actual apology. "I would've wanted to know instead of being a fool."

"I wasn't a fool for not suspecting my partner of stepping out on me."

"But it feels like you're one when it happens."

His nod was faint, then curiosity filled his gaze. Crap. I said too much, and it was the last thing I wanted to air out in front of him, or to commiserate with him. I could shoo him away and keep up the animosity, but I needed the sugar high before I faced the mess behind me. All I had was a water bottle and a ton of evaporated alcohol.

"Thanks." I reached for his offering.

Just as I was taking the bag, a "Yoo-hoo" rang out.

I snatched the sack from Teller in case he got distracted and forgot about forcing it on me. He dropped his hand, not giving me a response.

Whoever it was had his hackles raised. His lips were flattened and he was stiff. I leaned out as Wilna rushed down the sidewalk. She was ninety-something, but I'd thought she was in her nineties most of my life. Her gray hair was pulled back in a tight bun and she carried a stack of papers.

Her eyes lit when she saw me. I was tempted to scurry away. Wilna had a way of putting everyone around her to work, and I had enough waiting for me.

"Oh, Madison. I'm so glad I caught you." She

whipped out a sheet of paper. "Can you post this in your establishment?"

"It's not open." When she blinked at me, I took a flyer anyway.

Next, she beamed at Teller and thrust a sizable portion of her stack in his direction. "Be a dear and distribute these, will you? Have to make sure everyone knows."

Teller frowned at the papers. Wilna shoved them at his chest. He automatically put his hand on them, then cringed.

What had I missed? Teller always had a retort for me, but a tiny nonagenarian had him silenced?

The sheet was a poster announcing the annual bachelor auction, a fundraiser for shelters and food pantries in the area. Wilna and her crew also organized scholarships for ranchers during bad years and students who couldn't afford college, and they put on holiday shindigs for the nursing home to ensure that any forgotten family members also got to celebrate.

A picture of Teller's handsome, scowling face was plastered right in the middle with the words *Bid on a Bailey*.

A chortle left me. "You're getting auctioned this year?"

A muscle jumped in his cheek. "For work."

I snickered. "No one's going to buy you for *work*."

Bachelors either auctioned off a day of labor or an actual date. Teller was the most eligible bachelor in the area. I wouldn't be surprised if women from as far away as Helena came down. The auction was going to make a killing from Teller.

His scowl deepened. I almost felt sorry for him.

He worked his jaw back and forth. "I'm giving away one free project. I'm not a date."

"No one's going to care," I said, starting to enjoy his discomfort.

His gaze sharpened. "Are you saying you'd rather buy me for a date?"

His voice was almost a purr and his little gotcha smirk slammed my guards back in place. I'd almost been congenial with him. I'd had empathy for him. And he was teasing me again.

"You're welcome to come bid on him," Wilna said. "I'm retiring. It's the last auction, so it'll be a full house."

There was no way I was fighting a bunch of women for Teller. Besides, every cent I had needed to go into this place.

"Two weeks." Wilna patted the papers Teller clutched to his chest. Her gaze jumped around me, trying to see inside.

Teller witnessing the mess was bad enough, but I was used to being inferior around him. I didn't need Wilna spreading the word about what little I'd done so far.

"Thanks, Wilna. Good luck, Teller." I shut the door in their faces.

I put my back to the door and sucked in a long breath. Teller showing up at my door had been unexpected, to say the least. My fingers tightened around the grocery bag. I still held on to the flyer. His brooding face stared back as if Wilna had surprised him like a paparazzo.

He'd brought me candy. Had he felt bad about chocblocking me?

I giggled. I liked chocolate too, but days like today called for straight sugar. Looking inside, I gasped.

Holy crap. I hadn't registered the weight, but he'd loaded up. Skittles, Sour Patch Kids, gummy bears, and a bag of Trolli. No Jelly Belly, but my mouth was salivating.

A smile tugged at my lips. Not even my ex had been this generous when I'd asked him to pick up something sweet for me. I mulled over which bag to devour first. The decision took my mind off figuring out why Teller had dropped it off.

Sour Patch Kids first. Then . . . whatever I had time for. I dug my phone out of my back pocket and checked the time. Shit. I had to get ready for work.

I tapped the back of my head against the door. So. Much. To. Do.

If only I could hire someone. Who could I trust not to screw me over? Between Scott and my mom and my dad when he'd been alive, my last name didn't garner trust, and I could not afford to fuck around. None of Scott's old customers were in construction, and I wouldn't trust them sober any more than I had when they'd been drunk.

I needed a boost in my income, like yesterday. I had to get Flatlanders back in business.

If only I could get some help. Someone who was trustworthy. Someone who wouldn't waste my last two cents. Someone who the town didn't scorn for their last name.

I went to stuff the flyer in the bag, paused, and then stared at it one more time.

CHAPTER TWO

Teller

The collar of my shirt chafed. This room was too damn hot. Wasn't the church's AC working? "Stop looking at me like that," I snapped at Tate.

He was grinning like a cat who'd got the chubbiest mouse in the barn, only we were tucked into a little room off the front of the church. I wanted to crawl under one of the three round tables. Hide next to the bookshelf. The other nine bachelors ahead of me lounged in office chairs and scrolled through their phones.

Deputy Nordstrum was auctioning off a day of yard work. He was in his fifties but newly divorced. Yard work was probably a euphemism. Then there was a delivery driver for the distillery and his buddy from Livingston. They were clear about wanting dates. The pastor always auctioned off a day of work. I recognized the others but had tuned out when numbers started getting pinned on.

I was ten. The last bachelor. My stomach would eat through itself before that happened.

The din from the sanctuary reached me. Feminine laughter and chatter. I cringed. I hated this. I didn't want to date. I had no idea who would buy me—or why. I offered one project and it didn't include orgasms.

I liked orgasms. Fucking loved them. But if I wasn't alone, they always came with trouble, and I was tired of the drama. I hated getting fought over like a prized stallion.

I wanted peace and calm, and a strong woman who didn't feel like she needed to parade me around.

Madison's soft hazel eyes flashed in my head. Only because of the grocery store incident. I was a little responsible for egging her on—a lot responsible—but the way her eyes flashed and the abandon with which she spoke her mind fascinated me as much as it perplexed me. Did she have to be so defensive?

Maybe with me, yeah, she did. Other girls never took what I said so personally, but Madison tossed my words back in my face and added her own. It was exhilarating, and I was a jackass to indulge.

"Testing . . ." Wilna's voice rang out over the sound system, obliterating the memory of Madison's tight ass stalking away from me.

The auction was starting. My stomach knotted. Was I really doing this? I tugged at the collar of my shirt. I shrugged out of my flannel and tossed it on a chair. "Didn't they turn the AC on yet?"

Tate's deep chuckle was low enough not to carry

through the room. "It'll be fine." He leaned close. "You can say no if your buyer wants more."

"Sure." It'd been a while since I'd had *more*. I might not pass up the offer. Though sex with someone I wasn't planning anything long term with had gotten old.

Once upon a time, I'd been a committed man. Then I'd been embarrassed and betrayed. After that, I had fucked around. A lot. I had gotten a reputation, and I hadn't liked it, so I'd stopped. Now I was a stud on an auction block, afraid to return to the days of messing around and breaking hearts.

Acid burned up my throat. I hated being a spectacle. People talking about my love life, speculating. What had I done wrong? What had I done right? Who was I going to settle with?

For the last few years, I'd given them nothing to talk about. Until now.

I pressed my fingers to my temples and paced in front of Tate. Tenor was with Ruby at Copper Summit, but I'd rather be closing down the tasting room. I'd made my sisters swear they wouldn't be in the audience, but Summer had joked there likely wouldn't be room for them anyway.

How packed was it out there?

"It'll be fine," Tate said only loud enough for me to hear.

The number of men in the room was dwindling. Both of our delivery drivers had been called out.

"Some older couple is going to buy you to remodel their bathroom," he assured me.

A chorus of woos and laughter made a cacophony in the sanctuary.

"How'd you do this?" I kept pacing.

My brother hadn't asked out his wife, Scarlett. She'd bought him at one of these damn things with the help of me and my sisters. To be fair, she hadn't known my sisters had bid under her name, but it had all worked out. Tate and Scarlett were happy as hell and so in love.

I was happy for him. I wouldn't want it any other way. That jealous tug on my heart said there was more. Like dangerous hope that this auction would turn out the same for me turned me into the fool my ex had made me feel like.

"It's for a good cause," he said in that calm, infuriating tone, rubbing a hand down his dark beard.

He was right. The money went to people in the community, and ultimately, that was why I had given in to Wilna. I'd also wanted to quit running from a ninety-year-old woman in the middle of the grocery store, but I couldn't refute her claim that I would bring in a windfall on the auction block. Maybe not the twenty grand we'd raised for Scarlett to buy Tate, but enough.

I pushed a hand through my hair.

"You're going to ruffle those luscious locks," Tate teased. "The bidders might offer more if they can do it instead."

I shot him a glare. I hadn't gone to a barber for a while. They'd been hitting me up for Wilna. She'd put plants all around town to cajole me into saying yes.

One by one, the remaining men were called out.

My nerves slowly untwisted. I was accepting my fate. I'd do a job, be a decent human, and weather any gossip that came after. Besides, the bidding couldn't get that contentious.

Tate slapped a hand on my shoulder. "I'll go out for the show." He paused. "Seriously, if the outcome is . . .

unwelcome, we'll bail you out." He went out the door, leaving me alone.

More tension eased. I had a whole family behind me. It'd be fine. My anxiety was for nothing. I had dreaded getting dragged into this for so long that I'd built it up as some big deal, that *I* was a big deal.

I wasn't. It was just some harmless fundraiser. There'd be no problems, I'd mow a lawn or paint a house, and if worse came to worst, I'd go on a fucking date.

One of Wilna's crew popped her head in, big smile in place, decorated with bright-pink lipstick. "It's time for the grand finale."

I nodded and followed her through the dim hallway. As I got closer to the wide altar, a sea of faces turned my way. There were a few men in the audience, mostly with their spouses, to bid on a handyman for a day.

"Finally!" a woman shouted and whoops went up.

Wilna grinned at me, dollar signs in her eyes, as I climbed the three steps to stand by her. The cheering got louder, growing so much that the walls shook.

A couple hundred women stared back at me and red bidding paddles waved.

Shit.

Madison

Teller squared his shoulders and faced the crowd. His expression was unreadable, but his jaw was carved from marble. His molars must be withstanding superhuman pressure. I could almost empathize. I'd already gotten a million cursory looks, some full of disdain, and I could hear their unspoken thoughts. *What the hell is Mad Maddy Townsend doing at a bachelor auction? Of course she'd have to buy a man. Her own husband didn't want her.*

I hid my paddle in my bag. Signing in had been embarrassing, but for the most part, I'd been ignored after their initial shock at seeing me.

Flipping my braid over my shoulder, I looked around. Some women around me were standing. Most of them were cheering while Wilna and her octogenarian posse smiled on. All of the women in the crowd were grinning and clapping.

I was not. I was here for one reason and one reason only.

No matter how much Teller irritated me, he was a man of his word. Scott had thought Teller had screwed him over, but he hadn't. Scott had been his own worst enemy. Next in line were our parents.

I hid in the last row, squished between an old lunch lady from the elementary school and a girl who could barely be over twenty-one. She had bid on two younger guys earlier and lost.

This whole show . . . I couldn't imagine being on display. I felt like I was at a livestock auction, watching ranchers bid on a bull. But it raised money. Four hundred dollars to go to Curly's for a date night? Eight hundred dollars to plant trees for a day?

Teller would sell for way more than eight hundred, but I was prepared. The amount I could spend made me nauseous. If I won, Teller would wish he could plant trees for a day. He'd even wish he had offered a date instead.

Wilna leaned into the microphone. "Are we ready?"

Another two minutes of straight cheering rang out. Teller's shoulders were impossibly immobile. Was he even breathing? He was stiff, like he hated the attention on him, and in that, I could empathize. I shouldn't. He didn't deserve it from me, but...he'd brought me candy. He'd blocked it, purposely egging me on, and I when I stormed out, he'd selected sweet treats and brought them to me.

I still wasn't sure what to do about it. Other than eat everything that had been in the bag, and think of him with each bite.

Ugh. Being here was a mistake, but I was a desperate woman, and I was used to losing face in this town. I had to try to win this bid.

Finally, Wilna tapped the microphone and people quieted. "Bidding starts at one thousand."

Before my heart could lurch at her starting the bid at more than any other bachelor had gone for, someone cried, "Five." A paddle waved from the front row.

Oh god.

"Six!" Four more paddles waved.

Disgruntled grumbles resonated. I continued running the figures through my head. I could go higher, much higher, but I had hoped not to. My hopes died with each thousand-dollar increase.

"Ten." Cassie brandished her paddle like a sword.

Teller cocked a brow, but relief didn't fill his gaze. Wouldn't he want Cassie to win him? They were friends, or more.

"Twelve."

I looked around for the bidder and my stomach sank. Riley Graves. The best friend of my brother's ex-wife,

Wendi. Teller's ex. My dislike for Riley was almost as intense as for Wendi. Riley was a user. She had helped Wendi almost drain my brother dry, and she blamed me for ruining her good time. Scott had been a stubborn bastard, but he'd sometimes listened to me, and I'd finally gotten through to him about his wife. But then, I'd had irrefutable proof.

"Thirteen," Cassie countered.

"Fifteen," Riley said smugly.

I couldn't see much of Cassie, but she bit her lip. "S-sixteen."

Heads turned to Riley. A bidding tennis match.

She lifted her chin. "Twenty."

I glanced at Teller. Was his face paler than usual? I had my own grudge against Riley, and Teller might likely have one as well.

"Oh, say." Wilna scanned the audience. "Another twenty-grand bid. How blessed are we? Twenty going once . . . Going twice . . ."

I ignored the press in my chest, slipped my paddle out of my bag, and waved it. "Twenty-one." My heart rate jumped. Breathing grew hard as my ribs shrank against my lungs.

The entire audience pivoted in their seats to look at me. My lungs struggled to expand, but I'd had a lifetime of looking unbothered until I snapped. I called on those skills, minus the temper. I kept my expression impassive and lifted my chin.

I dared a peek at Teller. His brows knit together as he considered me.

"Oh." Wilna's breath gusted over the sound system. "Say."

"Twenty-two," Riley said, her voice hard.

Now I was part of the tennis match. Heads turning from me to Riley.

Teller subtly arched a brow. A challenge.

I flashed the paddle. "Twenty-five."

Riley's snarl rang through the crowd. Murmurs grew louder. "Twenty-six."

Teller stiffened, but his gaze didn't leave mine.

"Thirty." I wanted to choke on the word. I had some cushion yet, but if Riley kept going, I'd leave with nothing, not even my pride. After everything I'd been through, I'd managed to salvage some of that. Today might shred it once and for all.

"Thirty-one." Riley's glare bored into the side of my face. Heat blasted across my cheeks from the attention in the room focused on me, but I held strong. I could do this. I had to do this.

I did quick calculations on what I could bid, but they all led to the same answer. I couldn't go over the amount in my account.

My gaze stayed on Teller and I summoned all the confidence possible to volley another bid. "Thirty-two."

"Thirty-five," Riley snapped.

Shit. She'd said that way too easily. I had more cushion, but I'd love to leave with some of it. Settling Flatlanders' debts had wiped out much of what Scott had left me, leaving a meager stash to get the bar up and running. "Thirty-six."

"Forty."

Instead of getting loud, the audience went silent.

I was inhaling through a straw. Small sips of air. My brain fogged. I couldn't do this. It was a lot of money for a man.

But I'd have to find another person to do the work,

and after trying to find a realtor to sell my parents' place, I could envision just how that would turn out. No one who was trustworthy would agree to a job at Flatlanders.

Teller's jaw was clenched. His gaze slid to Riley and the crease in his brow deepened. He returned his attention to me, but his eyes lightened.

No other contractor would bring me candy. "Forty-five."

The tightness around his eye eased. I must be imagining things. There was no way he'd want me to win. Unless he assumed that there would never be anything between us. He was right. Just like guys like Teller didn't joke around with me, they also weren't interested in me. The one time I thought I had a decent guy, he'd shredded my trust and my heart.

The crowd waited for Riley.

"Forty-six." Her reply wasn't as bold as before. I knew the feeling.

Teller's cheek twitched.

My heart clattered against my ribs. I needed this to be over. "Fifty." I wished I could proclaim it loud and proud, but I feared it wasn't enough. If Riley could eke out one more dollar, I'd be done.

"Oh my god," the old lunch lady said next to me. "I never thought I'd see a Townsend spend a dime on a Bailey product, much less try to buy one. Bet he'll be the highest quality thing you've ever bought."

Okay, ouch. But true.

"I'd pay a hundred grand to date him," the young girl on the other side said.

I didn't want a date. No date I'd been on had ever been worth fifty dollars, much less fifty thousand.

Teller's chest rose like he was inhaling for the first time in a long time.

"Fifty-one." Riley's return lifted over the crowd.

Fear filled her eyes. She was a hairdresser with a salon in her house. Was she going to take out a second mortgage to pay for this? A home equity loan? She couldn't truly think there was a future between her and Teller.

Unless she was like me. Did she plan to have him remodel her salon?

That wasn't Riley though. She was bidding fifty grand in hopes of gaining access to his millions.

I bit the inside of my cheek. It was done. I'd lost.

Teller jutted his chin out like he was encouraging me to keep going. I squinted at him. I had to be seeing things.

A second ticked by. Two. He tilted his head to the side. I shrugged with no other way to convey that I had no more money. I'd love to ruin Riley's night more than anyone else's and extract some long overdue revenge, but I couldn't afford to. It was a balm to see someone detested her as much as me. That it was Teller was surprising.

"Wow," Wilna said. "A historic bid for the last year of the auction. That is something. Fifty-one going once."

His eyes flared and he cocked his head some more.

I couldn't.

"Going twice . . ." Wilna's words were a taunt. Everyone's eyes were on me, the weight heavy, but I was focused on Teller. His gaze repeatedly darted to Riley, darkened, then swung back to me. He tipped his head toward her again, urging me on.

I'd gathered fifty thousand dollars. Why couldn't I raise two thousand more?

Wilna leaned in. "Going . . ."

"Fifty-five." I whacked my leg with the paddle when I lowered it. I should smack my head. How the hell was I going to raise five thousand extra dollars? My next paycheck was barely five hundred.

"Wow, Mad Maddy," Riley sneered. "Even that much money won't get a man to stay with you."

I flinched, her words bitch-slapping me across the face as snickers rippled through the crowd. Teller's brows crashed together, but I dropped my gaze to my hands.

The former lunch lady chuckled. "Mad Maddy. I haven't heard that one in a while. Remember when you dumped spaghetti in Josh Tucker's lap when he called you that? Riley's almost as upset."

Josh had grabbed my boob, but I had gotten in trouble for the food. Not a memory I needed when I didn't have enough to cover my bid.

"You couldn't pay me fifty-five grand to let Riley put highlights in again," the girl next to me muttered. "I hope you win."

I snorted before I could smother my laugh. She would be the first. Riley shot me a glare.

A gavel pounded against the podium. "Sold to Madison Miller—oh, sorry—Townsend for *fifty-five* thousand dollars."

My heart stopped and it wasn't because she'd called out my married name, the one I'd changed as soon as the ink on the divorce papers was dry. My chest constricted, trying to resuscitate my heart. I was down fifty grand and five grand in the hole. What did I do?

Riley stomped over everyone in her pew on her way out. Then she flipped her middle finger at me as she wove toward the exit.

The roar of the crowd was growing. I couldn't sort my thoughts.

Wilna clapped into the microphone. "If everyone who won a bachelor can meet me in the pastor's office, we'll take your payment. You can make arrangements with your bachelor after we're done."

Shit, shit, shit. How could I get five grand between now and the twenty-second walk to the office?

Everyone filtered out, but I took my time, lingering in the pews, avoiding others' gazes. People were stopping to congratulate me as if I'd won Teller for life and not for the duration of the bar repairs. Some people even gushed about my generosity, shocked, like they didn't think I'd ever donate a dime. I'd never had money to give away. So I edged toward the side of the room, leaving others hanging mid sentence.

After a long stretch of time, the sanctuary cleared out. Auction winners exited the hallway on their way to discuss terms with their bachelor.

I had fifty grand. I could pay most of my bid. Would Wilna let me make payments on the last five grand? There was only a little more money in the bar's name, but that had to go toward supplies and materials.

Dammit. My feet were leaden as I walked down the hall. I passed the room of bachelors. Even that had emptied out. I didn't bother to look inside.

Tate waited outside of the pastor's office. "Hey, Madison."

Teller was close to forty with a good eight years on me, and Tate was the oldest Bailey. He'd never talked to me. Our paths had never crossed. I'd made sure of it. "Uh, hi, Tate."

"Good bidding out there. I didn't think you were going to get it."

My laugh was nervous. What did he think of my triumph? Had he been hoping Riley would win his brother? Her project would be easier and probably include less clothing. "Neither did I."

I walked past him to turn into the office, and he leaned forward. "Make him earn every cent."

Startled, I looked at him, but then the big man bending over the desk snatched one hundred percent of my attention. Teller's wide back was to me, but his ass was on display. Blue denim molded around a perfectly muscular butt. One knee was bent as he wrote something on the desk.

I stopped in the doorway. What now? I gawk at him while I wait to pay fifty-five thousand dollars to make him my bitch at the bar?

Wilna spotted me. "Hello, big spender. Come on in." Her face creased with her wide grin. "Your generosity tonight is astounding. It dwarfs even this man's."

Teller looked over his shoulder, his dark gaze pinning me. "I'm throwing in my own share."

"What?"

Wilna nodded. "He's kicking in some of your bid. Isn't that nice?"

"Excuse me?" My emotions were poised on the edge of a precipice. Stark relief on one side, utter humiliation on the other. "Why do you think I need help?" I did, but I was tired of being underestimated, and that it was by this guy stung more.

"It was the least I could do. Since you were so

gracious as to keep bidding." He tossed the pen back into a cup on the desk.

"You seriously paid for some of my bid without asking?" Indignation choked me. I should be relieved, but of course the mighty Teller Bailey would assume I couldn't cover the total.

I was supposed to finally have some leverage, and he was taking it away.

"Why would you do that?" I snapped.

He gave me a confused look. Wilna watched us, and Tate was probably outside the door listening in.

Teller stepped closer to me. I had to tilt my head back to meet his gaze, and god, why was that so hot?

He didn't move away. Neither did I. "Why don't you settle what's left and then we can talk?"

"*Or* you can answer me instead of expecting me to jump to do what you say."

He leaned a little closer and my traitorous body wanted to sway forward and close the distance, to feel how warm that big, hard body was. "I'll wait outside the office, Madison," he finished on a purr.

My thighs quivered. Then he was gone, taking that delicious heat and his enticing woodsy citrus scent with him. My world tipped sideways, and I covered the dizziness by facing Wilna. The sooner I was done dealing with this payment and *that man*, the better.

I'm supposed to dislike him, but my hormones hadn't gotten the message.

I'd never wired money before, but Wilna walked me through everything. The nausea returned through the process. For a brief, blissful moment, I'd had over fifty grand in my account. Now I was back to twenty bucks until payday.

I'd had less before.

In the hallway, Tate was gone. Teller was in his place, reclining against the wall. He propped a cowboy hat against his leg with one hand. My brain took a snapshot in case I needed to know what kind of guy was out of my reach. I was about to spin in the other direction, but after the money I'd spent, I needed what I'd paid for.

"When can you be at the bar?" I asked.

The corner of his mouth lifted in a tease. "You didn't bid so high for a date?"

"Disappointed?"

"Depends on what dating you is like."

His answer caught me off guard. "Not exciting." I inwardly winced. I didn't mean to say that, but it wasn't like my history made guys line up to ask me out.

"Hmm, I feel like that's not true."

Is he joking again? "Well, you're not finding out."

He held up his hands like he gave up, and a small part of me withered. "The bar? That's the project? That shithole?"

I bristled. *That shithole* would be everything I had once my parents' property sold. "Yes. Hope you're up for it."

I breezed past him just as he said, "Being up is never a problem."

His wall of heat stayed at my back, wreaking havoc with the interest my libido had with his comment. The church was empty as I marched through the sanctuary to get to the exit on the other side.

"What's your issue?" he demanded from behind me. "We're going to be working together."

I kept walking. As if I hadn't heard that question so many times before.

"Jesus, Maddy."

"You should watch your mouth in church." The glass doors were in front of me. I pushed out of them, but Teller was so close they didn't shut in his face. "Even us poor people have some manners."

"Are you that upset I helped with the donation? I could tell fifty was your stopping point."

This time, I spun. He pulled up short but not nearly far enough away. "You didn't think that if I came up with fifty grand, I couldn't cover five more?"

"Could you?"

I clamped my mouth shut. "I would've, yes."

"Life insurance?"

I stiffened. Guilt fed into my anger, diminishing it. "None of your business."

"A lot isn't my business, but it sounds like that bar is now. Wendi fought you for it, didn't she?"

I scoffed, but I hated hearing his ex's name come out of his mouth. "She fights for everything that isn't hers."

He huffed and nodded. "Ain't that the truth. Best decision Scooter ever made was divorcing her."

A lump formed in my throat. My brother hadn't had a choice, but I didn't want to get into it. I opened my door and scrambled in. Teller wedged himself in the opening. His torso was within touching distance.

Seriously? That was where my mind went?

"Move," I said through gritted teeth.

He clasped the top of the pickup. He'd also stuffed his hat on his head and the brim shadowed his eyes. I had a stubborn cowboy facing off with me, but my pulse didn't spike with fear. Heat wound through my veins, curling down farther, whispering steamy suggestions into my ear. Ideas that Teller was probably good at. Excellent even.

"It was a thank-you," he said.

I heaved my mind out of the gutter. "What was?"

"You saved me from Riley."

Oh. The money. So I had read him correctly. "Yeah, well. I can commiserate." My grudge against her knew no bounds. "But I could've covered it."

"You weren't prepared to spend over fifty."

Damn him. "I was too," I said stubbornly.

He gave me a flat look.

"I don't appreciate that you thought I needed saving." I stared out the windshield. He was overpowering otherwise. His size. That determined look in his eye. The way we seemed to be on the same wavelength during the auction. I had nothing in common with him but cheating exes.

Teller Bailey was a sexy man. A fact I'd never been able to deny. My hormones might've shut off when I had learned of my ex's betrayal, but my arousal argued otherwise. Damien and the duds I had dated before him had given me a soft spot for hardworking, honest men intent on taking care of their loved ones. Bourbon Canyon was too small not to notice those traits in Teller.

If I hadn't had to move back home, I could've kept my grudge against him fueled with nothing but memories of his outburst from years ago.

"Well, like I said, it's a thank-you," he said gruffly.

I could give him that. If I had to spend a day with Riley, I'd cough up five grand to skip it too. I kept my gaze hard when I faced him. The same fire wicked up my spine as it always did when I was this close to him. "Fine."

His grin was slow.

A million butterflies took flight in my belly. How bad of a mistake had I made?

"When do you want me to report, boss?" That low growl of his . . . He was potent. Too alluring for his own good. And he knew it.

"I work the night shift, so I sleep until one."

He frowned. "What time do you get off work?"

"Seven."

"And you only sleep until one?"

I was perpetually tired. What could I say? "It's only three twelves." Three twelves per week that banked each other and became six twelve-hour shifts in a row, but it gave me a good stretch off to do things like renovate a bar I'd never planned on running. "And then I pick up extra hours if I can."

"Right. You're a nurse."

"I'm not a nurse." I swallowed my usual shame when I had to correct people. "I'm a CNA."

He gave his head a brief shake.

"I help nurses." And I got paid half of what they did.

"I thought you were in nursing school with Wendi."

"I was." My stomach cramped. And there was the reason for my mortification. Being a CNA was fine. It was hard, backbreaking work, but it was rewarding. It just wasn't my choice of a career, but then nursing school hadn't been either, and leaving school had been my decision. Ultimately.

He waited, but I didn't elaborate. There had to be some limit to looking like an idiot around him.

"I work all weekend," I said, "but if you want to stop in anytime between two and six, then I can go over what needs to be done." I gave him a tight smile. His scent filled the cab to haunt me later. I'd have to drive with the windows down for a week to forget how good he smelled.

"You work tonight?"

My scrubs were in the back. Buy a bachelor with all my money and head to work. A normal day. "Yes. So, if you'll excuse me."

He let go of the frame of the pickup. "Monday. I'll be there after work on Monday."

"As long as it's after two."

He dipped the brim of his hat, and for some reason, my sex drive reminded me that it'd been a while since I had orgasmed.

I had to get away from this guy. "Monday." I swung the door shut and fired up the engine.

Teller didn't move as I backed up and drove away. The strong, straight-legged way he stood with the sky and trees would be etched in my brain forever. Each block I put between him and me left me as light as marshmallow fluff. I was finally making progress. I now had a contractor, and it was thanks to my brother's life insurance . . . and the bourbon cowboy in my rearview mirror.

CHAPTER THREE

Teller

"You're doing what?" Tate asked. He sat across from me at the big conference table in the top level of Copper Summit. "Flatlanders?"

My sisters gawked at us. Tenor had his laptop open, but he was as invested in my answer as the rest of them. Just my luck our monthly meeting was the Monday morning after the bachelor auction. No, it wasn't luck. Wynter had planned it that way.

I pressed my fingertips together. "It's a fucking mess in there. She probably left it for me." She should leave it for me. The night of the auction was the first time I had noticed the fatigue etched into her pretty features.

"For fifty grand, she should," Junie said, tucking a strand of hair behind her ear. She'd piled the rest in a blue-and-pink bun on top of her head. Apparently, each of her stepdaughters got to choose a color.

Wynter ran a hand over her pale braid. "For fifty grand, I'd make more of a mess."

Just like me, the whole town had likely peeked through the windows of Flatlanders. The damage Scooter had left behind had far outlasted the man. What had made him rage? Would he have done anything differently if he'd known he was leaving it all behind for Madison?

As for her . . .

When she'd bid on me, I hadn't believed it. Had she been passionate about the charity? I'd heard her family had been on the receiving end a few times—until her mom had gotten pissed and chewed out Wilna, telling her to stick her canned goods and winter coats "where the sun don't shine."

Then Madison had kept bidding, all the way to fifty grand. She'd sat in the back, waiting to see how high it went before jumping in. She had to have known the ruckus it'd create. But she'd had the money, most of it. She'd planned to win me.

Thank fuck Riley hadn't won. I'd nearly had a coronary when Madison had quit bidding. I'd had no idea if she could read my cues. I'd have kicked in all my retirement to keep from spending a day with Riley.

Perhaps my curiosity about why Madison was bidding had been just as strong. We couldn't seem to get along, but she'd forked over a tidy fortune that could've done a lot for Flatlanders without me.

Of course, I hadn't gotten much for an answer. Frustrating woman.

"You should've seen the bidding war," Tate said, clasping his hands behind his head and leaning back in his chair. "Riley Grant almost got him."

Autumn made a growling sound. "I don't like her."

"None of us do," Summer added.

"Her salon is tanking." Tenor closed the lid of his laptop like he knew we weren't getting to our meeting agenda for a while. "She called Ruby to ask for free social media tips, then chewed her out when she gave her a quote for consulting."

"Ugh. I can hear her do it too," Wynter said, her tone dripping with derision.

Summer smacked her lips. "That woman is always in the thick of trouble."

"So . . . Madison . . ." Junie cocked her head. "How's that going to go?"

Tenor snorted.

I glared at him. "Care to speak your mind?"

He spread his hands apart. "Judging from your interactions with her last summer? Everything you say is going to piss her off."

Everything I did would too, and I'd get to witness that fire blaze across her face. She was a passionate woman, and what if that energy was directed somewhere else— No fucking way was I going there with her. I wasn't one to waste my time on a dead end. She was attractive, gorgeous if I was honest, but she was also a land mine of emotions, and she was *not* interested. Besides, the bar was my job, and that was all I had to do with Madison Townsend. "That place was ruined. She's going to have to gut it."

"*You're* going to have to gut it," Tate clarified.

Yep. Me. Would she be there while I was working? Why did I hope she was? "You guys mind covering for me with the ranch?"

"Already talked to Mama," Tenor said. "Cruz and

Lane are back for the month, so they can fill in. How long will it take?"

"I don't know." I shrugged. "I could set up card tables, and it'd be just as nice as before." I didn't know Madison well, or at all really, but she deserved better than getting left with that.

Tenor shook his head. "It wasn't that bad."

Wynter smirked. "Because you finally proclaimed your love for Ruby there. You have a soft spot for it."

The lovesick look on Tenor's face made me look away. I was the last single sibling. Tenor's wedding was next month, then I'd be the only Bailey bachelor. Even Cruz and Lane, honorary Baileys since they were Wynter's in-laws, would soon be leaving Bourbon Canyon for good.

"Good. Everything's covered," I said. "I wish I knew more about the timeline and budget. I don't know how Mads is going to be about it."

"She might be a dick if you keep calling her Mads." Autumn tied her long red hair back and secured it with a band from around her wrist.

"It's Mad Maddy she hates," I pointed out.

"Yet you call her that too," Tenor said.

She fit the name. Madison had a permanent scowl and was hard as a nail. When she broke bad news, she just fucking dropped it on a guy. Hit him right in the face with *Your girlfriend is fucking my brother*.

As much as I had resented Madison for opening my eyes and crushing my dreams, I respected her for it. She hadn't reveled in it. "I don't say it to be mean." I said it to watch her blast out of that hard shell she'd formed around her.

"Everyone else does," Autumn said quietly. "It's not

as bad as it was when she was in school, but she's still Karl and Cheryl Townsend's daughter. Scooter's sister. She'll never outrun her family in Bourbon Canyon."

Regret tugged at my chest. Was that why I'd nearly had to toss the candy into the bar and run in order for her to take it? She just assumed the worst of me?

Why wouldn't she?

Are you enjoying this, Mad Maddy? Did you look forward to it? The first time I had really talked to her, and that was what I had said. That and more. Yet I couldn't quit digging under her creamy, smooth skin since then.

"I'll know more tonight. I'm stopping there after work to get an outline of what she expects." I spread my hands. "Sorry, guys. I had no idea this auction would take me out of commission."

"Oh no," Junie said with false sincerity. "You'll have to do something else besides work here or at the ranch. What will you do?"

Tate snorted and the rest tried—and failed—to smother their chuckles.

"Haha, fuckers." I liked my jobs. My work kept me out of trouble and stopped me from noticing how empty my house was. "Let's get this meeting started."

We made it through the whole meeting without delving back into the subject of Madison. I'd face her soon enough. When we were done, I all but ran out of Copper Summit, propelled by curiosity. How much backbreaking work did I have in front of me? How much fire would I get to see in her?

I strode to the parking lot and hopped into my truck. The trip to town took minutes and then I was parked in front of Flatlanders. I tried the front door, damn near excited to start backbreaking work. It was locked. Was she in there?

I knocked.

She couldn't be avoiding me when she paid that much to boss me around. I peered through the window. Shock had me pressing closer. This wasn't the same view from last week. She'd cleaned up all the debris. Sure, it'd been two weeks since Wilna had given her a flyer, but she could've left it all if she was hiring someone.

Why hadn't she actually hired someone? She could've gotten a contractor for cheaper than she'd bought me for. Scooter couldn't have caused that much damage. She couldn't be getting back at me for being a dick, could she?

She was a Townsend. They held grudges.

No movement inside and no lights were on. I took my phone out of my pocket. Damn. I stuffed it back in. I didn't have Madison's number.

Her truck wasn't parked out front. She must go through the back.

Jogging around the corner, I hoped the back door was unlocked. Her pickup was parked in a nook made by the two bordering buildings. I bypassed the dumpster and tried the heavy metal door. Locked. I knocked.

A minute passed. What the hell, Madison? I had other things to do.

I knocked again.

No answer.

Now worry started nagging at me. Was she as unpredictable as the rest of her family had been?

"Mads?" I called and pounded on the door. "Madison!"

"Holy shit, Teller." Her voice came through the metal

door. A bolt flipped on the other side. Her normally braided hair was pulled back in a low ponytail. She was smoothing strands back and blinking at me. "You're going to wake the neighborhood."

"It's four."

She rubbed her eyes. "I thought you said after work."

I studied her. She wore cloth shorts, and goddamn. She had long, tanned legs that looked even better bare than when they were in jeans. Her T-shirt was baggy, pooling around hips that would be perfect to hold on to while driving in—

Lust punched low and hard, but I shook it off. It had just been a while for me. That was all. "Did you just wake up?"

She wrinkled her nose and looked away. "No."

"Do you sleep here?"

"*No*." She crossed her arms, and fuuuck. She wasn't wearing a bra. Her nipples poked at the fabric, begging to be caressed—by my fingers or tongue.

I lifted my gaze to the sky before I could sport a public erection. "It's fine if you do. I'm sure it's better than the drive to your family ranch."

She didn't respond. I dropped my attention to her. Her brow was creased and she was shifting from foot to foot.

"Don't you live there?" I asked.

"It's none of your business." She straightened to her full height, and goddamn, I liked it. I liked not having to crank my chin down when I talked to her. I didn't feel like I could break her.

"Mads, it seems a lot of your business is overlapping with mine."

Her jaw remained set.

"Gonna tell me what you paid for me to do?"

"Yeah." She spun around and strode down the hall, her flip-flops slapping against the floor.

I stepped in and let the door shut behind me while admiring the long-legged sight in front of me.

"You can leave the office alone," she said as she went and I followed. "The bathrooms need work, but I want the main area repaired before I budget for the bathrooms."

She pivoted again and I had to stop before I stepped on her feet. I nearly swallowed my tongue. Her toes were painted the daintiest shade of pink. Tough-as-steel Madison Townsend had pink toenails. I'd noticed how beautiful she was—who wouldn't? But this little tidbit wiggled through my blood, heating as it went.

"That will be your job," she said, ripping my attention off how much I wanted to see what other surprises she had. More things that weren't my business. "To oversee the bathroom repairs. Unless you're a plumber in addition to a rancher and a distiller."

"Master distiller, and I can do rudimentary plumbing, but anything major in this old building should have an expert or be looked at by one first. Who do you want to use?"

"You choose. No one will screw you over." She turned again and continued to the pool table area. "Consider yourself a contractor and a project manager." She propped her hands on her hips. "Make this look like a bar again."

I studied the space. No more splintered wood shards littered the floor. The cords hanging from the high ceilings had no light fixtures at the end, but she'd cleaned all the glass debris too. The mirror behind the bar was gone. The cabinets and busted shelving needed to be removed. So did the bar and countertop.

It was a lot of work, but she'd done the brunt of it. Cleaning up destruction was never fun. "I know it's none of my business, but what made Scooter trash his own place?"

She sighed and I expected another *it's not your business*. "I don't know. I'm just glad he wasn't drinking."

"Why'd you clean all this? You had to know fifty grand made my labor guaranteed."

"And you assumed I'd leave the pigsty for you."

Didn't that make me feel like shit? "No one would've blamed you. It's a lot of money. *I* wouldn't have blamed you," I added when her brow ticked up. Suddenly, I wanted to stay on her good side.

She rocked back and forth on her cute little feet. "I need this done as quickly as possible."

"You know who could do that? A professional whose only job is to renovate your bar."

Her expression shuttered. "Everything's so easy for a Bailey."

Defensiveness heated the back of my neck. "We work hard for what we have."

"You don't think I work hard?"

"No, it's not that—"

"Because I do." She prowled closer, and my fingers were twitching to grip her waist. "I work all the fucking time, and I've had to because people try to take what I have away."

"I didn't mean—"

"Everyone thinks we're shit, so they treat us like it." She got into my face and her minty breath crested over my chin. "I've done nothing but stick up for myself and

I get insulted and used. But a Bailey can tell someone to fuck off for doing nothing but telling the truth. When a Bailey tells it like it is, they get praised. A Bailey gets used by a cheater and he gets the sympathy of the town, but that same bitch sleeps with my husband and I get left with his law school debt. I go to work every day and my boss threatens to kick my mom out."

Her words raced through my head, jumbling together and straightening out. A hard task when she was standing so close. I had told her to fuck off, not in those words, but the rest? Was it true? "Wendi slept with your husband?"

"After he finished law school." She snapped her fingers. "No." The apples of her cheeks were flushed. "It was after he got a decent job."

"A better-paying one than a bar brought in?"

She nodded. "She didn't just sleep with him. She took him." Folding her arms again only pushed up those fleshy breasts that demanded my attention. "I just wish that if Wendi was going to cheat, she would've done it before my nephew was born."

I hated to look away, but I did. Wendi and Scooter had Logan a couple of years after she left me, and it sucked watching a cheating bastard get the family I thought I'd have. The kid must be around four by now. "It's hard on him?"

Her jaw tightened. "I assume it is, but Wendi isn't really open to letting me visit him."

"That fucking sucks." Her ex had no taste, and apparently, mine didn't either. "Your boss is threatening to kick your mom out?"

Her expression turned impassive. "I'm dealing with

it. Anyway, get this place looking exactly as it did before."

My mind spun from the subject change. "Exactly like it was? It's yours now. You can do whatever you want with it."

"And I want it to be selling drinks and making money."

"It can do that with another plan. This is the chance for a rebrand."

"I'm not rebranding."

And here I had started not to mind her stubbornness. "Then make the reopening a thing. You could advertise—"

She tugged on her ponytail, her features hard. "Just fix the damn bar, Teller." The red was back in her cheeks.

"Don't you want better—"

"None of that is your business. I hired you—bought you—to get this place going again, and that's all you need to know."

Her shields were slammed back into place, and goddammit, I did not like being locked out on the other side. Butting heads wasn't going to help.

I held my hands up. "Okay, okay. You're the boss."

"It'll be easier if you remember that."

"I have some experience in bars, just saying. You have me at your disposal." I couldn't help myself. I knew things and most people deferred to me, but not her.

"I have experience too."

I tipped my head back and let out a frustrated growl. "Christ, Mads. You can let a guy help once in a while."

"Nothing good has ever come from that."

I snapped my gaze to her. She'd said it so matter-of-factly. From what I remembered, her dad had been a piece of shit, running around on her mom and getting into fights. Scooter had had his issues, and while he might've loved his sister, he'd been selfish to a fault. Then there was her ex.

No. Men hadn't helped her a whole lot. And here I was, swaggering around and expecting her to be grateful for my manly knowledge. All after doing nothing but put her on edge whenever we crossed paths since she'd moved home last year.

"All right," I relented. "I'll restore this joint back to its dive bar glory. Except the countertop won't be sticky." That earned me a glare, but I only grinned. There was the fire I thrived on. "I should have keys to the place."

Her eyes flared. "Oh. Um . . . yeah. Hold on."

I didn't. I followed her all the way down the hall. I was leaving after this anyway. I needed to look up contractors and carpenters. I could demolish and install a lot myself. Time would be an issue, but I'd make it work.

She went to a room across from the office, shot me a warning glare, and slipped inside, shutting the door behind her. What was in there?

While I waited, I poked my head into the office. I smirked at the empty bag of Skittles in the trash and the open bag of Trolli on the desk. My candy stash hadn't gotten tossed after all.

The door behind me squeaked open. She jiggled a set of keys. "I'll tell you when my days off are, otherwise don't come before one in the afternoon."

"Shouldn't I wait until four? Seems like you needed the nap." As her eyes narrowed, I chuckled. "I'll be here after five. I can work weekends and evenings."

"I picked up a couple of shifts this weekend."

She should be drooping from how much she worked. I wanted to go tuck her back in wherever she had been sleeping and tell her to rest, but she'd likely bite my head off. I snatched the keys from her and leaned in. "I need to do some research first, so give me a few days. I'll be back Friday. With more Skittles."

She inhaled sharply.

I grinned and pushed out the door.

It didn't shut behind me. "It was the Jelly Bellys."

I stopped. "Jelly Belly?"

"That day in the store, you were blocking the Jelly Belly display."

I would've grabbed anything she had asked for that day, but she had refused and fled. It was amazing I was even let into the bar.

She trusted me.

Humbled, my throat grew thick. I'd been stoking her, firing her up, and still she'd turned to me only by the grace of my last name. She'd left me in the dust that day, and then she had taken a huge gamble on my ass, helping me in the process. I couldn't let her down. "What flavors?"

"Is there a bad one?"

"Yes. Buttered popcorn."

"You got me there. Red apple and root beer. Skittles hurt my teeth." She disappeared inside and the door closed. The bolt flipped.

Red apple and root beer. As long as I worked on this bar, she'd never be out of them again.

Madison

I suppressed a yawn as I clocked in on the nurses' station computer. It was my last night of work before I got four days off. My body might not function the best from seven p.m. to seven a.m., but it was nice to work without my superiors breathing down my neck. I was less likely to say something to get myself into trouble.

No one here would tolerate me talking to them the same way I spouted off to Teller. Yet Teller didn't go away. He didn't back down, and I thought he might even enjoy riling me up. I didn't enjoy it. Except a little bit when his pupils dilated and the faintest flush stained his cheeks. I'd never seen him react that way to anyone else.

He had an obligation to fulfill, but when he had looked at me when came to the bar, I didn't feel like some dreaded responsibility. He even asked about my favorite jelly bean flavor. No one had ever paid attention to what I ate unless it was to tell me to back off, but he did.

I couldn't look too far into it. Maybe he no longer felt like my personal nemesis, but we weren't friends. We weren't even colleagues really. What were we?

Raquel, the nurse in charge, stopped next to me, her eyes sympathetic. "Your mom asked to see you."

Shit. That obliterated all thoughts of Teller. Mom did not ask. She'd probably ordered my supervisor to tell me to get my ass there as soon as possible. "Okay, thanks. I'll make it quick."

"We all try to," she said, knowing I felt the same way and it wasn't so I could return to work quicker. "Also, Ramona's on a rampage."

My stomach dropped. Ramona was the director of the nursing home. I'd paid for the next month before I'd bid on Teller, and I was keeping a few months in reserve until her house sold. Technically, it was my house, but I refused to live there. "Because of my mom?"

"Because she's Ramona."

I bit the inside of my cheek to keep from laughing. I already had one big Cheryl Townsend strike against me. If the director thought I was laughing at her, I could lose my job. Other than our small clinic, there was nowhere else to work as a CNA in town, and I doubted I'd get hired for home healthcare if I was let go from here.

I slowed my usual hurried walk as I approached Mom's door. Cheryl Townsend wasn't an easy resident, and she refused to have me help her with anything. I took the reprieve where I could, and the other staff paid the price.

Turning the corner into Mom's wing, I jumped. Ramona was leaning against the wall, her reading glasses perched on the end of her nose, and she was scrolling through her phone.

"Madison. Good." She tucked the phone into the pocket of her gray cardigan. Ramona never wore scrubs, despite being a nurse. Most of her work was admin and complaining to me about Mom.

Not good. "Yes?"

"Your mom swore at Joseph today."

Hopefully, she hadn't called him a cunt. Though he could be. "She swears a lot."

"We've given her warnings."

"I can talk to her again." Twice already, Mom had been threatened with removal, and she'd known enough to settle down. Her pride wouldn't allow her to live with me. She'd rather die on the street than seem weak in front of her daughter.

"I can have her removed."

"I know." I'd learned shortly after I started here that agreeing with Ramona was the best tactic. She hadn't hassled Scott like she did me, but Scott's lawyer used to be one of his customers. If the lawyer wasn't also an abusive dick to his kids, I'd probably give him my business. "I appreciate your patience."

"Mmph. She's on her last warning." Ramona sauntered away.

Mom had been on her last warning since my first day of work.

Sighing, I continued on my way. Mom's room was in the far corner of the east wing, where she couldn't be as easily heard cussing out the staff. The doors I passed were decorated with artwork from kids and grandkids, cutouts of handprints, and happy photographs. When I reached Mom's door, there was nothing but her first name.

I knocked. "Hey, Mom. Can I come in?"

"'Bout damn time. You shouldn't be late for work."

"I wasn't." I was never late, but I was never that early. We couldn't clock in more than seven minutes early, or we'd have to be paid for a whole quarter hour.

"What's this about you and that Bailey boy?"

Lead formed a ball in my gut. I should've anticipated this, but the work to be done on the bar and dealing with my sleazy real estate agent had demanded my brain space. "I hired Teller as a project manager."

"You bought him from that stupid bachelor auction. Fucking Wilna." The corner of her mouth curled up. The other side was weaker from the stroke, and the effect only deepened her sneer. She'd done only enough during her rehabilitation to keep that poisonous tongue of hers strong, but not her limbs. "Why the hell would you think he'd help you?"

She knew all about gambling, and I'd taken the biggest bet out on Teller. "I needed someone for the repairs and he won't screw me over because it's for charity."

"You should've sold that goddamn place instead of your childhood home."

"The sale isn't done yet." She was lucky I didn't burn my childhood home to the ground. The property and house were technically mine, thanks to Scott, so I could demolish it all. But I was better than that. I had a reasonable and responsible plan: sell it to pay for Mom's care.

She grunted her acknowledgment. *Don't count your chickens before they're hatched.* She'd taught us that. Mostly, it was to expect to get screwed over by people, and since life had only reinforced that thought, I took the lesson to heart. The sale was pending. I'd had little leverage and it had sold for less than the land and house were worth, but I'd already lost two buyers trying to negotiate.

"You shouldn't have used Sal as your agent," Mom grumbled. "The sale would be over by now."

Sal Longwood was a seedy prick who stared at me like he was picturing me naked, but he'd been the only one to call me back during my real estate agent hunt. No one in a hundred-mile radius wanted to work with a Townsend. I just shrugged.

"How much did you get for it?" she asked.

"Like I said, the sale isn't done." I wouldn't tell her anyway. She'd berate me. She knew damn well how much land was worth this close to Bozeman. She didn't know that even millionaires looking to escape their metropolises wouldn't pay premium for a house that needed to be condemned, not when it was surrounded by pastures still recovering from overgrazing.

She smacked her lips. "I don't expect you to be able to negotiate the deal. Sal's only going to screw you over."

I'd tried to haggle, but Sal said it was a buyer's market. "He did okay." The guy knew real estate and I didn't, but I knew how much of my debt that house would pay, and how many years of Mom's care it would cover, so I stuck with that.

She ran her tongue over her teeth. She was missing a bottom tooth and a couple of molars. "I would think by now you should be able to identify cheating men."

My defenses were clicking into place, but I couldn't help but compare how she lacked all faith in me to how Teller offered his expertise. He was bewildered I hadn't taken him up on it, but he hadn't insulted my intelligence or alluded to how he thought I couldn't do it.

"Scott would've been able to get a lot of the money for the house," she continued, "but he wouldn't have had to sell in the first place."

I bit the inside of my cheek. I would disagree, the bar wouldn't have been able to sustain her care, but I knew better than to provoke her.

She turned her gaze out the window. "He should be here."

Yes, he should.

Just as I was getting choked up, she pinned me with her hard gaze. "He should be here and not you."

I recoiled. Whoa. That last part was new. I'd been compared to my brother all my life. I hadn't been as clever as him, as ambitious, or as talented. He'd gotten all our parents' love and devotion. But in the six months since he'd been gone, Mom had never said *that*.

Why was I surprised? Yet my throat burned as much as the backs of my eyes.

"Good night, Mom." I spun on a heel and left.

Tears threatened to gather. I could not want someone like Ramona to see me crying. She'd hold it against Mom and there that last warning went.

This wing had a small party room that should be empty by now. The light was off and I ducked in, leaving the space dark. I tucked myself in the corner and inhaled a shuddering breath.

Get it together. I hated to cry in front of people. Weaknesses got exploited and tears only framed them with a neon sign.

I blinked and sniffled, but my vision continued to blur. *Don't cry, don't cry, don't cry*.

"Madison?"

I jumped and pressed my hand against my mouth. Who was in here?

A shadowy figure walked into the light filtering through the door. Mae Bailey. The corners of her kind eyes were creased with concern and she held a plastic tray with a lid. She set it on the table we used for food when there was a party and came closer.

"Are you okay?" Her warm smile was a balm for my grief. "It's a silly question, isn't it? But it's hard not to ask."

Her gentle voice soothed some of the hurt, but it didn't chase away the embarrassment of getting caught hiding and crying. "You mean most people don't tuck themselves into a dark corner when they're happy?"

Her chuckle was just as calming as the rest of her. "I was known to do that so I didn't lose my ever-loving mind when the kids were young and the house was louder than usual."

Her dark hair, streaked with gray, swirled around her face. She was younger than my mom, but not by much. Where Mae and her late husband had started their family young, my parents had waited. And then, according to Ma, kept going for one kid too many.

"After Darin died," she said, "I started doing it again. Otherwise the kids worry."

The differences between our families grew starker. She'd probably never called her kids stupid.

She patted my shoulder. If I leaned in, I'd be encompassed in a giant bear hug. I pressed myself against the wall, yearning for that feeling while also not trusting it.

"The loss of your brother is still fresh," she said, "and for years down the road, it'll feel startlingly raw. Sometimes, you just want your grief to be private."

Tears streaked down my face. "I don't have a choice but to keep it private." Shame burned through me. How could I confess something so personal to someone I barely knew?

Her arms surrounded me and I was pulled in for a fierce hug. "You've had a tough go of it, dear."

I nodded, grateful to be seen. Someone understood. It was my bad luck that it was a Bailey. My shoulders shook as I tried to gather myself, to regain some composure before a long shift.

"It's all right, Madison. Let it out."

I relaxed into her soothing words, letting the grief have its moment. When the worst of it was over, I pulled back and searched the dark room for a rectangular shadow that might be a box of tissues. Mae brandished a tissue in front of me.

I accepted it and wiped my face and nose. "Sorry." How were all the Baileys so damn nice? Even when Teller was poking and prodding at me, he treated me with more respect than a lot of people. And he'd apologized.

"Don't be. You know, I've always admired your strength, but I know it's hard."

That wasn't how people usually saw me. Angry. Stubborn. Inflexible. Others would call it standing up for themselves, but when it came to me . . . "Most people call it rude."

Mae was silent for a moment. The silence should be uncomfortable, but it gave me a chance to gather myself and dry my tears.

"All the fosters Darin and I took in over the years," she said almost hesitantly, "they were also called rude. People aren't wrong. The way one person sets a boundary can be insulting to another. Both can be true, and it just seems to change by the decade who we're upset with. But that's not what I meant. Several of the kids I had the privilege of taking in grew into angry adults who lashed out."

"Angry like my brother?"

"I didn't intend to include him," she said gently, "but yes. Others, like Wynter's husband, Myles."

All I knew of Wynter's husband was that he was a stupidly successful distiller in his own right, owning and running Foster House Whiskey. I'd also heard he used to foster at the Baileys' when he was a teen.

"Myles could've been a right bastard." She chuckled.

"Some might say he was, or is, but I wager he gets more leeway because he's a guy."

I huffed out a breath. "No kidding."

She patted my arm again. Then she picked up the container she'd been holding when I first came in and opened it. "I had forgotten this. It's what I came back for." She handed me a cookie. "They're oatmeal chocolate chip. The last time I brought oatmeal raisin for poker night, I almost caused a riot."

I laughed despite the roller coaster of emotions I'd been on and accepted the cookie. "Raquel thinks raisins are the ultimate dirty prank."

"Can't say I disagree." Mae withdrew a cookie and took a bite. "But I had raisins to use up that day."

I found a napkin on the table by the wall and wrapped my cookie. I slipped it into the cargo pocket of my scrub pants.

"I have to say that I hoped to find a slice of that coconut cake left over." She exhaled a regretful sigh. "I'm not a criminal, but I would've stolen that."

I'd made that cake and there was not one crumb left. That recipe was my favorite. I was allowed to use the kitchen here if I made something for all the residents, so I did it as much as I could. Once upon a time, I dreamed of making a living from my love of baking, but my parents berated that idea out of me. "I missed out. Darn it."

"I only had two slices." She chuckled. "So, I hear Teller is going to be helping you get the bar ready."

Abashed heat flooded my cheeks. I'd bought this lady's son to use him for backbreaking work. Worse, I wanted to watch her son do the backbreaking work. A girl needed inspiration for the lonely nights. "Yeah."

"Smart move. He'll do a good job." Mae took another bite of her treat, then lifted the container and wrapped her arms around it. "He knows a little something about sales, but he also knows people. Might be worth talking to before the deal closes on your house."

I stiffened. How had she known about that? I hadn't had time to get a sign up. It'd been word of mouth, and Sal was taking care of all that. "What do you mean?"

She tilted her head from side to side. "No one gets a good deal with Sal but Sal himself."

"Mom doesn't want me to use him either."

"One of your mom's underappreciated traits is that she knows when she's getting taken advantage of."

"She'd be surprised to hear you say that."

Laughter gusted out of Mae. "I told her that once. Her reply was colorful." She gave me a once-over. "You must just be coming on shift."

Crap. Work. "Yes, I should get going before they send a search party out for me." Or Ramona hunted me down herself. I'd have to stop in the bathroom first and check how blotchy my face was. I might need a cold-water splash. "Um . . . thank you."

"Anytime. Oh, and, Madison," she said as I rushed to the door. "Get your money's worth out of Teller. Every penny."

CHAPTER FOUR

Teller

I let myself in through the front door of the bar. It was just after one on a Friday, and the nagging sense I should've waited wouldn't leave me. Madison had said she was working the weekend and not to come before now. Technically, I should be fine. But hell. Didn't she need more sleep?

I lowered my toolbox to the floor. I had more supplies in the box of my pickup. Over the last few days, while I'd had some downtime in the office, I'd researched contractors, cabinetry suppliers, and renovation concerns on old buildings.

The main conclusion I had come to was that this place shouldn't be returned to its former glory. It should be restored farther back, to when the old brick walls could be shown off. The place should have new light fixtures that complemented the original look instead of the cheap, small-town-bar appearance Scooter had maintained. It hadn't been his fault a previous owner had slapped on whatever cheap woodwork had been available, but since Scooter had uncovered some of the beauty underneath with his destruction, it'd be a shame if Madison covered it back up again.

I went to a wall and ran my hand over the exposed brick. A few nicks had been taken out in some spots, but it added to the allure.

A door squeaked open and I leaned over to catch her attention. Madison exited the bathroom in nothing but underwear and a bra. I tried to duck back, but my boot scraped on the floor and she spun with a yell.

"Oh my god!" She held her hands in front of her black sports bra, dropped them down to cover the triangle her pink underwear made, then up again. "Shit. I forgot you have keys." She pushed back into the bathroom.

"Ain't nothing I haven't seen before," I called, and winced when I heard myself. *She* wasn't someone I'd seen before. From her powerful body, lined with muscle and generous padding in all the right places, to the way her hair cascaded over her shoulders, thick and wavy, no. I'd have remembered someone like her.

A guy could bury his hands in that hair, and those curves? Her thighs were lush while still looking like they could crush a guy's head. My heartbeat pounded behind my zipper as I tried to control the lust coursing through my veins.

How long had it been since I'd had my head between a woman's legs?

My brain quit working, overwhelmed with images of her long limbs and breasts that'd fill my hands.

The door cracked open. "Can you turn around?"

"Like a full three-sixty?" I should've been a gentleman and put my back to her, but the desire to see her again was too strong.

A moment of silence went by. "Seriously?"

I chuckled and turned to face the front of the place. "Done. Your modesty is once again safe."

She scurried to the room at the end of the hall. *One, two, three, no erection for me.* I steadily inhaled and exhaled. When I had myself under control, I continued to roam the room, making mental notes of what I wanted to talk to Madison about. Mostly, it helped me tuck away the idea of that waterfall of thick hair draped over my chest.

She swept out of the back room, dressed in jeans and a hastily buttoned flannel. Did she realize she was one button off? She was putting a loose braid in her hair as she walked down the long hallway. "Sorry. Um . . . maybe you should call before you come."

"And miss my chance at seeing that again?" I tsked. "It'd be a shame. Besides, I don't have your number."

She stared at me, studying me like she hadn't understood a thing I'd said. "Okay . . . I can give you that easy enough." She narrowed her eyes. "My *number*," she clarified.

"Like I said, damn shame. I know you insist it's none of my business, but I guess I'm a nosy bastard. Why are you staying here?"

"I'm selling the house." Her scrutiny increased. "Didn't you know that? Your mom did."

"You talked to Mama?" The thought pleased me. I couldn't figure out why. I should be worried Mama had gotten a tongue-lashing from Mads, but no. Madison only stuck up for herself when she thought she needed to, and Mama would never make her feel that way.

Her expression turned guarded. "She was at the home."

"Ah. Poker night. Back to the sale—no. I didn't know. Can't you stay at the house until closing?" The old Townsend home up for sale should've been bigger news. Though people had seen Madison going to Sal's office and speculated. The news *hadn't* come from any For Sale signs in the yard.

"Convenience," she said lightly and tied off the end of her hair. She left the braid hanging over her shoulder. "So. Where do you think we should start?"

Her house was a sensitive topic. Knowing her family, the place likely wasn't full of happy memories.

I looked from her to the room in the back. If she got off work at seven, then had to decompress, she would be lucky to get to sleep by eight. If she woke at one, then I had two questions. "Do you shower here?"

The color in her cheeks deepened. "I do that at work before I come home."

Made sense. So that left the other question. "Have you eaten yet?"

She frowned. "I'm fine."

Her stomach chose that moment to growl.

She wasn't going to work short on sleep and with no food. Not on my watch. "Come on. Let's grab something to eat."

She drew back, offended. "I have food."

I scanned the place. "There a kitchen hiding somewhere?"

"It's been built over. It's now the storeroom." She folded her arms in front of herself, which only made me recall how full her tits had been in that bra. "I have a microwave and a dorm fridge."

It'd been never since I'd lived on so little. What in the hell could she make with that? Little plastic tubs of food that barely tasted better than the container it was nuked in? "Well, I'm hungry." That wasn't a lie. We'd had a breakfast potluck at the office, so it'd been hours since I'd eaten.

"So go eat. You make your own hours."

Her brush-off scraped against my skin. Dammit. I dug out my phone. "What do you want from Curly's?"

"Nothing."

"If you don't tell me, then I'm ordering for you and you can't complain about my choice."

"I'm not eating your food."

"I'm ordering for us."

"Teller."

"I always get a steak. Curly can be a dick, but he knows his beef." I tapped in my order and doubled it. "I requested extra buns."

"I'll eat my own stuff."

I hit the button to finalize the order. "Too late. Two rib eyes will be on their way as soon as I contact Seb." I typed out a quick text to him.

She gawked at me. "Who's Seb?"

"A kid I hired as my personal DoorDasher. He does all the runs for Copper Summit in the summer. I have him on retainer."

"You have food delivery on retainer?" She shook her head, erasing her incredulous expression. "I'm not taking your food."

"My treat."

"No."

My patience snapped. There was being stubborn and there was hurting herself, and I was too damn certain of what she was doing. I advanced on her. "If you're not turning that sweet ass of yours around to get more sleep, then the least you can do is eat a good meal."

Her red lips turned down on *sweet ass*. "I said I have stuff to eat here." She stood her ground, and normally, I admired that about her. If she continued, I'd hold her down to eat and food would be the last thing on my mind.

"Is it good quality shit that'll help offset the four hours of sleep you're short?"

"I-it's fine," she sputtered.

"Is it meat?" I asked, towering over her. I lowered my voice since I didn't want to be intimidating, but I also didn't want to back away and lose that soft, linen-fresh scent of hers. "High-quality protein? Seasoned to perfection and cooked to a perfect medium rare? Do you have sweet potatoes with bourbon cinnamon butter? How 'bout steak fries? Because I got those too. And remember, extra buns."

Her stomach growled and she scowled.

"Thought so," I said, triumphant.

She licked her lips, and goddamn, her tongue was almost my undoing. I was close enough to capture her mouth, to pull her to me and bend her back until she completely submitted to me.

"Why are you doing this?" she asked in a ragged voice.

I snapped my restraint back in place. A missing puzzle piece she seemed to unknowingly control. "Doing what?"

"Being nice to me. I hired you for a job. That's all. And I need it done as soon as possible."

The distrust in her gaze unraveled me. So did her dread, like she was just waiting to be hurt or insulted in some way. I didn't draw back. I leaned in closer, my mouth to her ear. "Because you're worth being kind to, Mads, and I don't care how tangled our history is, I'll never treat you otherwise."

A nervous breath stuttered out of her. "You don't like me."

I pulled away far enough to look her in the eye. "Seems that I like you just fine, Mad Maddy."

She jolted like that nickname was a downed wire, and the green in her hazel eyes glowed brighter. "Don't call me that."

"Why not? Mad Maddy's cheeks get flushed and her eyes spit fire. I'm starting to wonder if people piss you off because you're quite the sight to behold when you're angry. Some guys might wonder where else you express that passion."

Her mouth dropped open.

Shit. I went too far.

"So whatdya say? Can we be friends or something?" The word was heavy on my tongue. *Friends*. I was starting to have some unfriendlike thoughts about Madison.

"My last friend was pretending so she could keep me busy while Wendi fucked my husband." Betrayal and embarrassment shimmered in her gaze. "It was Riley."

Shock zapped me. Goddamn, I was not prepared for that confession. How much shit had this woman gone through? She might be tough as steel, but she was full of dents.

"Jesus. She did that?" It was everything I could do not to trace my fingers down her cheek. She didn't wear makeup and she didn't have to. She had cheeks that reddened with a thought, and thick, dark eyelashes. Was her skin as soft as it looked?

She nodded, pain scrawled all over her pretty features. "So you see why I don't have friends."

If I could, I'd massage each tense muscle she had. Yet she was on edge. If I put one fingertip on her, she'd shut down. She'd think I was using her like everyone else. "What about Ruby?"

"I hired her for consulting."

"But you're friends."

She screwed her face up, and damn it was cute. "No."

The trust issues went deep. She trusted me as a Bailey and with the bar. She didn't extend that feeling to her, but I wouldn't give up. I'd start with a damn good meal. "So you gonna eat my food then? We both have some long hours of work ahead and I need to talk to you about what we're doing with this place."

Her frown was back, like it was her default expression. "I thought I told you that I wanted it restored to the way Scott had it."

"You did, but I have some ideas. It's not what you paid the big bucks for, but I'm asking you to hear me out. Just give me a little time to explain."

She ran her hands over her braid, but the heaviness of her expression lifted. "Is this the first time you had to ask for a girl's attention? You gonna be okay?"

A smile played over her lips, and I lifted a brow at her levity. Now that was more like it. "I have four sisters. I know what it's like to be ignored by women."

She laughed, a pleasing chime that should be heard

more. "Why don't you program my number into your phone so you don't walk in on me again?"

"You're not giving me a good reason to give you my number."

She rolled her eyes, but I caught the smile ghosting over her lips.

"I can walk around in my underwear to make it even," I offered.

Her blush returned. "I don't believe in an eye for an eye. Keep your pants on."

"If you say so." I didn't quit grinning.

She couldn't hold back her smile. "Fine. Tell me what you're thinking."

My current thoughts would make her demand the keys back and lock me out forever. As it was, I wasn't sure what to do about the desire flooding my brain and my body. Madison didn't just possess an underappreciated sexiness that her fucknut of an ex-husband had squandered, but she also had a personality I was quickly becoming obsessed with.

No, I wouldn't tell her what I was thinking. Because I wasn't sure myself.

Madison

All weekend I had pondered Teller's ideas. They were good ones. He'd painted a picture of a bar that would still fit the name and brand of Flatlanders Prohibited but would also give it an inviting character. If I approved some of Teller's suggestions, Flatlanders would no longer only appeal to the dive bar crowd. It'd be worthy of being featured in those tourist packets distributed by the chamber of commerce. Flatlanders would be right next to Copper Summit as a sight to see.

Ultimately, his plan to leave the brick exposed and restore the floor wouldn't take more work and it wouldn't add more cost. Since he would have to pull out the remnants of the booths to clean and inspect the brick, I'd said I'd think about it. I couldn't sense an ulterior motive, but I had learned that lesson the hard way. The guy worked fast. He was nearly done dismantling and hauling out the old twenty-four-foot bar and the busted shelving for the bottles.

I had a decision to make.

I didn't work tonight. I was on my stretch of days off, and fatigue pulled at me. I hadn't slept today, pulling an all-nighter so I could sleep tonight. Though lately, I could probably sleep anyway. Sometimes, even the curb looked comfortable.

Teller was hauling scraps of wood out the propped-open front door. He'd stripped down to his black T-shirt, and with each board he held, his biceps bulged bigger than ever. A squiggly vein lined each side. I wanted to trace it with my tongue.

I'd been fine admitting that Teller was an attractive man. Tall. Bearded. Fit. It didn't help that he was also a nice guy. Now he was being nice to me.

Because you're worth being kind to, Mads.

He was more than kind. He saw *me*, and that was terrifying. The worst thing I could do was admit I was attracted to him. Maybe I could do it in an observant, objective way.

No. How I felt around him was very, very subjective,

thanks to him asking about my sleep, ordering extra buns on top of the most amazing meal I'd had in months, maybe years, and then dropping off a small pack of red apple jelly beans on the desk in the office without needing thanks or fanfare.

That man was supposed to be infuriating. I wanted to hate him, to lump him in with everyone else who'd been an asshole to me in my life, but he was inching himself out of that category, and he probably wasn't even aware he was doing it. He was just being nice. Like a goddamn Bailey.

I went out the door and swept up the mess behind him, making sure each nail was picked up. I refused to be blamed for someone getting a flat tire driving by my bar. My phone buzzed, but I didn't look. My job likely wanted me to fill in again, and while the extra paycheck would be helpful, along with the overtime pay, I was running on empty.

Teller and I continued to work and my phone stayed quiet. Unusual, if it was one of the nurses desperate for a CNA. I pulled out my phone.

Ruby: If you're not already, you should take pictures of the process so you can make teaser posts leading up to your reopening.

Ruby, Teller's soon-to-be sister-in-law, worked in the marketing department of Copper Summit, and she'd given me some tips when I'd been trying to help Scott pull this dump off the ground. She was nice too, with a youthful innocence and enthusiasm that made me feel ancient.

"Hot date calling?" Teller asked as he swaggered back in from hauling out a load.

I shot him a playful glare. I was getting accustomed to his teasing, taking it less personally each day. He did it with everyone. The postal guy had stopped in the other day to drop off a load of bills and estate papers I still had to settle for Scott, and Teller had joked around with him. I'd never seen a postman giddy, but he'd about skipped out of here after some attention from my bachelor.

"It's Ruby." I tucked my phone away. "She said I should take some pictures through this whole process for a grand reopening campaign."

"When is the grand reopening?"

I lifted a shoulder and looked around the empty place. "I dunno."

His brows crashed together. "Do you have a strategy for opening? Events to hold to get people in?"

"The same regulars will probably come back." They'd been enough to keep Scott afloat. Somewhat.

He blinked. "You need a plan, Maddy."

I stiffened. "I have a plan."

"Me?"

I ground my molars together but couldn't bring myself to look at him. I wasn't done taking everything personally. "I'll figure it out." A tiny pile of dust gave me enough of an excuse to turn away from him to clean it up.

His boots were heavy behind me. "If I'm your plan, can you let me help?"

I didn't answer. I squatted to capture the barely perceptible debris with my dustpan. I nearly ran into him when I turned to find a trash bag to dump my pile into.

He didn't move. "I've been making and selling spirits over half my life. Almost as long as ranching. I help out with the animals, but my day is spent keeping the doors of Copper Summit open."

"This isn't Copper Summit." I tried to sidestep around him, but he did the same, blocking my path.

"I'd hate to do all this work and then the business flounders because there's no business strategy in place."

"I said I'll figure it out."

"I can help." Frustration filled his voice.

"I don't need your help."

"Not to boast, but I'm an expert at this, Mads."

The fine wire of my patience snapped and embarrassment flooded in. "And I do what? Just clean butts and bedpans?"

Confusion filled his expression. "No—"

"I'm just the help? I'm supposed to shut up and spoon-feed someone's loved one until you're all done?"

"I didn't say—"

"And then what? You tell everyone how you did all the work because I was too inexperienced?"

"Madis—"

"I might not have finished college, but I'm not incompetent." Heat burned across my eyes and my vision got blurry. Dammit. Crying around his mom was different and it'd been about my brother. *This* was my humiliation out there for Teller to witness.

He gripped my shoulders. "I never said you were incompetent." He ducked his head to look me in the eyes. "I want to work *with* you, not bulldoze over you."

I fought back the tears, but one escaped. The hot drop rolled down my cheek. Teller captured it with the pad of his calloused thumb, a gentle touch, but brushfire swept through my body. *More.*

I tried to draw back, but his hold was too firm. Both hands were back on me and he wasn't releasing me. Nor was I fighting to be set free. I was really damn tired, and I soaked in all sorts of comfort from him touch.

"Can we talk about this?" he asked gently. "Like really talk, where I tell you what I can offer and you consider it while trying like hell to keep that impressive baggage of yours from interfering?"

"Impressive baggage?" Apt description.

"Listen to me, Madison." His voice was a low growl. "I'm not any of them. The people who hurt you. We had some issues, but you and I are in a new place, and they're not with us."

Tension vibrated through my body. I wanted to put miles between me and him, but I also desperately wanted to close the last few inches between us. "I know," I said quietly.

I'd bought Teller for fifty grand, and he hadn't gotten a cent of that money. He probably didn't need it, but that was beside the point. He was working for free. For charity. Also, for me. I was a charity case whether I liked it or not.

I could set some of my baggage aside and quit tripping over it. He deserved somewhat of an explanation. I licked my suddenly dry lips. His gaze dropped down to my mouth, tracking my tongue. The air between us thickened, but it had to be my nerves.

I swallowed the lump in my throat. "Do you know why I didn't go to nursing school with Wendi?" She had gotten her degree and moved back to Bourbon Canyon to work at the clinic. To date Teller.

He shook his head. It was still the two of us, standing in the middle of the bar. The sun was dropping lower in the sky outside. It'd be dark soon.

"I met Damien my sophomore year." Heat wicked up my neck. My cheeks would be blazing soon. "He was a poli-sci major and he had plans for law school. I was . . . " Enamored. Starry-eyed and infatuated. "Impressed. He was nothing like what I had grown up with. The more serious we got, the more we talked about the future. Planned it out. Including debt."

Anger blew his pupils. "He convinced you not to finish school so he could afford to go."

"I told him I'd make good money as a nurse. It's why I picked that profession—I could get away from home and work anywhere. But he claimed we'd have two large student loans before he even got into law school." I fisted my hands. "I was so proud of going to college, but I had no help. We were newlyweds and the debt was scary."

It had been nothing like what I'd been left with in the divorce. The school loans were considered our debt.

"So I quit and worked as a CNA instead, plus picking up odd jobs here and there." I flexed my hands and fisted them again. "Then, after my divorce, I tried to help Scott with this place, but he knew better. He always knew better."

"Why didn't you stand up to him like you do everyone else?"

"He's my brother. He helped me after I moved home." Scott had been the only one there for me after the divorce. He'd found me a cheap rental and finally let me help him with Flatlanders' social media and a little more.

"You should've been free to tell him that he wasn't listening to you."

My temples throbbed. "Once you quit thinking my family is like yours—"

"Jesus, all I'm saying is that you make yourself heard. There's a reason you earned the name Mad Maddy—"

"Don't use that name." It made what he said before sweep through my head. Made me wonder if he was one of the guys who wanted to know where else I was passionate.

He stepped closer. My chest was nearly touching his. "Maybe if you heard it more, you wouldn't lose your temper each time someone said it. *Mad Maddy*."

"Stop it."

"Mad Maddy." He dropped his voice to a low level that vibrated right through my belly, lighting up nerves along its path. "Mad Maddy. Mad Maddy."

"Knock it off." My demand lacked force. He could tell me to fuck right off in that voice and I'd ask him to say it again.

He lowered his head, his lips a whisper from mine. "Mad Maddy." The slight tickle of his breath along my skin filled me with an aching need. "Mad Maddy," he said with a whisper. "Is that better?"

"No." My answer came out hoarse. It was not better. My breasts ached and my heart beat between my goddamn legs. I was horny. Because of him. "You need an annoying nickname."

"I look forward to what you come up with, Mad Maddy."

"Oh my god, Teller—"

His lips brushed against mine, the softest of touches, a slight tickle from his beard, and my vocal cords froze. I couldn't speak. I couldn't move. He added more pressure and a whimper escaped me, going right into him.

I could crawl onto him, into him, just to get more. *More*.

A horn blared outside, and I jumped away from him with a gasp. "What are you doing?"

What was *I* doing? I hadn't smacked him away as soon as he touched me. I'd wanted it. Dammit, I'd been dreaming of it if I had to be blunt with myself, and I had to be. Teller had nothing to lose. I'd lost almost everything already. I couldn't risk the rest.

I pressed my fingers to my temples. "You can't do that again."

"I'm sorry." He folded his arms and dropped his chin.

I tried to summon rage. He'd kissed me without asking.

Could he do it again?

Crap. I already couldn't quit thinking of him. Now I wished he'd done more than put his mouth on mine. I had a lot of other ideas. No. This wouldn't do. "It's over."

"Mad—"

I smashed my hand against his mouth, his whiskers scraping against my palm, sending shivers over my skin. His dark brows skyrocketed.

"Don't you dare call me that again." My voice was the only part of me that was steady.

His blistering hot tongue licked against my skin. I yelped and jumped back, cradling my hand against my chest like he'd burned me—and I liked it.

His grin was shameless. "I was going to say Madison."

The teasing flipped me around and turned me inside out. I couldn't take it. "Give me your keys. You're done here."

"No, I'm not."

My blood pressure crept higher. "I'm in charge."

"Then you know you can't fire me. I'd hate to tell Wilna I couldn't fulfill the deal and she had to give the fifty grand back."

Damn. The money. The work. There was so much more to do. "You can't kiss me again. You can't touch me again."

Instead of looking ashamed, his expression turned smug and his goddamn eyes twinkled. "I won't—unless you beg me to."

I scoffed, but he didn't laugh. He was serious. As if I'd beg. A tremor raced down my spine and my lips still tingled.

"I'm finishing this job," he said with a note of finality. "I'll do the work however you want, and I won't interfere—"

"Ha!"

The corner of his mouth lifted. "As long as we understand each other. I'll be back tomorrow. I just ask one thing."

"I can't wait to hear it." I managed to sound derisive instead of breathy. My mind wanted to be guarded; my body wanted to hear exactly what that one thing was.

"You think about what I said." He spread his arms wide and all I could do was look at his body. "This place is yours. You said you didn't want to be dictated to by others anymore. Then don't be. You can turn the building into anything you want. Is that really Flatlanders?" A mischievous glint lit his dark eyes. "Mad Maddy."

That low growl. I almost moaned.

He strode toward the front door, his boots hitting nice and steady. And then he was gone, leaving me alone in a building that could be anything. Unlike me.

CHAPTER FIVE

Teller

"That place could be anything." I paced in front of Tenor's desk. On the other side of the wall of windows, the distillery was bright. Sunlight filtered from the many windows around the building. It wasn't five o'clock yet, but I had to leave soon. If I sat at my desk, I'd nod off. After a restless night of sleep, worrying that I'd over stepped— No, I had pushed it and I knew it.

It would have been easier to stop breathing than it would've been to not kiss her. Yet I worried I'd lost the trust I was trying to build with her.

The taste of her though. She'd had a handful of jelly beans before I'd kissed her, and she'd been a sweet dessert I wanted to devour. A mere whisper of a touch, and it had me wound up a million different ways inside.

"She doesn't want it to be anything," Tenor said for probably the third time.

"The building has it all. Do you remember, before Scooter put in a bar, that place was a restaurant?"

The corner of his mouth twisted up. "One we feared getting hepatitis in. That's why it was shut down."

I sank into the chair across from his desk. "No, it was closed because the guy who bought it from the original owner had a record."

Tenor snapped his fingers. "That's right. He was a sex offender, and he was hiring nothing but fifteen-year-old girls. Scooter got a helluva deal on that place."

I grunted. "She doesn't want to run a bar."

"What makes you think that?"

"There's no passion."

He pushed his glasses up. "And you know what she's like when she's passionate?"

She got a flush on her cheeks, and the more worked up she was, the farther down her neck it went. Those hazel eyes of hers spit fire, just like they had each time I had said her hated nickname. Only she didn't hate it. Not when I said it. And that was what she disliked. Her blush told me so.

Tenor sat forward, his mouth dropping open. "You and Madison?"

"No." I laughed. If Tenor had seen the way she'd leaped away from me, he'd chortle too. "I've just gotten to know her. She's no-nonsense and she's defensive as fuck, but there's something she'd rather do in life. She's never had a choice, but she does now. The bar is stripped down, but it's got an office and bathrooms. It's as close to a lump of clay as it can be."

"So what would the obstacle be?" He scratched the back of his neck. "The two biggies for people are time and money."

"She works long damn hours at the home, but she has a stretch off. If she wanted to open a bare-bones bar, she could do it before your wedding."

"So it's money."

"She paid fifty grand for me." And she'd said it was so she wouldn't get screwed over. Had she worried about hemorrhaging cash for poorly done jobs? Or that she'd get overcharged? Most people worried about that, but they didn't go and buy a bachelor to coordinate much of the work. "If she'd ask me for advice, I'd be able to help her better. Fuck, I'd be able to help at all."

A slow grin spread across Tenor's face. "She's hurting your pride left and right."

"No." Yes, goddammit. I had so many damn ideas. We could talk budget, business strategy, and goals. Yet she kept me damn near in the dark. Did she even have a plan beyond Make It Flatlanders Again?

Tate pushed into the office. "Thought I'd catch you two. Scarlett's been asking wedding questions and I don't have answers."

Tenor's grin stayed in place. Mention of Ruby or his upcoming wedding tended to do that. I'd been the lone single Bailey for almost two years and I hadn't gotten less envious of my stupidly happy youngest brother.

"Just show up," Tenor said. "That's all we're asking."

Tate's mouth flattened into a line. "And you are clearly not married with kids yet. You can't just show up, and Scarlett will sit out the end of the world if she doesn't have clear instructions for who needs to wear what."

Tenor and Ruby's wedding was next month, but it was purported to be a low-key affair. Instead of having it at Mama's place, they were doing it at Tenor's house. I was wearing what I'd worn to the rest of my siblings' weddings. They'd all been casual affairs at their homes or at Mama's.

"Two o'clock." Tenor hooked his fingers behind his head and reclined in his chair. "Church casual since I know Scarlett won't feel comfortable sending kids to a wedding in jeans. Curly's is catering so Mama doesn't have to cook."

"Mama wants to cook," I said.

"I know, but then everyone will be rushing to help her with food. Ruby wants relaxed. She wants guilt-free." His grin widened. "She only wants me."

I didn't bother holding back my groan. "Fuck, you're pathetic."

Tate slapped me on the back. "You will be too one day. Happens to all of us."

It had happened to all of them. Every single one of my siblings. Even some of the fosters my parents had cared for over the years, like Myles. But the one time I'd been in love, my heart had gotten ripped out, and Madison had known before me.

"Teller's pissy because Madison won't stroke his big, thick ego." Tenor's eyes twinkled. Bastard.

Tate's laugh boomed through the room. The packagers downstairs and across the building could probably hear him over the whirring of the equipment.

"You both suck," I muttered. "I'm just trying to do the job she bought me for."

"You want to do it like *you* want it done," Tenor pointed out again.

"Ah." Tate's shit-eating grin was still in place. "You're not the boss over at Flatlanders."

"It shouldn't be Flatlanders," I snapped. "They put a

dress on ET, but he was still a wrinkled little bugger. Giving Flatlanders a facelift won't help. People will show up wanting the dive bar. They'll expect Allen to serve them and not give a fuck. Everyone's going to expect mixed drinks that have only a drop of soda, but Allen moved to Washington. Madison is too smart to load her drinks up with the most expensive ingredient, so at the minimum, she'll charge more. And that'll piss people off from the start."

I was breathing heavily after my rant.

Tate crossed his arms and studied me. Tenor had unhooked his hands from behind his head and leaned forward. They exchanged a look, then pinned both of their stares back on me, each with a brow raised.

"What?" My crankiness knew no bounds.

"You're worried about her," Tenor said.

Irritated, maybe. Frustrated. Vexed. Yes, I was goddamn worried. "The bar isn't going to run like it used to, but she's convinced it will."

"You don't give a damn about the bar," Tate said. "You're worried about her."

"Why wouldn't I be?"

"It's Madison," Tate insisted, his gaze appraising.

"I never hated her." My attitude during my run-ins with her over the last few years streamed through my head.

Tenor tapped his fingers against his desktop. "Everything you said rubbed her the wrong way."

Tate smirked. "But I think you want to rub her the right way."

"Jesus, Tate." The sight of her in nothing but a sports bra and underwear flashed in my head. There'd be so many right ways with a body like that. She was strong, and for once, I wouldn't have to hold back— No. I was not looking for a fuck, and definitely not with the prickliest woman I'd ever met.

My brothers shared another knowing look.

"You two are pissing me off," I growled.

Tenor kept tapping his fingers.

I pushed out of my chair and stomped toward the door, but Tate sidestepped, blocking me.

"Let's talk about this," he said gently.

I straightened to my full height, but that was the same as Tate's and he'd never been intimidated by me a day in his life. "There's nothing to talk about."

"You care about Madison and you're worried she's making the wrong decision." His calm tone should be infuriating, but goddammit. He was right.

"I know she is." I ran my fingers over my short beard. "This makes me sound like a prick, but she doesn't know enough about the business to pull a dive like Flatlanders out of the hole it had likely been operating in."

"She had enough money to buy you," Tenor said.

"Life insurance," I answered.

"Didn't any go to her nephew?" Tenor asked.

I shrugged. "Maybe there's a trust or something."

"Everything was left to Madison?" Tate said, a crease forming across his brow. "The bar, the life insurance, and even their parents' old place? From what I heard, a lot of people are pissed they didn't know it was for sale before she accepted an offer."

All of her neighbors would've put an offer in. "Who's she going through?"

Tate's lips pressed together like he tasted something sour. "Sal Longwood."

"Fuck." Sal was slimier than a northern pike and his

teeth were just as sharp. For someone who didn't trust easily, she'd gone for the least trustworthy guy. "Why the fuck would she use him?"

"Wasn't he friends with her dad?" Tate asked. He thought for a moment, then shook his head. "I'd have to ask Mama."

"I've gotta talk to her." I tried to step around Tate, but he stopped me by pushing his fingers into my chest.

He didn't let me pass him. "You're going to go charging in there, demand to know why she's working with a sleazeball like Sal, rant about the mistakes she's making with the bar, and then you're going to wonder why the hell she's upset and won't talk to you?"

My chest rose and fell under his quelling hand. That had already been happening, minus the Sal business. "Maybe."

"Remember when Madison's dad lost his shit at a parade and punched a horse?" Tenor asked.

How could I forget? Punching a horse had made Karl Townsend an instant villain, as if we hadn't known he was before that. The guy had yelled instead of talking. He had sworn like he'd been getting paid per "fuck." Several businesses in town had banned him from entering, thanks to his legendary temper.

Tate grunted. "He said we shouldn't complain since he hit animals instead of his worthless kids."

I had winced at that, in the middle of the parade with over half the town watching. A young, doe-eyed Madison had shrunk against her mom, only to be shooed away.

Well, hell. "She had a shitty upbringing. No wonder she isn't staying at that house."

"She might need the money." Tate scratched his beard. "I hate to spread gossip—"

I guffawed. "Oh my god, you love it. Don't think I haven't seen you hanging out in the gas station, getting your morning coffee so you can keep tabs on the town."

The gas station had a breakfast nook that was full of old farmers and ranchers and retired business folk each day. Sometimes, I'd been half tempted to linger myself.

Tate smirked. "Dad used to say if you wanted real news, find out where the retired people hang out." His grin turned affectionate. "Scarlett also pays in kisses per rumor. But anyway, when Madison moved back to town, the old bank president commented that she wouldn't find a place to live. Her husband left her with a shitload of debt."

"School loans." Since the asshole had let her support him through law school.

Tate nodded. "That and credit cards. Auto loans. He said the asshole was driving a seventy-thousand-dollar truck."

"Bet the fucker is still driving it too." Madison's old beater had probably come off the family property. "Divorcing a lawyer couldn't have ended well for her."

"Ruby probably knows her better than anyone in town," Tenor said, "but she says Madison is hard to get to know. She's all about business and won't share much of herself."

Guilt wound its way through my gut, leaving an inky feeling behind. She had no one, and she'd been used and discarded by everyone. I was a bossy asshole who made her defensive.

How did I change that?

Madison

A small bag of root beer jelly beans sat on the pool table. Teller had pulled up two of the nonbusted barstools for us to sit on. He had papers spread out on the green felt, each sheet filled with his chicken scratch.

That was too harsh a term. His handwriting was strong with slashes. Even his print resonated confidence. This man didn't question a single thing he did.

"So those are our options for plumbers." He shuffled another sheet of paper on top of his pile. It listed plumbing companies, one local, two from Livingston, and three from Bozeman. None of them had called me back when I had tried to get someone out to help replace leaky faucets in the house before I put it on the market.

One of the guys in Livingston had told me that he wouldn't touch my house if my mom crawled to him on her hands and knees to apologize. Another said she still had outstanding invoices my mom had disputed.

I studied the list, rife with rates and timelines. "You didn't tell them where it was for, did you?"

"That's why there's only six."

He'd used his name, and he'd probably done it without second thought. For me. He'd do it for anyone, but he was here, throwing the Bailey name around for me.

He tapped another list. "Here are the electrician estimates."

I picked up that neat list, hyperaware of his proximity. The heat between us from yesterday was gone. He was professional, kind, and efficient. It was irritating.

I refused to become one of Teller's many fangirls, but here I was, wishing he'd look at me with a spark in his eye.

Dropping my attention to his notes on electrical estimates, I choked. "Oh my god. Are they rewiring the building?"

"No, it's just that expensive."

Despair weighed me down until I worried I'd crash through the wooden floor. The bathrooms would need new toilets, sinks, and partitions and cosmetic work. "What if they find issues while doing the work?" My question came out more frantic than I'd intended. I didn't have the funds for more. As it was, I was waiting for the house sale to close so I could have enough to cover what I needed. The money shuffle was the cost of bidding on Tenor.

His gaze stroked across my face. "You'll have to plan a buffer. Always overestimate because there will be delays and problems."

I sucked in a shaky breath. My stomach heaved. How the hell was I going to do this?

"You forget you paid a considerable amount of money for my work."

I wasn't forgetting much when it came to him. Most of it came back to me when I was trying to sleep.

He dug a small notepad out of the pocket of the flannel shirt he'd draped over the other end of the pool table. "I can replace toilets, Maddy. And sinks. I made a list of supplies I'd need."

"What about awful wallpaper that's probably been peed on?"

The corner of his mouth lifted. "I don't know about the women's restroom, but if pee is all that's on the walls of the men's room, I'll be surprised."

My laughter took some of my stress with it. Another reaction he didn't have a problem coaxing from me. "I didn't mean . . ." He'd been nothing but a decent man. He might've taunted me with Mad Maddy, but he'd left me wanting to hear him say it again. I thought I'd get thrown in jail if I heard someone utter that awful nickname at the wrong time, but now it turned me on. He might be a bastard for that, but only because I needed to sleep, not masturbate. "I didn't mean for this to be immense. Project managers make bank."

"I already make bank." He tossed the notepad onto his shirt. Then he pointed to the roof, the walls, and the floor. "The basics are good. The electrical hasn't caused issues up to this point, so I don't anticipate an electrician finding something. Same with the plumbing. This building has been through a lot, but it's been kept up."

The nerves in my stomach calmed. "I just need it to make money."

"Other than because life is expensive, is there another pressing reason?" He gathered up the papers with the estimates he'd collected like he was giving me space to answer. Or he was preparing to get his head bitten off.

I ran my bottom lip through my teeth, debating how much to share. His collection had to have taken a good couple of hours. I owed him something and I had little more than words. "Just Mom. Long-term care is ungodly expensive. It's why I used the fifty-grand for you. It'd buy only six months, and I needed long-term. But it's better than living with her again."

His look wasn't pitying, and for that, I was relieved. "I understand." He fell quiet for a moment, his forehead wrinkling. "Can I ask you something?"

I wanted to smooth my fingers over those lines across his brow. He was one of those guys who got better with age. If he started graying, there'd be a rash of silver fox obsessions popping up all over Bourbon Canyon. "I can't promise I'll answer."

He grinned and it shot straight to my belly, curling and winding, yearning for his touch. "If I know anything about you, it's that. Mad Maddy."

I shot him a glare, but I preened inside. He kept smiling and stoking that fire only he lit inside me.

"Why did Scooter leave everything to you? Or did Wendi and their kid get something?"

"Logan has a trust he'll get access to when he turns twenty-five." My brother had called me drunk one night after the divorce and told me that he was changing everything so I was his beneficiary. "I'd like to leave this bar for Logan when I'm gone."

"You miss him?"

"He's one of my only family members left." I had my nephew and my mom and that was all. "I wish I could spend more time with him, but I refuse to use him as a pawn in Wendi's games."

"Her games can wreck a person. I doubted my decisions when it came to women a long time after her. How could I have been so clueless?"

"Sex does that to a man." I was only half teasing.

"Did it to me then, and I'm not about to let it happen again."

"You've never let anyone close after her?" He'd asked probing questions and I'd told him none of it was his business. He had every right to do the same. Had he been struck with this same yearning to learn more when he'd been bugging me?

The shake of his head was small. "I went to the far extreme of no attachments until I had to finally admit that I was becoming the bad guy. Just because I claimed I didn't want commitment didn't mean that I wasn't fully aware the girl I was dating wanted more. Then when I finally did want more . . . Eh, it's a small town. The dating pool is a koi pond."

"Nothing but orange speckled fish?"

"Nice enough fish, but none I'd build a pond for in my backyard." Why was that so satisfying to hear? He glanced out the window. "It's getting late. Since tomorrow's Sunday, I can be back after I help with chores."

The reminder that he worked two jobs weighed on my conscience. "No rush. Really. You need to rest too."

He rose. "I get into trouble if I'm idle. That's what Mama used to say."

"Used to?"

He chuckled and I went to the front door to close the cheap-ass blinds I'd bought for the windows while we were renovating. A light rain fell outside and the streetlights glared off the pavement. I almost didn't want this night to end.

There was no almost about it. He'd leave for the night, but I'd sense his presence everywhere.

An engine revved from a pickup turning the corner.

A "woo-hoo" rang into the night a millisecond before something crashed through the window. I cried out and jumped back as glass rained down at my feet. Another crash sent me scurrying back. Then another. Something grazed my leg as I jumped back again. I hit a hard chest.

Teller gripped my shoulders and hauled me to the side, behind the protection of the door. He spun me around, held me at arm's length, and searched my body. "Are you all right? Did it hit you?"

I shook my head. My heart beat in my throat, a rapid thump that made it hard to speak. "N-no. I don't th- think so."

He dashed toward the door as the roar of the engine grew fainter.

Once again, glass covered the floor and there were gaping holes in the front windows. Three bricks rested among the shards. Someone had thrown them at my bar.

Just once, I wanted something in my life to go right. And if it went wrong, I didn't want Teller Bailey to witness it.

CHAPTER SIX

Teller

I sprinted outside in time to see a dark pickup with a dented rear fender fishtail around the corner.

"Fuck!" I raced inside.

Madison stared at the mess, her hands pressed to both sides of her head. Her eyes glistened. An angry red painted her cheeks. Her gaze jerked to mine and she trembled as she drew herself together, sucked in a deep breath, and puffed it back out. "I'll get a broom."

She stomped away, her shoulders drawn and her head down. I wish I'd gotten a plate number, but no such luck.

As I surveyed the damage, my heart sank. Two panes of glass had three large holes, and shards covered the floor. The third was untouched, but since they were all old, all three would likely have to be replaced to fit together and look decent.

Goddammit, she didn't have the budget for that.

I went to the broom closet by the bathrooms. As I got closer, her sniffles became audible.

I cleared my throat. She didn't want me to see her cry and I'd give her that. "We should call the police."

"No."

"Mad—"

"They won't do a damn thing but blame me." Her voice echoed loud from inside. "They'll ask what I did to piss someone off. They'll insinuate I asked for it."

Dammit, she was probably right. The history in this bar was too strong, and the police hadn't witnessed her devastated reaction or the way she was trying to hide how much it bothered her. "Hey, uh, I can call Tate and he can bring a couple of sheets of plywood—"

"No, it's fine. I can get some."

"Do you have a woodpile at your place, or is that getting sold with the house and property?" I hadn't meant to sound so sarcastic, but when she spun out of the closet, her eyes sparking, I was grateful I could give her a target.

"It's none of your—"

I crossed to her and gripped her shoulders. "Like it or not, *you* are my business. I'm not willing to leave you alone. I'm calling Tate, and we'll clean up until he gets here."

Her wide eyes took me in. I didn't let her go. It was all I could do not to hug her to me. Her fear, her despair, gutted me.

"It's late and he has kids." She gazed forlornly at the mess behind me.

Her consideration for my brother caught me off guard. Life had battered Madison but she was concerned about bothering someone else? I dropped my hands before she distracted herself by getting upset at me. "He won't mind. I'd call Tenor, but he lives farther out of town, and Tate's got nice wood."

A giggle burst out of her. She put the back of her hand against her mouth. "Stop it," she said against her skin.

Her emotions were all over, but I'd take manic giggles. "He'll say his wood's bigger than mine, but he's lying."

She gaped at me a moment before she turned around, her shoulders shaking. "This isn't the time to be funny."

"You're the one who's laughing. Do I need to change your nickname? Because Giggly Maddy doesn't have the same ring."

"Don't you dare."

I came up behind her and put my hands on her shoulders again. I could get used to touching her. "It's going to be okay."

She sighed. "It never is."

"I promise this time it will be."

"You can do a lot of things in this town, Teller Bailey, but you can't work miracles."

"So you admit I'm pretty impressive?"

"Oh god, will you stop?" She looked at me over her shoulder and grinned.

Relief pounded through me. For a woman who used to slither under my skin, her tears bothered me.

If I wasn't careful, the whole woman would become my weakness.

Madison

Tate helped Teller board up the windows, then left. I'd offered to pay him, but he'd given me an *Are you serious?* look that lacked the scandalized flare others usually gave me with the same stare. All he'd said was, "Put it on his tab and charge him double."

That was it. No bargaining. No negotiations. Tate had lent his assistance and I wasn't out any money or property. I tried to recall when that had ever happened in my whole life and blanked.

Teller inspected the secured plywood, then ran his boot over the floor like he was looking for specks of glass. We'd swept and vacuumed before Tate had arrived.

Turning, he pinned me with that dark, brooding gaze of his. "Grab your things. You can stay at my place."

Air whooshed out of my lungs. Stay with Teller? No. Absolutely not. "I'm fine here."

He knocked on the plywood. "This isn't enough security."

"It is," I insisted.

"Nope. Get your things. I'll wait." He strode toward me and my heart crawled into my throat. His powerful steps and intense expression said he wasn't going to drop the subject. "I'll do it for you if you don't."

Alarm spiked hot in my blood. "You are not going to touch my stuff." He didn't need to see how little I had.

"Then pack. You can follow me home." He got a sly grin. "Unless you've been spying on me and already know where I live."

"I have no idea where your cave is." I almost snorted. No Bailey lived in a hovel.

"You got somewhere else to stay?"

I had two things—this shitty bar and my pride. Tonight, I felt like both had been busted.

"Your mom's old place?" he asked quietly.

"The sale is pending. The place is cleaned and empty." Clean was a stretch, but I'd done what I could and it'd been enough to finally get an offer that stuck. I hadn't gotten a good deal, but at least I was getting something. Once the sale was done and Mom's care was secured, I could relax just a little.

"You're using Sal?"

My nod was jerky.

His lips flattened. "Look, I'm not leaving you alone here. We don't know if that was asshole kids or if someone has it out for you."

If Flatlanders wasn't being targeted because of me or Mom, then it could be lingering resentment toward my brother. Scott had burned bridges. The cause didn't matter. Dealing with the effect did.

"I don't need protection," I said stubbornly. I could not take more of Teller than I was already getting. Teller in his jeans and tight shirt working. Teller with his jokes and ready smile. Teller and those lips that had been on mine.

I went to sleep with his image burning the backs of my eyes. I did not need to see how he lived. I didn't need to witness the class divide between us. My family was on the wrong side of the tracks. The Baileys were in the castle on the mountain.

"All right." He scratched the side of his face with a knuckle, fatigue in his eyes.

Guilt returned, cloying and powerful. He'd been

working his ass off here, and he had other jobs, more obligations. "You should go. Get some rest."

"I'll crash on the pool table."

"What?" I screeched. My heart hammered against my ribs. Why wouldn't this guy give up on me? Everyone else would've by now.

"You're not coming with me, so I'll stay." The weary lines around his mouth grew deeper as he eyed the pool table behind me. "I can run home and clean up in the morning."

"You're not— You can't sleep here."

He went around me and ran his hand over the felt surface. "I might have to borrow a blanket."

The infuriating man hoisted himself onto the table and rolled to his side, his back to me.

"Just hit the lights when you turn in." He curled his arms under his head.

I wanted to run, but there was nowhere to go. Not only was Mom's place empty, but the water had been shut off. Same with electricity. I couldn't go there. I couldn't stay under that roof and get a lick of rest. Memories would assault me until I wished I was being haunted by real ghosts instead.

I exhaled a frustrated sigh. "I'll get my things."

CHAPTER SEVEN

Madison

To make this night sting more, I was in the same pickup as Teller. I'd hated to leave the bar looking like no one was there, so he'd told me to choose which pickup we took. He had a lot more to lose with his truck if it got vandalized. I'd barely be able to tell if anyone tampered with mine.

He could also buy another one easily enough, while I wasn't sure I'd get a loan, much less afford another monthly payment. Besides, I hadn't wanted him to see the holes in the seats, the sun-faded dash, or experience the lack of air-conditioning or a fan of any kind.

So I got to ride in luxury. God, I could sleep in this seat. It was like my ass was getting a hug. I rested my head against the passenger window and gazed at the dark trees we passed. It was better than watching his strong profile and wishing I could run my fingers over his short beard. Was it soft?

Not my business.

But I was his business. Why did that declaration make me want to smile and kick my feet?

He stayed quiet and so did I, but it was a peaceful silence. We were both tired, and I was anxious about seeing his house.

My family's ranch had been southeast of Bourbon Canyon, while Teller had grown up tucked into the valleys and foothills of the Bridger Mountains. All of the area surrounding Bourbon Canyon was gorgeous, but there was something extra special about the land the Baileys owned. Sprawling pastures, wide valleys, all backed by white-tipped peaks, there was nothing that wasn't breathtaking.

I hated how much I was anticipating viewing everything in the daylight tomorrow. The trees and grass would be a vibrant green. Some of the wildflowers would be blooming, a sprinkling of yellows, blues, and purples. I'd missed this during the years I had lived in Missoula. That area was gorgeous too, but I'd been working too much to enjoy it.

He turned down a long gravel drive that wound around what must be a draw in the landscape. Nothing but darkness was visible for several seconds before his yard came into view.

"Jesus," I breathed. The lone light in the yard illuminated a shop that had more aesthetic appeal than any home I'd ever lived in. The rectangular building had wooden supports around the entrance for an overhang that must shade a concrete pad. But it was his house that stole all my words.

Even in the dark, shadowed by the yard light, his log cabin stared back at me, majestic as fuck. Two levels lined with windows that must have such an impressive view he wouldn't need any artwork inside. Just nature, gazing right back. A wide porch ran the whole length from one end to the three-car attached garage.

He punched a button on the dash and the garage door closest to the house started to rise.

"Oh my god, are you serious?" A cynical laugh slipped out. "I've never even stayed in a hotel this nice." I thrust my hand toward the button he'd just pushed. There was no separate opener. "Or a vehicle."

"Didn't your ex get himself a vehicle fit for a lawyer?" He sounded like he knew Damien had done exactly that. I'd never gotten to drive it, and by then, he'd quit trying to take me on dates or spend much time with me.

"He likes to think he's a big deal, but even I know that he's the bottom of the corporate ladder."

"What do you mean 'even you'?" He pulled into the garage and hit the button again.

"You know what I mean," I said, irritated. I shouldn't have to explain it.

"You're an intelligent woman, Madison, and I think people underestimate you, but I don't think you should underestimate yourself." He killed the engine but didn't move to get out.

I wasn't some intern or whoever he mentored at Copper Summit. He didn't have to be patronizing. "You don't think I'm smart." My wonky sleep was charging up my crankiness, fueling the stress of being a pauper in this prince's carriage. "You think I'm doing the wrong thing with the bar. You think I'm wasting my time and my money, and who knows what else you think I'm doing wrong since you run a bourbon empire for a living.

And you also think I'm a fool because I'm not siphoning as much knowledge as I can from you."

I couldn't look at him, but the brush of heat against my cheek told me his gaze was on me.

"I think you've been dealt an awful hand," he said gently. "I think you're between a rock and a hard place and you can't see the way out. I think you haven't had the ability to ever bet on yourself because there's never been a safety net, so you're doing what's tried and true. I think you're not hitting me up for information because you're afraid I'll use your trust against you."

He said it matter-of-factly, but I heard the hint of consternation. Everyone trusted Teller Bailey.

Did I? His reaction after the bricks came through my windows came to mind. His first instinct had been to check on me. To cover me and protect me. To gauge my well-being. And then he'd continued to take care of me.

"It's not that I think you'll hold it against me." I twisted my fingers together until the bite of pain told me to keep talking. "If I turn Flatlanders into something else, what kind of business do you think I'll get? Who's going to buy cheerful cookies from Mad Maddy? Who's going to say, 'Hey, sorry for teasing you about your frayed pants that were too small in fourth grade? Can you put *Happy 6th Birthday* on the cake?' Or 'Remember when we pushed you into the mud puddle? Good times. I'd like four dozen snicker-doodles.' "

Surprise rippled through his expression. "You want to open a bakery?"

A bakery and candy shop. "It's just an example."

"A pretty specific one."

I loved baking. It was one of the few things I had

gotten compliments on in my life. "The world doesn't need more bakeries."

"That sounds like Damien's bullshit, and it's not allowed on my property or when I'm with you." Before I could react at his surge of protectiveness or tell him it was my dad's quote, he opened the door. "Let's head in. I'll show you the guest room."

I followed him through the pristine garage, which smelled faintly of paint and exhaust, into the house.

He continued through an entry that was larger than either of the bathrooms in Flatlanders. "You can leave your shoes on. Don't worry about it."

I did worry about it. The dark-stained hardwood floor was cleaner than the garage, and his boots left dusty prints. I wiped my feet off, taking in the sizable laundry room to my right and the expansive kitchen to my left.

"Seriously, Mads." He had stopped and was frowning at my shoes. "The vacuum will clean up the dust tomorrow. It runs every day at eleven."

Of course he had a robot vacuum. That wasn't his only toy. A double oven was proudly mounted on the far side of the kitchen with a microwave next to it. The matching French door fridge stood across from it and acres of counter space circled the room. In case that wasn't enough, an island with its own freaking sink bordered the dining room on the other side.

"Holy crap." The farther in I went, the more I spun in a slow circle to take it all in. A restaurant-worthy exhaust hood? Envy beat deep in my chest. Talk about the haves and have-nots. Teller had all the toys. "This kitchen is wild."

"I don't use it much."

"How could you not?"

"Cooking for one isn't a lot of fun." He opened a wide fridge door. "Are you hungry? Mama made me some smothered pork chops."

My stomach growled. The damn thing wouldn't shut up around him. "No, I'm good."

He arched a brow and cocked his head toward a rectangular table with a black resin strip down the middle. It was masculine and simple and fit the rest of the vibe around the place. He hadn't overdecorated, that was for sure. There were no stuffed animal heads mounted on the walls. My dad had loved to hunt, and while I didn't care about trophy heads, I hadn't liked them staring at me or the allergies I had developed.

"Sit," he commanded. "I'll heat up some food."

"I had dinner."

"We've been working all evening." He shrugged out of the red flannel he'd tossed on before we left the bar. He was still in a black shirt, but I'd never tire of that chest. "Besides, I've gotta ask you to hang out here for a while in the morning while I help with chores and haying." He sent me a sidelong glance like he was waiting for an argument.

I was supposed to be irritated. I had work to do at the bar and someone had just vandalized it. But his house was clean and quiet. All the chairs, tables, and windows were intact. His toilets and sinks probably weren't even cracked.

The peace soaked into my body and I craved more. "I won't steal your silver."

He flashed a smile that lit up the whole night. "I'd hate to have to frisk you." The deep timbre of his voice rumbled over all my nerve endings, caressing them and exciting them at the same time.

He saved me from making a fool of myself by turning back to the fridge.

I shamelessly wandered through the main level. A flight of stairs with the plushest carpet I'd ever seen flanked the other side of the kitchen wall. The carpet color was like cream and light gray had a baby, and the way it curled around each step reminded me of a shallow creek trickling over rocks.

Down a hallway next to the stairs were a few doors. Probably a bathroom and a den. His bedroom? My pulse sped up. Upstairs or down, how had I ended up this close to Teller Bailey's bedroom?

Teller appeared by the island, and I let out a startled cry. I slapped my hand over my racing heart. It wasn't just the surprise. He fit this house. It was like the place assembled itself around him. "How does such a big man move so quietly?"

"Dad was a mellow guy unless we made a lot of noise while hunting." He lowered his voice to a gruff growl. " 'Jesus, boys, there'll be no deer left in the western hemisphere if you clod around like that.' "

I smiled. I hadn't known Darin Bailey other than by reputation. Everyone had liked him except for my parents. Once I was older, I'd realized that was often a testament for the other party. "Your sisters didn't hunt?"

He shook his head. "They learned how, but they'd rather not hang out with 'a bunch of stinky guys' in a deer stand." He stuffed his hands in his pockets. "Time to eat."

I should be used to eating around Teller. He supplied me with jelly beans regularly, sometimes brought Curly's, or we each munched on our separate lunches and dinners when we could. This time was different. I was in his domain, and while he hadn't cooked for me, it was his personal food he was serving me.

I could not view it as more than it was. He was a nice guy. He'd no doubt fed every woman he'd brought over, only he hadn't directed them to a guest room and told them good night at the end of the meal.

Running my hand over the table, I sat. "I've always loved this style."

"Jonah made it."

Summer's husband made the most beautiful furniture. I'd never be able to afford his work.

Teller set a piping-hot dish down. When he took the cover off, I was greeted with smothered pork chops and cubed potatoes. Another dish of diced squash was next to it. Not even Curly's served food this good.

I accepted the dish from him. "I've admired the pieces he has in Eats and Seats." Jonah had been another guy Scott had disliked, but then Jonah and Teller used to be best friends.

"He's only getting better and more in demand since he doesn't have the time he used to."

A wistful hand wrapped around my throat. I didn't know Jonah or even Summer, but there was a time when I had hoped to be that happy couple growing a family. I'd been determined to do things differently. I'd be nothing like my mother, and Damien would be the opposite of my father.

Turned out, he'd been very similar. A user and a cheat.

I stabbed a potato. The buttery, savory flavor of the food carried me away. I moaned around my mouthful and shoved a forkful of pork chop in. "Oh my god. This is amazing."

Teller was frozen, his fork poised over his plate. Hunger raged over his face, but he paid no attention to the food, his focus on me.

Nervous, I concentrated on the meal in front of me. I had to be wrong. At the very least, he wasn't thinking about *me*. Teller was a flirt. He made everyone around him feel special. So in that regard, I wasn't special, but I was grateful I was no longer on the outside looking in.

After we were done eating, I helped him clean up the dishes and admired his dishwasher. He caught me inspecting it, gave me an amused twist of his lips, then left me alone to fondle his appliances.

"I didn't know you had a thing for ovens," he said.

"I have a major thing for ovens. Especially when you have more than one."

"A fan of multiples?" When I rolled my eyes, he smirked. "I can show you to your room." He went to the entry and retrieved the bag I had packed.

"Oh, I can carry that."

He ignored me and started for the stairs. I couldn't follow him. At the bottom, I toed out of my shoes.

He looked over his shoulder from three stairs up.

"I'm not touching that nice carpet with shoes," I explained.

"Suit yourself."

I did—I stared at his hard ass all the way up.

"I'm right here." He pointed to the room closest to the stairs before pushing into the door across from it. "And you're here."

That close?

"The next door is the bathroom. I have my own, so don't worry about running into me."

"I was more worried about your beard trimmings in the sink."

He winked at me. "That's not all I keep nice and trimmed." I made a choking sound and he laughed, dropping my bag on the bed. "Get some rest, Maddy."

I stood at the entrance. The room was as lush as the carpet. A queen-size bed with a polished wooden head-board darker than the logs of the exterior walls was surrounded by matching dressers and nightstands.

"Good night," I said woodenly, humbled by a room that was calling me poor.

He came within inches of me as he exited. "Sleep tight."

I would with that voice still in my head.

CHAPTER EIGHT

Teller

I stepped into Mama's house. Wynter was sitting on the counter with her feet swinging. Myles crowded close to her, and I was one hundred percent sure they'd been making out before I'd entered.

"Careful," I warned. "You might get pregnant again."

"Teller!" She laughed. Myles didn't bother to hide how satisfied he looked with himself.

Someday I'd quit being envious of my siblings, but today was not that day.

I dug through Mama's freezer just as Tate pushed through the back door.

"Did you get any answers on that brick business?" he asked.

Myles propped a hand on his hip but didn't leave my sister's side. The Bailey grapevine was in full force. I had kick-started it. News would be around town soon enough. The asshole who'd done it would be bragging, and then I would catch him. Madison didn't want to go to the police and I wouldn't charge through her boundary. But I could get around it.

"No," I said grimly, removing a tray of burritos. Would Madison moan over these like the pork chops last night?

"Did she go to the police?" Tate asked like he knew the answer.

"Doesn't trust 'em." I had to set the burritos on the counter before my fingers froze. "I didn't push her. It's not like they'll care about Flatlanders." The bar was probably the last business law enforcement wanted to see resurrected.

"Officer Tom is a good guy," Tate argued.

"But he's glad not to have so many drunk drivers to pull over with Flatlanders closed." I shrugged. "Plus, he's nice to us. How would he be to Maddy?"

Tate frowned, but Myles nodded. He'd had a different upbringing than us. Myles would get how Maddy felt.

"Myles has a window guy," Wynter offered, rubbing her husband's back. "He hooked us up with the house. He supplies all the McCountry Mansions getting built in Jackson Hole."

I had a McCountry Mansion.

"I'll send you his info," Myles said.

"I'll take it, but I'm not sure it'll be a good fit." My sister and brother-in-law hadn't built on a budget. The land had been gifted to Wynter by our father like mine had been. Myles was wealthy from his own distillery and investment endeavors. Madison didn't have their means.

Everyone was looking at me, waiting for an answer, but I wasn't outing Madison's financial issues.

"I'll check a little more local," I said.

Myles's eyes narrowed. "Smart to save on transportation costs."

Wynter gasped. "Ohmigod. I'm sorry. Of course she's going to be cost sensitive. She had a dump dropped on her."

"It's not that bad. I just wish she'd turn it into something she wants." She claimed the bakery was an example, but from the way she ogled my kitchen, I had my doubts.

"She was turning Flatlanders around," Wynter said. "Just by listening to Ruby and working on the socials. And I heard her cousin moved, so there'll be no bartender staring at boobs."

"I'm sure she'll do fine." I meant it, but I'd rather she worked on her own dreams, not someone else's. I picked up the burritos. "Anyway, when I get home I'll ask her about any changes she wants to make and get a budget for the windows."

Tate crossed his arms, Wynter's brows lifted, and Myles's lips quirked.

"When you get home?" Tate asked, the corner of his mouth tilting up.

"She couldn't stay there last night," I argued. "It's not safe."

"Wait." Wynter waved at the air in front of her like she was swiping my words out of the way. "She's living at the bar?"

Fuck. "She's private. I don't want to spread her business around."

"We're not just anyone," Wynter said, her mouth in a pout. "We don't spread other people's gossip. Outside our circle," she amended. "I heard she gave up her apartment, but what about her parents' place?"

"Sale's pending," Tate answered for me. "Not safe, huh? You keeping her nice and secure at your house?"

"It's not like that." Her wonder when she'd soaked in the guest room had eaten through my chest all night. I had built the home of my dreams, but I hadn't considered it'd be anyone else's fantasy. Yet I had wanted to give her a tour, to see the amazement on her face with each of my design and style choices. "She's going through a rough time, and I'm not letting her go back until windows are installed and a security system is put in."

"Might take a while," Wynter said with mock seriousness.

"Those windows don't get put in overnight," Myles added.

I waggled a finger between them. "That's not what it's like."

Tate clicked his tongue. "Better get those burritos back to your girl."

"She's not my girl." Those words tasted sour. Madison was strong and attractive. I couldn't keep my eyes off her butt, and the vision of her in her bra and underwear tormented me in the dead of night and sometimes in the shower.

I gave them all a hard look and marched out of the house. Tenor was just pulling in next to my pickup. He got out and looked at his phone. As soon as I saw his shit-eating grin, I knew what he'd seen on his screen. The Bailey text thread was burning like a wick.

"Don't start," I warned.

"Got a guest?" He eyed my container of food.

"You're not one to talk since you had a pretend girl-friend staying at your house for several weekends."

"And I know exactly what we were doing."

I shoved a middle finger in the air and kept walking to my pickup. Ten minutes later, I pulled into my garage. Once I got in the house, I tucked the burritos into the oven, turned it on, and set the timer. They were frozen, but hopefully Madison wasn't in a hurry.

I jogged up the stairs. I had an idea for today, but I didn't know if she'd go for it. "Hey, Madison?" The guest bedroom door was closed. She couldn't still be sleeping, could she? It was almost noon, but then her hours had to be fucked up with her night shifts. "Maddy?"

I was about to knock again when the door swung open. Madison blinked at me from behind a curtain of glossy hair. Her yellow pajamas were as sunny as the day outside. My blood pumped hot through my veins. I nearly took a step forward to push her back into the room and onto that rumpled bed that was probably still warm with her body heat. I fisted my hands to keep from burying them in those silky strands, tipping her head back and claiming her mouth.

She screwed up her face. "Shit, I overslept." She pushed her hair off her face and her tight little nipples pushed against the fabric of her yellow pajama top.

Fuck me, she wasn't wearing a bra, and her tits were as lush as I remembered. My mind fogged over with arousal. Then she turned and presented me with her full butt cheeks, barely covered with thin, pale yellow pajama pants.

"I'll get dressed and be ready in twenty minutes. Sorry." She bent over the bed to tug the covers in place.

When she was about to turn, awareness slapped me

across the face. She was going to constrain that hair in a strict braid and dress in those jeans that could just as well be body armor.

I couldn't have that. "I was thinking we could stay in, go over some numbers. Find a window contractor and talk about security for Flatlanders."

She straightened and faced me, the dots of her nipples still poking through her top. Another minute and I'd sport a raging erection that would be impossible to hide. "Can't you do that when I'm working?"

Yes. "I haven't had a day off in a while."

Guilt flashed across her face. "You can drop me off. Or I can call for a ride." She wrinkled her nose.

There were no cabs in Bourbon Canyon. "I could call Seb. He also does Uber— No, wait. He teaches swim lessons on the weekend. Don't worry about it."

She chewed the inside of her cheek. When was the last time she'd just rested and hung out? "I hate to burn a whole day."

"We'll still be working. Besides, I've got burritos in the oven." She inhaled like she was going to argue. "They're Mama's, and I'd like to see if you let out that sexy little moan when you taste them."

Her mouth dropped open and I deliberately let my gaze fall to her chest. Then I turned away. I was playing with fire around this woman. If I kept going, out of everyone in town, only I would know the real reason she fit her nickname. Madison Townsend was going to drive me out of my mind with desire.

Madison

. . .

I had told Teller I'd be ready in twenty minutes, but since he'd said he was cooking something, I hadn't been able to resist the shower. I stood under the strongest stream that'd hit my skin in . . . ever.

Blisteringly hot water cascaded over me. At the nursing home, the locker room had an old showerhead and it took five minutes to get hot water. I hadn't known what I'd been missing. A shower was a shower, but not all showerheads were made alike. Water beat at my skin, massaging out knots that had been there for years.

I let out a long moan. My eyes flew open. Could he hear?

His comment about my sexy moan should've been embarrassing, but when he'd followed it up by staring at my breasts, embarrassment had been the last thing I'd felt. This time, he hadn't been surprised by me walking out in my bra and underwear like before, but the heat in his eyes had been the same.

Teller liked what he saw. And I liked that he liked it.

I shook my head, sending water droplets flying. I was being absurd. It was the proximity. That guy had his choice of women, and it would not be me. How many ladies had enjoyed this shower?

A depressing thought filtered through. They'd probably enjoyed the luxury of *his* shower—and him.

I was not made for jealousy and I didn't have time for it. I had to finish washing up and get to work. The bottle of three-in-one made me smile until I put a dab on my palm and the woodsy, citrusy scent of Teller rose up in the steam around me.

When I was done, I towel-dried my hair. I couldn't

find a hair dryer and there was no Betty Sue down the hall to let me borrow hers like at the home. I squeezed as much water as I could out of it and got dressed in jeans and an old maroon University of Montana shirt. I left the flannel shirt I used for working in the bar on the dresser.

At the bottom of the stairs, I could see Teller's head tipped back on the couch. His feet were kicked out in front of him. I circled around and pressed my fingers against my mouth. The space in my chest expanded, filling with affection.

He'd fallen asleep. His boots were off and set by the corner of the couch. His feet, in pristine white socks, were crossed at the ankles. I took the opportunity to look my fill.

The way his mouth puffed open with each exhale was adorable. His arms were crossed at his chest and even in slumber his biceps were big. The narrow waist to thick thighs was apparently a thing for me. Like a perfect seat.

I pivoted before I had any more inappropriate thoughts about a sleeping man. The savory smell of the burritos curled around my nose and my stomach clenched. I concentrated on hunger versus my arousal and went to the kitchen. The oven timer was about to hit zero. I shut it and the oven off. Digging around in the drawers, I found a silicone oven mitt.

With the delicious-smelling burritos cooling on the counter, I went back to the living room. I stood away from Teller as if he'd wake up and bite me—and I'd like it.

"Teller." I twisted my fingers together. I didn't want to get closer. What I really wanted to do was climb onto his lap and kiss him awake. "Teller," I said a little louder.

His brow scrunched. I'd never associated Teller with being cute or adorable. He was manly. Larger than life. Brooding at times, usually toward me. That is, until he'd started working for me. Right now though, he was downright cuddly. The yearning to climb onto the couch next to him and fit myself to his side was strong.

"Teller," I snapped. I couldn't stand here and lust after things that were never meant for me.

He turned his head to the side like he was burrowing farther into the cushions. How tired was he?

The guy had been working three jobs. I should let him sleep, but it also felt wrong to enjoy his mom's food when he'd already done manual labor this morning.

I crouched on the edge of the couch next to him and pushed at his knee. "Teller, wake up. It's time to eat."

His eyelids fluttered open and a soft smile graced his face. "Hey," he said in a raspy, sleepy voice that called to every feminine molecule inside of me.

"Food's ready," I said quietly. "I didn't want to eat without you."

He trailed the backs of his fingers down my cheek. "I didn't miss the moan?"

Heat pulsed in my cheeks. "No."

He spread his fingers out and cupped my face. "I want to hear it again." I was frozen, afraid he'd stop, terrified he'd keep going. "I really want to kiss you," he said in that low, drugged voice.

"No, you don't."

"You seem to think you know a lot about me," he murmured, his eyes still on my mouth.

Nothing existed around us. Just him and me in this small bubble. The whole world was blocked out. Why couldn't I kiss him again? "I do know a lot about you."

His mouth pulled up in a lazy grin. "Yeah? Tell me."

"You're used to everyone liking you, but you don't care if they don't. You're used to women throwing themselves at you, but you don't care if they don't. You want to do the right thing, but I suspect that deep down, you don't care if you don't. But you do care that others will care."

"Damn, Mads. You lay it all out there." He brushed a few stray strands behind my ear, then ran his hand down my braid, draping it over my shoulder. He gave it a gentle tug. "Let me give it a try. You've had to be tough all your life, but you're soft inside." He trailed his finger across my chest, over the crest of my breast, stopping over my heart. "You have an independent streak a mile wide, but I bet you wish, for once, you could depend on someone. And you pretend you don't care about anything when, in fact, you care. Very deeply. And that's how people hurt you."

Each insight stripped away a layer of the brick wall I'd built between myself and the world, leaving me raw and exposed. "That's not—"

"True?" He curled his fingers around my braid and pulled me closer. "It's absolutely true. I bet that you'll want to fire me after this. Cut your losses with the donation. Kick me out. Demand your keys back."

Another row of my wall shattered. The spark of those thoughts had started to smolder. "You don't know me," I whispered as he reeled me even closer. I wasn't resisting.

"I want to."

"You date all the women, but you never settle down. She broke your heart." I flattened my hands on his chest. When had I gotten this close? When had I adjusted my position until a few small movements would have me straddling his lap?

His eyelids grew heavy-lidded. "Your lips are too sweet to be talking about that bitterness." He was stroking my face again, rubbing his thumb over my bottom lip.

"You don't know how my lips taste," I whispered. I was so close now, all my nerve endings were alive, waiting for the tickle of his beard, the soft pressure of his mouth. My breasts felt heavy and need coiled low in my belly. He was the polar opposite of me, yet it was like we were magnets. I couldn't quit getting closer to him.

"Let me find out."

It wasn't a question but more of a plea, and I gave in to my own curiosity. I touched my mouth to his. The shock of my lips on his almost had me pulling away, but he curled his hand around my head and took the kiss further and faster than I could've imagined.

He licked along my lips and I automatically opened for him, then he was twining his tongue around mine. I whimpered, and he dragged me onto his lap like I weighed no more than a throw blanket. I draped myself over him like I was one.

He held my head still so he could devour me. I was on top of him, but he was in charge, and maybe I was just like he said. I wanted someone I could depend on. Someone who could take the reins. Teller was doing that now.

I straddled him and did what I refused to admit I'd been dreaming of doing for weeks. For years, even. I buried my hands in his thick hair. Soft strands caressed my palms and I dragged my fingers over his scalp.

A greedy moan rumbled from his chest and into

mine. I widened my legs so I could straddle him lower. The hard ridge of his erection ground against me, and damn, that felt good. How long had it been since I'd been with someone? I rocked back and forth over him and pleasure sizzled through my veins. It'd been so long.

Just as long since I had realized there was no one in my life I could trust or rely on.

I yanked back with a gasp and nearly tumbled off him. He caught me, but I wrestled away from him. He released me immediately and I nearly flopped backward. I managed to get my feet under me.

"What's wrong?" he asked. His cheeks had a flush I'd never seen before. Plenty of other women had.

I didn't hold his dating against him, but he didn't commit. It was why his ex eventually cheated with my brother. She got tired of waiting. I knew how this would play out—with me on the outside looking in. "You're what's wrong. I don't want to get my hopes up, or to get strung along."

He scrubbed his hand down his face, and despite his nap, he looked tired. "I told you I'm not that guy anymore."

I pushed a hand through my hair, tearing at the bound strands and disrupting the braid. He didn't know if he was that guy or not. He'd said he quit dating. "No, but you don't want to be the bad guy. You'll be nice about when you want to be done with me, but the ending will be the same."

His jaw hardened and he looked away, his dark eyes tortured.

"It's like you said." I shouldn't say this much, but I was as transparent as a rainbow to him. "I pretend not to care, but I do. And that's how people hurt me."

A play of emotions I couldn't identify ran through his expression. He sat forward, wincing. If he was still hard, that was some ridge to hunch over. He pressed down on the fly of his jeans.

More heat spread through my body. No more thinking about his size or girth.

"You want to leave, don't you?" he said.

No. I didn't want to leave this house with its enviable kitchen and cozy bedroom and warm water. I didn't want to leave the feeling of being surrounded by nature and solitude. "You can just give me a ride to town. You're clearly tired and need a day off."

He didn't say anything, and I started to squirm under his direct stare. Could he see that my nipples were still hard? They would be every time I thought about that kiss.

"Or," he said slowly, "you could stay here and we could go over some plans and the budget."

I was rebuilding that wall he'd destroyed, only to have it crumble again. I had just told him that he could really hurt me and he was still trying to do the work I'd bought him for? "You don't have to keep doing this."

"I'm going to see it through." He rose. I didn't move away, but I had to tip my head back to meet his determined gaze. "If only to show you that I can commit to something." He sidestepped around me. "I've gotta check on the burritos."

"They're cooling on the counter," I said numbly. He committed to work more than anything in his life. It was women he couldn't commit to, and nothing in his declaration had included me.

CHAPTER NINE

Teller

I punched numbers in my calculator. I'd taken my research, brochures, and estimates from my office and spread everything on the table. It might not be the wildest day, but Madison hadn't demanded I drive her to town, and I got to sit close enough I could smell my shampoo on her.

Madison stared at the data, eyes wide, sometimes unseeing, like she was getting lost in her head about the magnitude of what was left. Meanwhile, I was lost in the kiss. How pliant she'd been. Responsive. How good she'd felt in my arms.

"I don't . . ." She shuffled through some estimates of windows I'd gotten online. "I don't have this much money."

"You paid too much for me." She likely hadn't thought the bid would go that high, but it had. I couldn't let her down. I also had to talk to her, lay it all out, and let her make the decisions. Too many of her options had been taken away, and I wouldn't be that guy.

She wanted me to quit kissing her, I would, hating every moment my lips weren't touching hers. She wanted me to quit helping her? Nope. As soon as she had waved that paddle for the final time, she was stuck with me.

"If Tate gives me a hand, we can install the windows." I pored over the very rough estimate sheet I'd made.

"He can't keep helping you."

"He'd be happy to. We can also install the toilets. If we get into old plumbing, and the project turns bigger than we ever thought, then we'll worry about it then. Otherwise, I can install toilets. Same with the sinks. New stall dividers are easy enough to erect."

Her expression grew more and more fraught with each task I was willing to take on. "That's backbreaking work. You can't keep doing all this." She pressed her hands against her face, covering those lips I had gotten to taste. "I should sell."

"And what? Have Sal screw you over on this too?"

"He's not screwing me over." At my dubious look, her brows pinched together. "Normally, I'd agree, but how could he?"

Good. She was letting me in, asking for my advice. I could puff my damn chest out. "What did you get for an offer? Or better yet, how well does Sal know the buyer?"

She blew out a disbelieving breath. "It's not like that." Uncertainty flashed in her eyes. "He found a buyer for a busted-down house and land that hasn't been cared for in decades."

"It's Montana. You've got property a short drive away from Bozeman. That land will sell and there are buyers who won't care about an old home because they have plans to build a two-million-dollar house. I'm just saying it's not too late to start asking questions."

She neatly stacked the papers with the estimates on them. "By the time the sale goes through, it might be. I need the money."

He was likely preying on her desperation, and I wanted to deck him. "You could get a lot more." I flipped through my little ringed notebook to a page I hadn't shown her yet, hoping this wouldn't slam her guards up against me. "I asked an old friend of my dad's who used to work in real estate what she thought your property could reasonably sell for."

I spun the page to face her. Color leached from her cheeks as her eyes grew wider. "That's not—" She sucked air between her teeth. "That's a joke. She was wrong."

"She was conservative. You have how many acres?"

She worked her jaw back and forth, her gaze on the figure I had jotted down last week. "It's not all good land."

"No, it's not the best for farming and it kind of sucks for grazing. Yes, your parents had property disputes, but that'd be taken care of with a simple survey. What that land is good for? Recreation, and there are a lot of people out there with a lot of money to spend on that slice of paradise." Madison thought everything her family had touched was worthless and no one had told her otherwise. I would not be another person in her life letting her think she wasn't invaluable.

"I just want it sold." Her lips formed a troubled line and doubt filled her eyes.

"Sal's a piece of shit." I didn't say it with heat or accusation. I stated it like a fact, like I was telling her it was seventy-eight degrees out. "He's screwing you, and I

don't have to know how. I just know he is. Because it's
Sal. He knows you're in a bind. You want that place out
of your hands and you want your mom to stay where she
is, but now's the time to be Mad Maddy. Now's the time
to let her protect you like she always has."

I tensed, waiting for that jolt of anger she often
lashed out with at that name. It was time for fireworks.
Instead, she worked her jaw back and forth. "No one
else returned my calls."

"Jesus." The vulnerability in her voice made me want
to haul her onto my lap. If I had my way, we'd be going
over these details in bed, after I got to see how much
she flushed when she orgasmed. "What about someone
out of town?"

"It'd take time." And trust, but she didn't add that.
Better the enemy she knew. "Everything was taking time
and it took forever to get out of probate."

She worried her lower lip while staring at the seven-
figure number I'd shown her. Sal hadn't advertised the
property. He'd probably made a deal with a buddy and
somehow they were both going to profit, probably by
getting control of it so they could sell for top dollar.

"You can get a line of credit with the bank using
Flatlanders and delay the sale. There are ways to make
sure you're covered, Madison." She could let me make
sure she was covered, to ensure no one fucked with this
woman. "Ways to ensure Sal isn't at the very least in a
conflict of interest with the buyer, who I'm guessing
knows this number and plans to use it when he flips the
property to sell, which I'm sure Sal will help with."

Anger darkened the amber in her hazel eyes. She was
running the numbers. How much she'd lose in whatever
bullshit closing costs Sal stuck her with. How far an

honest sale would go to help with long-term care for her mom, who did not deserve her daughter's diligence. Madison had to see just how many opportunities she had.

"You're not like the rest of your family," I insisted, "but one thing they always did was stand up for themselves. So maybe it's time for you to be a little bit like your parents."

A laugh puffed out of her. "No one's ever encouraged that before." Her smile faded. "I've worked really hard to be better than them."

"You are. Standing up for yourself doesn't mean you have to call Sal a cunt—but you'd be right if you did."

Just as she sputtered with more laughter, my phone buzzed.

Tenor: Cows got out in the north pasture. You free?

Damn. "I've gotta round up some cows. You wanna come with?"

"You'd bring me to your ranch?"

"Why not?" Maybe because I never brought women there, but Madison wasn't just some woman. "Mama leaves the cattle rustling to us and she loves company."

"I like your mom," she said, almost shyly. Shit, this girl could get to me like no other. "What would your family think?"

Ah. There was no way I was telling her my family was likely taking bets on how fast and hard I'd fall for Madison. "We'll tell them the truth. You're staying with me because Flatlanders was vandalized, but you're not comfortable in my house alone."

Her gaze swept over the living area where we'd made out on the couch, then pretended it hadn't happened. I'd never forget that kiss. She'd been warm and soft and so damn sweet. Longing filled her expression as she took in the place from the peaked ceiling to the oak hardwood floor. She didn't even let her eyes stray to the kitchen. "They will not buy that this house isn't comfortable. It's the most luxurious place I've ever stayed. I've never used appliances as expensive as those."

"You can touch my appliances all day."

She shot me a mock scowl that went straight to my groin, but the color returned to her cheeks. A playful Maddy was disarming. Not many people saw her like this, but I got to. "Tell them you don't trust me to be home alone in your house. Or that I don't have a car, and if there's another attack on the bar, someone will be around to drive me to town."

If that got her to come along, I was tempted to tell them whatever she wanted, but I wouldn't tell them I didn't trust her. "Let's load up."

Madison

My stomach was a tangled mess by the time Teller coasted down the sprawling driveway to a log home that was bigger than his. My breathing was shallow as I took in the outbuildings. The giant cream-colored shop, the large red barn, another smaller shop, still well cared for, and a small shed that resembled a tiny home. Red and white chickens darted around the exterior. There were a couple of other sheds, all in excellent condition, their purpose unknown to me.

On Townsend land, there was nothing but sagging roofs and crumbling walls.

"Welcome to Bailey Beef," he said.

"My dad is clawing out of his grave," I muttered. I'd always felt different from the rest of my family, but this would be going too far in all their minds. If Mom found out, there'd be hell to pay, and I'd endure the cost on each shift I worked.

My concern diminished the closer we got to the house. The Bailey home sprawled in front of me, the house that seven Bailey kids had grown up in, the house that several more foster kids had found refuge in. My parents used to gloat about how miserable those kids must be in the giant Bailey crew. They hadn't cared why the kids had been yanked from their home or what they were going through otherwise. Just that it must be miserable with the Baileys.

Teller parked in front of a garage door, and we walked across a rock path toward the back door. I couldn't escape the sense that I was one of those displaced kids. That I was getting farther from where I'd grown up because it was no longer habitable. My home had never served me, it had never been meant for me, and all my attempts to make one for myself had failed.

He opened the screen door. I tensed at the creaking sound it made. My surroundings had seemed surreal until that very ordinary noise. Mae was at the sink, her hands in soapy water. She beamed at me, and my heart caught in my throat, cutting my air off. Was this what it was like to walk into a real home? To have someone happy to see me?

"Madison," she said warmly. "Welcome. Tate told me about last night, and Teller said he'd be bringing you."

She dried her hands and came toward me. Instead of encompassing me in a giant hug like when I'd broken down in the party room, she put an arm around me.

"You don't have to chase cattle. Why don't you hang out with me? Give me someone to talk to while I'm getting dinner ready. You're staying, right?" She glanced from me to Teller. I relaxed at her not-a-question. We were staying because she'd said so. Politely.

Teller lifted a brow. If I wanted to leave when the cows were secure, he'd make it happen. But I didn't want to. Mae's home was different than his. Inviting in a different way. Warm and bustling, even though she was the only one here. Her kitchen was large and open, but the massive table was lined with chairs. Glasses and fruit bowls littered the counters. The top of her cupboards had decorative plates she'd collected over the years, a couple of bushy ferns, and the silver fridge was covered with family pictures and grandkids' art.

"I can help you cook," I offered. "I could even bake something for dessert if you don't have that planned yet."

Teller tipped his head to study me. The softness in his eyes did things to my belly and summoned the memory of me grinding on his lap. "All right, then. I'll saddle up and find Tenor."

I wasn't impressed by a guy on a horse, not after growing up with my dad and brother, but I so badly wanted to see Teller doing cowboy things. Especially after he gave his mama a kiss on the cheek and stuffed a tan cowboy hat down on his head.

My world tilted, just a little, but enough to give me the sense that I was sliding off. I should've stayed at his place. Better yet, I should've stayed at Flatlanders. Since last night, ten more cars could've driven by and tossed bricks and I wouldn't know. Part of me wanted to remain oblivious too.

Mae smiled at her son's departure. "So you bake?"

I would happily bake for hours if it gave me time to straighten my chaotic feelings. "Yes, and if you have the ingredients, I know just the thing."

CHAPTER TEN

Madison

Three hours later, I marveled over the speed and efficiency with which Mae could whip up a large meal. She'd made a delicious-smelling pulled pork roast and homemade buns. It'd been too long since I'd gotten to bake buns or bread. I hadn't been able to keep up my sourdough starter once I moved into the bar.

Mae assembled tin pans full of food. "We can haul this outside. Tate said he'd get his boy to help him set up the tables in the shop."

"The shop is nice enough to eat in?" I hadn't meant to sound so astonished. Weren't there mice? Bird nests? Feral barn cats?

"Oh, yes. We have enough get-togethers that it stays presentable." Her smile was understanding. "At least the front half, where we can party, and we do like to party." She drizzled a honey glaze over the carrots. "I can't believe you can make that coconut cake on a dime. It tastes like it takes hours to whip up."

I'd found all the ingredients. Mae did enough cooking and baking that she'd had the pudding mix and buttermilk, a few bags of coconut, and I'd found enough other supplies to make a chocolate cake for the coconut haters.

Did Teller like coconut? He'd said he liked baked goods, and I had thought of him and what he liked the whole time I whipped up the goodies.

I'd needed two cakes as soon as I realized she was inviting more than me and Teller. Apparently, Cruz and Lane were in town. They were out helping the guys. Since they were around, Mae said Myles, Wynter, and their kids would come over. She had called Tate and asked him to let Scarlett know about dinner, so Scarlett and their other two kids could come. The oldest boy was out helping with the cattle already.

And well, since everyone else was here—Mae's casual words of warning—she might as well let Autumn, Summer, and Junie know too.

The entire Bailey brood was having a gathering and I was invited. Hell, I was more than invited. I was involved. All those people, all one happy family, and then me. My pulse kicked up and nervous energy zinged up and down my spine. I was the oddball, and I had no escape. I didn't have a grudge against the family, but what if someone said something I took offense to? And then I ran my mouth? I shook my hands as if that'd help shed the anxiety. "Are you sure two cakes are enough? I can make some cookies."

Mae looked like she was about to shake her head, but

her gaze dropped to my hands. I had started clenching and unclenching my fists. "Cookies are never a bad idea."

"I've never been able to perfect your chocolate chip recipe."

Surprise flitted through her expression, and she reached into a drawer next to us. She withdrew a small cookbook that was full of stains. "I don't have to look at it anymore, but that recipe is on page nine. Help yourself while I finish setting up the buffet."

Delighted, I paged through the book and hit the recipe. At last! I frowned. Nothing in the ingredients stood out. Maybe it was this kitchen. I glanced out the window and my anxiety spiked. Pickups were pulling in.

Would Teller regret bringing me? Was he embarrassed? No, a guy like Teller owned what he did and that included bringing a stray home. And if that stray made some excellent cookies, that'd help offset anything I said.

My gaze landed on the chickens. That was it. Her farm fresh eggs. That was the missing key.

The back door opened.

"Knock knock." Ruby entered. "Hi, Mae. Madison!" Her voice held so much enthusiasm it was my very own pressure valve. She rushed toward me but didn't tackle me with a hug. "How are you? I heard about the bar. How awful."

The good thing about my business spreading like wildfire was that I didn't have to repeat stories. "Yeah, it's not an expense I needed."

She stuffed her hands on her hips. "Did you get pictures? I bet you could make a post with something like hashtag *setback* or *vandals* or *didntneedthis* and leave it at that, and you'd get some outrage. The public might flush out who did it."

Ruby was only five years younger than me, but her innocence was a breath of fresh air. "I don't think the public will care that much. It might give people more ideas."

"I don't know. Flatlanders is part of Bourbon Canyon." She went to help Mae cover the food with aluminum foil. "I don't mean to sound callous with my marketing brain, but you can build this into your story. Make it a comeback thing."

"I'll think about it." I actually would. Surprised, I started digging through the cupboards. My first instinct hadn't been to brush off her advice. She feared it was callous, but what it was was calculated. I had a shuttered business I was renovating to turn a profit. Ruby hadn't steered me wrong yet.

"Ruby," Mae said, "can you help haul these outside, and then would you mind seeing if Madison needs a hand with the cookies or the cleanup?"

"No problem."

I kept busy while they transported the trays of food to the shop. No help was needed; I could make cookies in my sleep. Did Mae see that Ruby made me more comfortable? The thought warmed me from the inside out, gave me an unfamiliar sense of security.

Ruby made one more trip before stopping. She kicked her hip against the counter. "How are things going with Teller?"

"Fine." I continued plopping globs of cookie dough onto the baking sheet.

"He's been decent to you? You two seemed to clash

before." Sincerity oozed from her. She didn't sound like she was asking to get the dirt.

I slid the baking sheet into the oven and faced her, adopting her position. "He's been good about backing off when I don't want his bossiness." Never mind the superior kisses I couldn't quit craving. I was already wondering how much better at other things he was. "He's honest, and I need that."

"Good. He's always been good to me at Copper Summit, and he's an amazing boss. They all are."

"The benefits of being raised by decent parents."

"I don't know what your parents are like, but you're a good person too."

I smiled tightly. "Let's hope I can be a good boss."

"You'll be terrific." She grabbed another baking sheet and we loaded it up with cookies.

What was it with this family and everyone associated with them? Endless optimism and they handed it out like candy. I happened to like candy, and their confidence bolstered me.

After we swapped out the next batch of cookies, Ruby leaned against the counter again. "Your invitation came back to me. I was going to stop by Flatlanders and catch you, and if that failed, I'd just text your invite. I hope you can make the wedding."

"You're inviting me?" Ruby and I had been friendly, but she was more like a contractor I had hired. The girl couldn't help but be bubbly and friendly, but to invite me to her wedding?

"Of course!" Her radiant smile lit the room. "I consider you my friend."

Didn't I just tell Teller I didn't have friends? But I'd

been baking with Ruby much of the afternoon. I was at a family party with her.

Holy shit, I had a friend.

The back door opened and Teller stepped through. His warm gaze immediately landed on me. "Smells good in here."

My stomach dipped and flipped. He made it sound like he wasn't talking about the food, but like I had splashed vanilla extract behind my ears and dabbed it on my wrists. "Cookies do that."

"And cake from the looks of it outside." He came closer to steal a cookie from the baking sheet. I scooted the pan out of his reach. "Hey now," he said, chuckling.

I grinned and then caught the astonished way Ruby watched us, a flicker of delight dancing in her eyes. Teller and I must be making a hell of a domestic scene.

I jerked my hand off the cookie sheet. Teller narrowed his eyes and snatched a cookie without taking his attention off me.

"Cows are contained." He chomped half the treat.

"Did you smile at them so they'd follow you anywhere?" I asked sweetly.

Ruby snorted. "No wonder they put the bulls in the pasture closest to your place."

Teller swallowed wrong and started coughing. He threw his arm over his mouth and turned, his shirt pulling at his waist. He smelled like sunshine and warm grass with the pleasing undertones of horse sweat. I inhaled deeper.

"Sorry," he rasped and grabbed another cookie. He handed it to me. "You tried one yet?"

"I made them."

"Then the baker should get a taste too."

Ruby's eyes burned into me as I accepted the cookie. I hadn't noticed the hunger grumbling in my stomach while I'd been busy in the kitchen. I took a bite and caramelized sugar and butter blasted over my tongue. My sweet tooth woke up and I moaned.

Teller stuffed the rest of his cookie into his mouth, watching me as I chewed.

I covered my mouth with the back of my hand. "I shouldn't ruin my appetite." I swallowed. "Your mom worked hard."

"So did you. Have the cookie. She's pretty damn excited about the coconut cake."

"She had all the ingredients."

"No way," Ruby said. "You made it? That cake is legendary. I even heard about it before today. I'll have to try some."

My cake had a reputation? People gushing at the nursing home was one thing, but something good related to me circulating through the Baileys of all people? What universe did I wake up in?

Teller was watching me, like he knew this was a momentous moment for me, and he hadn't heard Ruby's declaration.

His name was shouted from outside. One of his brothers. "I'm needed." He snatched two more cookies and rushed out the door, and didn't that fill my chest with all sorts of warm goodness.

The beeper on the oven went off.

I wiped the crumbs off my fingers. "Oh, good. The batch is done. Should I put them on a plate and take them out right away?" I retrieved the perfectly browned rounds and set the pan on a trivet on the counter. "I don't want to ruin Mae's routine."

"I think Mae will let a lot ride. Especially when Teller looks at you like that."

Heat exploded in my cheeks. "What?"

Ruby touched her fingertips to her lips. "I shouldn't have said anything. God, how awkward. I'm not usually like that, but then I've never seen Teller like that, and I've spent a lot of time in the tasting room with him. Oodles of women gawk at him, hit on him, practically flash him, and he's aloof. The way he acted just now took me off guard."

"He's just being professional at work, but he's a natural flirt."

"I think he's a learned flirt—except when he's with you. It's natural." Ruby ran her lower lip through her teeth as she considered me. A divot formed between her brows. "Sorry. I'm just rambling. I'll text you that invite. I really hope you can make it." She scurried out the door.

What the hell? Teller didn't look at me differently. Sure, there wasn't the annoyance anymore. And sometimes, he got that concerned crease when he was worried about my safety. Then there was the humor. His seriousness, like when we were discussing his expenses. The perplexed encouragement he'd given me when he'd tried to talk to me about making Flatlanders a bakery.

What exactly did Ruby think she saw?

The memory of him calling me Mad Maddy while a breath away from my mouth surfaced. His low voice when referring to my moans. His hooded eyelids when I was straddling him on the couch. Those moments were each a fluke.

Flukes weren't supposed to happen repeatedly.

Even if Ruby was right, I wasn't interested in being

temporary. I wasn't going to be just another date. A fling. Anything more than that left me with a pounding heart and flashbacks to catching Damien with Wendi in our bed, her mouth wrapped around his cock.

I'd had my trust broken countless times. My heart too. There wasn't enough of it left to survive Teller's interest.

Teller

Having Madison at the family gathering fucked with my mind. My attention kept homing in on her. My personal beacon.

She was nervous, her hands so tightly her knuckles turned white as she chatted with Mom, Wynter, and Ruby. Summer, Autumn, and Scarlett were part of the girl group too, but they were chatting among themselves. Everyone had a piece of coconut or chocolate cake. Both were about gone, and they'd been fucking delicious. Myles and Wynter's little girl, Elsa, was wandering around with chocolate frosting smudged over her chubby cheeks. Chance had inhaled most of the cookies and was getting himself another plate of pulled pork.

Now Madison was fiddling with the end of her braid. She glanced around, saw that flies were loving the empty container of veggies, and she jumped to roll it up and throw it in the trash. From there, she didn't go back to the group but scurried around and rearranged food trays, consolidating them or stuffing them in the trash. I paid close attention when she was bent over the garbage bin, making sure it wasn't overflowing. Her ass was cupped nicely by her jeans.

"I think we've lost him." Tate's words tugged at my attention.

"He doesn't even know how lost he is," Tenor replied.

I scowled at both of them. "What the hell are you two going on about?"

"I was asking you if the shipment of rye showed up on time or if you're still expecting it."

"It'll be here Monday." The pull to watch Madison roam the shop was strong.

"Third time in a row it's been late," Tenor pointed out. "Might be time to look into it more."

It was on my to-do list. The supplier was as local as we could get for rye, and we were all about weathering the storms of family issues, climate change, and business hurdles, but three times was becoming a pattern. Especially when there was little communication and we were left hanging. If it wasn't for Tenor's tedious inventory programs, we might have gaps in our supply. "I'll talk to them this week."

Tate's girl, Brinley, skipped to Madison and tugged on her hand. Madison's expression transformed from determinedly busy into a radiant smile. She even kneeled down to Brinley's level and propped an arm over her knee to chat with the girl. I heard Brinley ask if she had kids. Madison told her she had a nephew that was around her age, and he'd think this picnic was fun.

"And he's gone again," Tate muttered.

"You and her a thing?" Tenor asked.

I gave him an incredulous look, but the feel of her lips tingled against my mouth and the taste of her danced on my tongue. Her weight had been pleasing while she'd been on top of me, and not because it'd been a while since I'd had a woman that close. Strength radiated from her, yet she'd been uncertain. She had crawled over my lap like she couldn't help herself, and for Madison Townsend to let me kiss her like that, to turn over the power while she possessed it all? Well, I was hooked.

However, the way she had scrambled off me, looking angrier at herself than me, didn't hook me at all. "No. There's nothing going on."

Both guys studied me. Myles and Gideon approached, each holding a glass with a finger of Copper Summit Original that Mama swore paired well with the coconut cake. She hadn't been wrong.

Myles was still dressed like the rest of us in his jeans, T-shirt, and cowboy boots. Same with Gideon. Two guys who had worn suits for their careers—Myles still did—fit right in. Meanwhile, Madison probably itched with the feeling of standing out. Until my niece had cornered her.

Now she was letting Brinley tow her away. There was a newly chalked, massive hopscotch board on the cement pad in front of the shop. Would Madison hopscotch?

I leaned over to see around Tate better and Myles chuckled.

Myles took a slow sip from his bourbon. "I'm not sure what you were talking about, but there is most definitely something going on."

"That's exactly what we've been saying," Tenor said.

I glared at them both, then at Gideon for good measure since he was nodding.

Gideon swirled the glass, then wafted it in front of his nose. "You should marry her and figure it out later."

"That only worked for you and Autumn," I said.

Madison tried to navigate the hopscotch board and lost her balance after three jumps. Brinley squealed with laughter and Madison tossed her head back, laughing.

Fondness filled Tate's expression as he watched his daughter coax the shyest party guest into trying again.

Elsa ran over, clapping her little hands together. Brinley put her hand up like a stop sign, but Madison said something I couldn't hear. Elsa jumped into her arms. Madison lifted her to her hip and then tried again slower, careful of jostling Elsa too much.

Delighted giggles rang from the group.

Junie, holding Emma, wandered over and got in line next. Emma waved a chubby arm at the girls. When Madison reached the end, she turned and surprise lit her face, but she smiled at Junie.

"Isn't there a saying about little kids?" Gideon asked. "That they can sense your energy?"

When we all stared at him, he glared at us. "Bite me. I'm married to a schoolteacher and babies everywhere adore her. We can't go to the grocery store without some kid giving her googly eyes."

"I think that's just you," Tate joked. "But, yeah. I've heard something about that too."

The kids were probably nicer and less judgmental to Madison than most adults.

Jonah carried Eliott to the edge of the cement pad and set him down. The toddler darted over to get in line.

"I hope you know, Madison," Jonah said, his tone

serious, "Teller holds the record for the number of back-and-forth runs on Brinley's hopscotch boards."

Madison lifted her gaze, catching mine. A smile curved her lush lips. "Is that so?"

The urge to impress her over a stupid kids' game that Mama would make sure generations after her knew how to play was strong. And I could be a competitive prick. "I'd tell you that it is, but I'd hate to intimidate you."

A dark brow ticked up. "Big words for a guy who's staying as far away from the game as he can."

A chorus of "oh" and "whoa" rang around me. Fuckers. The challenge was one I couldn't resist, and they knew it. I'd jumped so damn much I could barely walk the next day, but I was the reigning record holder.

Good thing I hadn't had any bourbon with the cake. I'd need every ounce of my balance for this. "Once Junie shows us that her agility onstage is nothing but a performance, I'll put you all to shame."

"I tripped once, Teller," Junie said with pretend outrage. She beckoned Rhys over to hand off Emma.

"Are we hopscotching?" Hannah called as she skidded to a stop next to her dad.

Rhys nodded. "Teller issued a challenge."

"Can we play nine square after this?" Bethany asked after she jumped into line. The PVC nine-square court was set up next to the shop.

I reached the group. "I'd hate to show everyone up in that game too."

The girls all started arguing with me. I wasn't boasting. My height gave me a wicked advantage in nine square and uncles weren't supposed to let their nieces and nephews win.

Madison handed Elsa to Wynter and finished her

run, making it down and back three times. She was grinning when she came to stand by me. With the sun
shining off her hair, giving it a blackened-brass luster, she
was as breathtaking as ever.

My heart stumbled over itself as I drank her in. She
was dressed more like me and the guys than my sisters,
who favored shorts and summer dresses, but I didn't
care what she wore. She was so goddamn beautiful it
hurt.

She hooked her thumbs in her jeans pockets. "You
talk a big game, Bailey. You gonna live up to it?"

"Since I ate half of that chocolate cake, I'm going to
have to." I winked at her and enjoyed when the blush in
her cheeks spread down her neck. How far down did it
go? "The real question is, what do I get if I beat you?"

"I'm not a betting woman."

My presence in her life said otherwise. "If I beat you,
then you have to make me a batch of cookies every week
until we're done with Flatlanders."

She clucked. "Punishments aren't supposed to be
something I enjoy. What if I win?"

"I'll name our next special batch after you."

Her lips parted and shock darkened her eyes. "You
can't do that."

"I'm the boss." I shrugged. "One of them. Wynter
won't mind. She and Ruby will figure out how to market
it based on the name."

We shuffled farther up the line.

Junie let out a whoop. "Five runs!"

"How would that work?" Madison asked, folding her
arms. Her shirt was thin enough I could make out the
outline of her bra. Was she wearing a black sports bra

like last time? "Copper Summit Townsend? Copper Summit Madison? Neither roll off the tongue."

She would roll right off my tongue, smooth and silky, as rich as our top-line Copper Summit Gold. "Mad Maddy Summit."

"*No*. You can't."

"It'll be robust, strong, and expensive. A quality bourbon. One of our finest."

Her mouth dropped open. She snapped it shut. "You're kidding."

"I'm serious. You can be there when we taste it." I swayed closer to her. "If you win."

CHAPTER ELEVEN

Madison

I stared at the pitched ceiling in Teller's guest bedroom. I would be making Teller cookies every week, but I could've had a bourbon named after me. After that irritating nickname I could no longer hate.

Would people have thought it was a joke? A way for Teller to make fun of me?

Yet why would a company put time and money into labeling a product with anything *Mad Maddy* if it wasn't serious? Why would they waste marketing dollars to make fun of me? None of the Baileys had given me a hard time. All except for Teller, and now that I wasn't so defensive around him, I could admit that had been more miscommunication between us thanks to someone who had hurt us both.

The edge I was on around him was no longer about defensiveness. The thrum in my chest that spread down to between my thighs, that was altogether different.

Thankfully, I had tried to kick Teller's ass so much that my left knee throbbed. An old horse-riding injury flared up if I ran. Made sense that jumping across a concrete pad would have the same effect.

I rolled to the edge of the bed. My shirt hung loose and I'd paired it with a pair of baby-blue shorts that were too short to wear outside of the house. I used to use them for gardening, but the garden and flowerbeds were no longer mine. Just a few of the things I had lost in the divorce.

I listened for Teller's movements, but he'd gone to bed an hour ago. I needed an ice pack.

Mostly, I needed a massage, but it was hard to get the right pressure myself and I'd left the metal scraper I'd bought online for fascia work at the bar.

The house was dark. Could I get ice and a butter knife without waking him? Would he care that I used the butter knife to rub all over my leg?

He didn't have to know. I could sneak downstairs, and in the morning, I could slip the knife into the dishwasher.

I slid out of bed, pausing only briefly by my suitcase. Should I throw a flannel over my pajamas or put a pair of sweats on? Deciding against it, I eased my door open. It swung open quietly and I tiptoed downstairs, marveling over how none of the floorboards creaked in the house.

At the base of the stairs, I pushed my hair back. A nearly full moon glowed through the window, bathing the main level in shadow. Paired with the yard light, I didn't need to flip any other lights on. I entered the kitchen and yelped.

I was met with broad shoulders and a chiseled, bare

chest. Teller stood next to the fridge, holding a glass of water.

"Oh my god!" I couldn't look away. Even in the dark, his body was mouthwatering. The boxer briefs he wore rode low on his hips, and that was all that was covering him. "I'm sorry, but god, you are so quiet!"

"I didn't want to wake you." He took a long pull of water. If there had been more light, I could have watched his throat work over the swallow. There was nothing on this man I didn't get tired of looking at.

"I didn't want to bother you." I hugged my arms around myself. I should've put on that flannel. I wasn't wearing a bra or underwear. With the pajama top and bottoms, I might as well be naked around him.

"Can't sleep?" His gaze trailed down my body, lingering on my toes and the polish I needed to refresh, then traveled back up.

It was too dark for him to see well, but I felt exposed. The dull ache on the outside of my knee reminded me to get the ice. "I fell off a horse when I was fifteen."

"Happens to the best of us."

"Your horse probably apologized and helped you up. Mine ran off and I had to limp two miles back home, only for Dad to lose his shit because Flight Risk was out."

"You had a horse named Flight Risk, and your dad was surprised he was a flight risk?"

That pretty much summed up my childhood. "Anyway, my knee still aches sometimes. It's why I'm not a runner."

"I'm not a runner because it'd involve running."

Unprepared for his frank response, I giggled. "Fair. I'm built for fight, not flight."

His grin flashed in the shadows. "What usually helps it? Ice?"

"That and scraping or a massage." Since I was busted and I didn't need my knee keeping me awake on top of joking around with a shirtless Teller, I would admit to my real intentions. "I was going to use a butter knife for scraping. It helps loosen everything."

He set his glass down and dug around in a drawer, withdrawing a plastic baggie. Then he sifted through another drawer and got out a butter knife. "Have a seat. I can help. We can try massage first."

"Y-you don't have to do that." My heart rate kicked into a climb. He was not offering. He couldn't be.

"Listen, if you're going to be making me cookies every week, we cannot have your knee hurting."

The humor amplified the heat building inside of me. What a weird turn-on, and still not appropriate. "You claim to not be a runner, but you dominated hopscotch."

"When you're the middle brother, you learn how to barter your way out of chores. Then when a ton of sisters show up, you realize you can dump a fuckton of work on them by betting on games."

"Sibling warfare?" A tug of envy and nostalgia hit me. "Scott used to get me to feed the chickens and horses after school by telling me that he'd do it in the morning, but then he'd sleep in and go to a friend's house and I was stuck with it anyway."

"Tate tried that on me a few times. I kept falling for it." He gestured behind me. "Have a seat somewhere and tell me what you need." He stepped closer and my breath hitched, but he reached over to the fridge to fill the baggie with ice. His body heat fought through the AC to curl around me. I could lean into him.

My need was the problem. "You're not massaging me."

"I've been told I have talented hands."

Arousal caressed my insides. The skin on my leg tingled, telling me just where he should put his skilled hands. "Teller, it's fine."

"I'm the one who made you jump all afternoon."

"I would've anyway." Today was the most fun I'd had in a long time. Teller's family gathering was everything I had dreamed of. Everything I had known I was missing. I shouldn't have experienced just how joyful and comforting it was. Now my early years seemed even more bleak.

"We had to jump for almost an hour. Sit."

"Really, it's fine." I started for the stairs.

"I didn't know you were such a chicken." Taunting challenge filled his tone.

I stopped. This distance between me and the bottom stair could just as well be miles. "Are we twelve?"

"I bet if you were twelve, you wouldn't run." He pretended to polish the backs of his fingernails against his chest. "I do realize how irresistible I've gotten as an adult."

He was joking, but he couldn't be more spot on. He'd only grown more appealing with age. His trimmed beard, rugged good looks, body honed by the outdoors, and the way his eyes saw right through people all painted a broad, handsome picture.

It was why his outburst all those years ago had warped my attitude toward him. How dare he lump me in with the rest of my family when he'd been so good about accepting others where they were? That dynamic had shifted over the last couple of weeks.

He was also correct that I was a chicken. What if he touched my skin, rubbed me down, and then walked away like it didn't affect him? I'd be crushed physically and emotionally. I was mature enough to understand that.

Then there was the flip side, and I couldn't go there. That was some other lucky girl's future. Not mine. "You don't think I can resist you?"

"Oh, Mad Maddy. I think you're doing very well at resisting me."

That stupid rumble sent shivers skittering over my skin. My nipples were hard, and dammit, I was glad the light was off. "Fine. But I'm not sitting on the couch."

"I'm that potent, I know."

He was so solemn I chuckled and shook my head. I went to the dining room table and pulled a chair out.

"Sit on the top so I can use the chair."

I gave him a look that asked him why the hell I'd plant my ass on his tabletop. He shrugged, the baggie of ice swinging from his fingers. "Give my back a break. I'm not twelve anymore."

He pulled out a chair at the end of the table where he usually sat and plonked his butt down. He used the butter knife to gesture to the spot in front of him.

My skin got tight as I scooted myself up. I kept my knees closed and hunched my shoulders so he couldn't make out how tightly peaked my nipples were.

He wiggled the butter knife. "What do I do with this?"

"Use the back of it and lightly scrape over my skin." I made the motion over the edge of my right quad.

"That's it?"

"I'm not a physical therapist. I'm sure there's more, but that was what YouTube showed me."

The corner of his mouth lifted. "Won't that chafe?"

"I mean, usually lotion is used, but I didn't want to get it all over your silverware."

He set the baggie down and withdrew an ice cube. "We can use this."

"Won't that be cold?"

He held my gaze as he cupped the ice cube in his palm and flattened it over my thigh. An electric jolt went through me at the brush of his heated skin and the shocking cold of the ice. I exhaled a shaky breath as my insides went haywire.

"Too cold?" he murmured.

Too warm. His skin was hot, and he was sitting close, his head tilted toward me and his chest only inches away. "No," I said, more than my voice unsteady.

I flinched again when he put the cool back of the knife against my quad and slowly slid it up and down. He worked like that, his concentration on the task. I raked my gaze over his hair and his broad shoulders. The way his abs crinkled when he sat and the man spread he had going on. Between his thighs was nothing but the dark shadow of his boxer briefs.

Each time he glided the ice cube over my skin, my flinch grew weaker. I began to anticipate it. His blistering fingertips danced over my skin. He wasn't working with just one hand, but both. When he wasn't holding the ice cube, he set it next to me. The wet spot shone in the darkness. Desire rippled under my skin, and I was only wearing pajama shorts. My body was primed, ready to have more than my knee worked on by those strong hands.

All he was doing was exactly what I would've done upstairs, but his method was utterly different. A slow, sensual float of the ice over my skin, and then his hands on me. The delicate slide of the knife, somehow knowing the right amount of pressure.

I tried to stay unaffected, to keep from trembling over the wanton need to scoot off the table and right into his lap. I pressed my palms into the smooth surface of the table behind me instead of gripping his shoulders or, worse, stuffing my hands into his hair.

What was he thinking? He was quiet, almost studious as he worked.

When he picked up the ice cube again, his fingers splashed into the small puddle left behind. The baggie was still sitting next to me, slowly melting, but he didn't reach for it. Instead, he put his damp fingers back on my skin. His heat. The coolness of the ice melting. How could steam not be rising?

"How's your knee feel?" he asked gruffly.

As achy and needy as the rest of my body. "Good." The word came out breathy.

"Good," he echoed softly as he brushed his fingers up and down my thigh. "Christ, Maddy. I'm dying to know if you're wearing underwear."

"No," I said before thinking. My brain was scrambled, focused only on where his touch was on me, counting each one of his rough fingertips.

"Fuck, you're not?" A long, low growl left him and he rose like a cobra, uncoiling to unleash all its power. His hips were kicked back and his forehead was close to mine. "My fingers were inches from that sweet pussy of yours and it's *bare*?"

His voice was strangled, matching the squeeze in my chest. He dragged those wicked fingers up my thigh.

"I said once that I wanted you to beg for me, but I can't let you." He swallowed hard. "I want to make you feel so damn good, Mads, and I don't want you to have to beg for it. I'm ready to drop to my knees and plead like the world is going to end if I don't feel how fucking wet you are."

My lungs squeezed tighter with each sentence. How had this happened? How was I in the dark with very thin clothes between me and Teller? How could he be so strong but so gentle too?

I licked my dry lips. "We shouldn't."

He lowered his head even more. "Why?"

"We're working together."

"The only thing this will change is that every time I see you bend over in those jeans, I'm going to want to grab your hips, wrestle those pants down, and thrust inside."

A quiver shook me. His mouth was close to mine. "You don't want to get serious, and I'm tired of men not taking me seriously."

That didn't get him to back away. "I'm very serious about your pleasure."

My body insisted that was good enough. My mind was not convinced I wouldn't get hurt when I moved away and Teller didn't ask me to stay. Yet, at this moment, I didn't want long term. Short-term pleasure sounded fantastic. "What about you?" I was stalling, but I also wasn't saying no.

He chuckled, the rumble pleasing and deep. "Getting

you off would very much be my pleasure." He placed a light kiss at the corner of my mouth. I was still leaning back, my weight on my hands behind me, afraid to grip his shoulders, or I'd cling to him like Saran Wrap. "Hearing those needy moans would very much stroke my ego. Discovering how wet you are for me? Very pleasing. Tasting you? An orgasm for my tongue."

My disbelief rose. "Getting me off would be enough for you?" I scoffed. I definitely wasn't asking to buy myself time, to reach the point where I was strong enough to push him away and say no. He was fooling himself.

Each second that had ticked by only brought the realization that I did not want to reject this man. In fact, that was the bulk of my issue. I had never wanted to push him away. I'd been wishing he'd close the distance the whole time.

He pulled back enough to narrow his eyes on me. For a moment, I wished a spotlight glared down on us so I could see the glittering of his dark eyes and determine whether he was lying to get into my pants. Men took what they wanted from others to feel good. Teller was no different.

This wasn't the time to remember that Damien was my only gauge for what men wanted. Him, my cheating dad, and a line of men doing stupid things for my ex-sister-in-law.

"Hearing you cry out because I brought you to orgasm would be enough." He placed a tender kiss on the other corner of my mouth. "Don't get me wrong, I would love to take things further. I want to bury myself deep inside of you, but only to heighten your pleasure and to know what you feel like coming from the inside out. But I'd go to bed happy with nothing but your cries in my ears."

A shudder racked my body. I couldn't take this man. His words made me swoon. I feared the power of his tongue. "I don't believe it."

"Let me prove it," he whispered and touched his lips to mine.

His kiss was light, but I surged up into him, hungry for more, starving to taste him.

He growled and wrapped an arm around me. My ass slid to the edge of the table and he deepened the kiss until I opened for him. A small whimper left me as his hot, velvet tongue stroked inside.

This time, I had to release the table and hook my arms around his broad shoulders. He invaded my mouth and I let him. He was strong but sensual, licking against my tongue with steady thrusts. My core ached in time with his movements. I wiggled to get closer to him.

"Let me," he said in between twining his tongue with mine, "prove it. Over and over and over." His hand was on my leg again, sliding up until his thumb crept under the hem of my shorts. He was millimeters away from my pussy, then he stopped.

Keep going. I needed more. Half drugged on the faint mint of his taste, my eyelids heavy, I got out a "yes."

His growl ripped through the night, but he didn't fall on me like a rutting stud. He kept it achingly, frustratingly slow. My shorts stayed on as he swept his thumb in half circles, creeping closer to my center. I spread my legs wider, nudging the cold bag of ice farther away.

He captured my mouth again, leaning me back with one of his arms anchoring me to him to keep me from tipping all the way. Just as I was going molten against him, he found my clit and stroked over it.

My knees drew up of their own accord. It'd been so long since I'd been pleasured, including by my own hand, but nothing had been like this. He was barely touching me and I was ready to come.

"You're so fucking wet," he said against my lips.

"Are you proud of yourself?" He'd done that just with his ministrations to my knee.

"Not yet." He circled my clit and my entire body shook. He smiled against my lips, his beard tickling the sensitive skin. "Getting there though."

Then he adjusted his arm, his big biceps flexing, and he slicked a finger through my seam, landing at my entrance. My mouth dropped open, the pleasure intense. Then he pushed inside.

"Ungh." My head tipped back. I was not in a position to rock my hips up, but if he hadn't been holding me, I'd have fallen backward and smacked my head.

"Does that feel good?"

"Yes," I whispered.

He pushed all the way in, then pumped in and out while lazily rubbing my clit with his thumb. "How about that?"

I rocked with his movements as much as I could. "You know it does."

His mischievous chuckle was only a turn-on. Teller knew what he was doing and I was grateful. No fumbling. No hesitancy. No regrets. "Teller," I whined. I would beg, but I didn't have to. He'd been the one to ask instead.

"You're close, aren't you? So damn needy that you're ready to come. Dripping wet in my hand."

I nodded, unashamed. If this had been years ago, I might've been approaching embarrassment, but not with Teller. This was about me and for me. He hadn't just told me; he was showing me. A flush of heat grew between my legs as energy coiled inside my belly.

"Not yet, Mads." He withdrew his hand, leaving me bereft. Until he kicked the chair farther back and dropped to his knees. He curled his fingers around the waistband of my shorts and tugged down. It wouldn't have mattered if I had lifted my hips, he was strong enough to get them off me.

I tipped back and caught myself as he dragged them down my legs. My bare ass was pressed against the table.

"So fucking pretty," he said roughly, his head between my legs. "I'm going to see this in the light of day, Madison." The way he said it was a promise. "I'm going to get you off over and over and over until you realize that I was not fucking joking. Your pleasure is mine. This pussy is mine."

I couldn't form coherent words.

"You'd better hold on." He wasn't slow or gentle. He descended on me, sucking my clit into his mouth.

"Oh my god!" My shout echoed in the empty house and I didn't have to worry about neighbors. The thought should alarm me, but I'd never felt safer. More supported. He was concentrating on me. He was consuming me.

I was at the very edge of the table, his arms wrapped under my thighs and holding me. That talented tongue of his licked and lapped, finding the right rhythm until I was grinding against him. My abs clenched and my legs spread, I dug my hands through the silky strands of his hair like I had wanted to for so long.

I hung on to him as the pleasure inside me grew and swirled, morphing into unadulterated ecstasy. My skin was shrink-wrapping around me again, holding in growing energy. It wouldn't be enough. The explosion was coming.

As much as I wanted to reach orgasmic heights I'd never experienced before, I didn't want this to end. He'd come to his senses soon enough. He couldn't really mean what he had said about my pleasure being enough. I could wait to find out and stretch this moment to eternity.

But he was too good for that. I hit my peak and toppled over, and even that was different. A gradual, more powerful fall that grew stronger and stronger. "Oh my god—Teller!"

He lapped at me as everything inside me went tight. I jerked on his hair, not meaning to but unable to let go. All the trembling from earlier roared back, racking my limbs as I shook and convulsed due to nothing but his tongue on my clit.

"Oh god, oh god, oh god," I panted, every muscle taut. Then languid heat spread through me, all the way to my toes. I released his head and my legs hung, only held up by his wide shoulders.

He kissed the inside of my thigh. "Fuck me, Mads. That was amazing."

He prowled up my body as he rose and claimed my mouth. If he didn't care about being covered in me, then I didn't either. I was still trying to catch my breath. His kisses were sensual, slow, searching, like he was asking me if I was truly okay.

I hung my arms over his shoulders. His erection prodded me through his underwear, but he didn't try to seek relief for himself. If he kept up with that mouth of his, I'd be seeking more real soon.

"Don't you need something?" I asked, sliding my hands down his arms, eager to take this further.

He gripped my hands, turned each one over, and kissed the palm of my right hand, then my left. "Another time. Right now, I need to tuck you into bed."

He released me and helped me to my feet. Then he grabbed my shorts off the floor and held them open for me to step in.

He seriously wasn't going to ask for more?

Okay . . . I gingerly put one foot in, then the other. He slid the shorts up my legs.

Awkwardness was setting in. I glanced behind me at the table. "I can clean up before I go to bed."

He rose and tipped my chin up, giving me another sweet kiss. "I'll clean up. Go. Get some rest."

Confusion swirled around my head. Uncertainty. There was more space between us right now than there'd been all night. Had I read everything wrong? "You sure—"

Another firm kiss. "I said over and over and over. This was once. I'm not done showing you that your pleasure should be a priority. And if you don't get upstairs, I'm going to bend you over the table and fuck you until neither of us can stand. I'm not a man who likes to go back on his word, Madison, but I'm still just a man. Save me and get that sweet ass of yours upstairs."

Oh. Energy sparked inside me and a comforting warmth filled my chest. "Good night, Teller."

"Good night, Mads."

CHAPTER TWELVE

Teller

Warm water pounded against my body. Last night, I'd thought I'd pass out from my erection. This morning, I was barely able to keep it under control. Just hearing Madison puttering around in the kitchen had been enough to propel me to the shower to jack off. Seeing her in the kitchen was going to do it again.

I shut the faucet off and stared as the last of the water circled the drain. Why hadn't I tracked her to her bed and plunged inside of her? She would've let me. We both wanted it, needed to succumb to this intense chemistry between us.

Part of me knew she'd be dangerous. I'd rushed into a relationship once and gotten slammed back hard. And publicly. The rest of me had gleaned enough from Madison's comments to know her shitty ex had been just as selfish in bed. But I cared for her. I was also insanely attracted to her.

So I wouldn't rush anything. Nor would I make any promises. She could be . . . She could be the one.

The one. I scrubbed a hand down my face, flicking droplets of water off. Fuck, I didn't know. I'd been single for so long, a bachelor most of my adult life. I'd resigned myself to being a bachelor forever. Finding what my siblings had, it had seemed like an impossibility. Then Madison had stomped away from me in the grocery store and consumed my thoughts since.

She'd been messed with enough. Used and discarded. I wouldn't be another asshole jerking her around. I'd give her all the pleasure she deserved until we figured this thing out.

After I'd dried off and dressed in my normal plain shirt and jeans, I went downstairs. Her back was to me at the stove. That damn flannel of hers was covering her ass, and I let myself mourn. I'd had the most spectacular sexual experience of my life last night and I hadn't been able to get a clear view of her. Her shirt had remained on, and I hadn't made out much of her sweet, wet pussy in the dark.

But I'd tasted her, and I had a new craving.

How did she feel? Did she have regrets? Had I incinerated all the trust between us?

I'd rather know sooner than later. "How much are you overthinking last night?"

She stiffened and peered over her shoulder while she continued stirring whatever was in the pot on the stove. Her curtain of hair was bound in the braid. How many people knew what she looked like with it down? Was I one of the few?

"I don't know," she said. "I might be underthinking

it." She turned away, hiding her expression. "I mean, it was just so-so. Not worth getting worked up over."

The tease in her response went straight to my dick. Everything she did sent my blood flowing south. "Is that why you hollered my name so loud?" I closed the distance between us and put my hands on her hips. "I bet I can make you scream louder."

There went my attempt at preventing an erection. Pressure built behind my zipper. Not even the sight of the oatmeal she was stirring slowed the buildup.

An exhale gusted out of her, and I slid my hand around to work the button of her jeans open.

"Teller? Here?"

"Why not?" I kissed her shoulder and slid her zipper down. I could've jacked off ten times this morning and it wouldn't have mattered. Arousal pounded at my temples.

"The oatmeal will burn." Yet she kicked her hips back into me, grinding against my hard-on.

A groan left me, but I didn't stop. "Keep stirring."

Finally, her pants were open. I tunneled my hand between her hot skin and her clothing, past her shirt and underneath the hem of her underwear. Then I hit her slick clit.

"You're already wet for me," I murmured against the shell of her ear.

A shiver traveled down her body, and I felt each inch. I flicked my tongue out, licking the delicate curve of her ear.

She groaned and flipped the oven off. She plopped the pot of oatmeal between two burners and braced herself on either side of the stove. Her head hung down, but she rocked into my fingers, covering me in her juices. "I can't believe you're doing this again."

"It's not every day a sexy woman is in my kitchen." An understatement. I twined her long braid around my free hand and gently tugged her head to the side. I laid kisses along her neck.

"Sexy?" she asked on a moan.

"So fucking hot." I stuffed my hand down until I could push a finger inside of her. She leaned harder on her arms, but I held her braid tight. There was no way she would jerk and burn herself while I was making her come.

My heartbeat pounded behind my fly, but I ignored it. I hadn't been lying to her. Getting her off was the ultimate pleasure. The way all that tension leaked out of her and she handed herself over to me. Madison didn't do that for anyone. She probably hadn't done it for her douche of an ex either because he hadn't known what he was doing or he hadn't cared. But she did it for me, and I didn't take her trust lightly.

"You know how tight you are?" I growled against her skin. She lifted her hand like she was going to reach back and grab my head or link her fingers with mine. "Hands on the counter while I'm inside you." I thrust in and out, straining to continue rubbing her clit within the constraints of her jeans.

She propped her hands back in place. "Teller."

"I've got you." Fuck, she was close. So damn responsive. Her heat branded itself into my hand. I'd never forget her taste or how she gripped me when I pushed farther in. Tension built in her and the rock of her hips got more erratic.

"Come for me." I licked a path up her neck to her earlobe.

"Teller." Her mouth fell open and she slammed her

ass back into me. I held her tight as she shook. Each scrape of her butt against my dick sent fireworks exploding behind my eyes.

After several moments, she sagged against the counter, but I held on to her, making sure she stayed safe. Mostly because I liked the feel of her in my arms. What would it be like to wake up to her? To roll over and snuggle against her back? To go to sleep with her?

Her breathing had slowed and she was steadier on her feet. I withdrew my hand, first from her and then from the snug warmth of her clothing. I let go of her braid and placed one more kiss at the crook of her neck. She tilted her face to peer at me. Holding her languid gaze, I put the finger that had been inside of her into my mouth and licked the salty, sweet taste of her off.

Her eyes flared and a blush blazed along her cheeks. "Jesus, Teller."

"Mm. Can't wait to have what you're cooking." I adjusted my painful erection with an exaggerated movement and forced myself to back away from her.

She dropped her gaze to my fly. "I can help with that."

"Over and over and over."

The blush didn't leave the crests of her cheeks. "You're really serious about that?"

"I'm serious about your pleasure. I'm going to show you that if a guy wanted to, he would."

Her lips parted, and I escaped to the quiet calm of my downstairs bathroom. If I went back out there before I calmed my raging desire down, I'd haul her upstairs like a goddamn caveman. I'd sling her over my shoulder and march away to claim what was mine. I probably wouldn't even make it to the stairs if she was as eager as me.

I splashed water on my face and glared at the droplets dripping off me in the mirror. Dots of water glistened on my beard. I hadn't looked much different last night. Haggard expression. Fevered gaze. Lust stamped into every line and crinkle.

I wouldn't do anything differently. I'd gladly weather a painful erection to hear her scream my name a thousand times. The only doubt I had was how soon I could do it again.

Madison

I walked into work, my body still humming, thanks to Teller. I had continued to stay at his place all week, but I was driving my own pickup. He'd shown up an hour before my shift and . . . Well, I wouldn't look at the pool tables the same again.

Now I had a full shift ahead of me while he was working on replacing the flooring in the bathroom before installing the new toilets we'd bought earlier in the week.

I was fifteen minutes early like I'd planned, but I slowed my steps as I walked through the nursing home side to the more independent wing Mom was in. I hadn't seen Mom in a couple of weeks.

I slowed to a stop in front of her room. The door was slightly ajar and the TV inside was blaring. She could hear just fine, she just hated the reminder of where she was. She'd lashed out at me the last time I was here, but I had to check on her. She had no one else.

I knocked lightly and pushed the door open. "Hey, Mom. How are you?"

She grunted and slid her gaze back to the TV. "The house sold yet?"

I'm fine, thanks. "It's pending." Teller's words played through my head. I really should ask Sal more questions. I had no idea what, and I didn't want to drag Teller with me like I was a woman who couldn't do anything without a man. I'd look like a woman who couldn't do anything without a Bailey.

Mom gave me another grunt. "How's Scott's bar?"

I bristled and brushed it right off. It'd never be my place, and since I was resurrecting the place as Flatlanders Prohibited, then it would always be tied to Scott. I didn't mind. I missed him. "It's coming along."

The brick was fully exposed and Teller and I had spent the last few days cleaning it.

"You seen Logan lately?" she asked.

I shook my head. "I messaged Wendi, but she hasn't gotten back to me. You know how she is."

"We can ask your ex how she is."

The sting from her words was fainter than normal. I'd been left for another woman, but thanks to Teller, I'd also been treated with respect, listened to, and then there were the orgasms. Hard to feel awful about getting betrayed after experiencing everything my marriage had been missing.

"I'll try again tomorrow," I said. "I'm sure she's just busy."

"That girl always thought she was too good for us."

"Agreed."

Mom turned her sharp gaze to me. Tension built behind my ribs and spread outward. "What about that Bailey kid? I've heard things."

I frowned and talked my pulse down. No one knew I was getting off with Teller. We weren't a thing. He was making a point about my pleasure and I was soaking up his attention. "I'm not sure what people are saying. He works at the bar around his hours."

"You're riding around with him."

Oh. The next part wouldn't go over well, but I'd rather she heard the news from me than catch me off guard and harangue me later. "The bar was vandalized, and it's not safe to stay in. I'm using a guest room in his house."

"Turned into a slut for a Bailey, did ya?"

My cheeks flamed. "Geez, Mom. No. The bar isn't safe."

She smacked her lips against her teeth. "Wendi took what you had, so you're taking what she had."

I wasn't. I couldn't see her with the Teller I knew. I had only known who Teller was when he'd been with Wendi. I had been married and living in Missoula, but I wasn't the same girl I was back then, and Teller wasn't the same guy. Wendi's leftovers weren't making me laugh or protecting me when bricks were thrown through windows. But I wasn't sharing any of that with Mom. "It's just for work," I mumbled.

"It's nothing for him. Remember that. You're not his type." She raked her gaze down my gunmetal-gray scrubs as if she were pointing out that the extra six inches of height would be gross for a guy. That my sturdier build would never be desirable compared to Wendi's petite curves or her long legs. I kept myself covered thanks to

Mom pointing out flaws all my life while Wendi dressed to express, and she had a lot to say.

"Well, it's business. I'm not worried." I was a little worried, but talking with Mom wouldn't assuage those feelings. I made a show of checking on the clock on the wall. "I've gotta clock in. Need anything from me before I go?"

"No," she said disdainfully, turning her attention back to her show. "You ain't got nothing for anyone."

Mom was a cat with a busted leg, swiping at whoever tried to help her, but this time, it scraped over me like 24-grit sandpaper, chafing against my pride. I had gotten good at letting it roll off my back. What was different about tonight?

All week, I'd marveled over how nice it'd been to hang out with the Baileys. Everyone had been so supportive of each other. Mae hadn't said one rude word toward her daughters—or anyone else, for that matter. The party had been full of mothers and daughters who loved each other, who'd been kind to each other. They hadn't even been separated, but when a kid had run to their mom, their mom had always been happy. It hadn't mattered which kid or which mom.

Loss tugged at my heart. I hadn't had that upbringing. Mom had lived a hard, loveless life. I'd at least gotten some affection from my dad's sister. Aunt Tilly used to encourage me to be better than my circumstances. That was what I was doing now. Being better to Mom than she'd ever be to me, and it was easier to do after Teller burst into my bar and my life.

"Night, Mom." I left the room on her grunt.

Now that I was done with my obligatory visit and not feeling utterly beaten down, the talk with Teller played through my mind—about the house, Sal, and the likelihood he was screwing me over.

I didn't know how long Teller would take with the repairs, or how long he and I would be messing around, but I wanted to absorb everything he was willing to give, and one thing was his support.

I took my phone out and sent a quick message to my real estate agent. If this panned out, Teller would earn out his bid several times over. And I'd have no idea how to repay him.

CHAPTER THIRTEEN

Teller

"I'm going to be late for work," Madison gasped.

"You'd better come, then."

Her legs were splayed on either side of my head as she was pressed into the corner of the spare room on the cot she'd been sleeping in at the bar. She arched her back and pushed her pussy against my face, and a blast of heat hit as she came. Fuck, yes. I lived for this moment. When she climaxed, there was nothing on her mind but how good she felt, and I was the one giving it to her.

She pushed at my hair, and I rose, licking my lips. Then I drew one exposed nipple into my mouth. A shiver racked her and her tits jiggled.

Her eyes were hazy, but she smiled. "You're so naughty."

I grinned and pushed up, taking in her long, nude body. Full breasts, strong hips, and a stomach that I had a hard time keeping my hands off.

She eyed the push of the erection at my jeans. "I can take care of you."

"I'm a man of my word, Mads. I don't need the pleasure."

She frowned and grabbed her underwear from where it had landed on the pillow. "But why do you need the pain?"

I sat back on my knees and nearly slid off the cot. I twisted to sit on my ass. If I watched her dress, I'd keep taking each article of clothing off. "It's not about pain." It was putting her first. Always. The way it should've been for much of her life. It was about showing her she was more to me than a good time, but if I told her that, she might start building a wall between us, brick by brick.

Her phone pinged. She crawled over the cot to peek at her phone. She had her bra and underwear on and was shrugging into her scrub top. When she saw who had texted, she yanked up her phone and growled. Then she tossed it back on the storage bins moonlighting as end tables.

Her frown deepened as she wiggled into her scrub bottoms. "I've gotta clean up before work." She popped up, stuffed her feet into slippers, and turned. "That was Wendi."

My ex's name took care of my erection. The blood reversed direction, retreating to keep from having anything to do with Wendi. "Not good news?"

"Is it ever with her?" We shared a smile, then she glared at her phone. "Logan's too busy this summer to come visit me."

In other words, Wendi was controlling and likely jealous of her former sister-in-law. She might sense

Damien still had some feelings for Madison. Or she might be jealous that Logan would be excited to see his aunt. Either way, it hurt Madison. "That's fucked up. I'm sorry."

"It is fucked." She rubbed a spot between her brows. "I told her I could drive out there. But nope. Too busy."

She disappeared. Moments later, the sound of a toilet flushing filled the silence. Then water running. Several minutes later, she returned, her hair in a refreshed braid. "I'm going to wake up early tomorrow since this is my last night for a week."

I'd be happy to have her to myself for a while. "Maybe we can grab something to eat when you get up."

Other than the cookies she'd made as part of our bet, I'd eaten like shit since she'd been working her six-day stretch of twelve-hour shifts. When she was off, she made oatmeal taste good with brown sugar and toasted pecans. For meals, she had tossed in roasts or cooked steaks. I'd thought Mama spoiled me. Madison took it to a new level. I could pay her back in more than orgasms.

"There's nothing to grab but a coffee," she said.

"We could go to Curly's."

She paused, grabbing her purse. "Like a date?"

"No," I said quickly, and she drew back. Shit. We were messing around, but she balked at the thought of being official. The sting to my ego gave way to logic. I couldn't assume with her. She was guarded for a reason. "It'd be more casual. We can ask Tenor and Ruby or something so it doesn't look like a romantic night."

She pursed her lips. "Wouldn't want that."

The more I was around her, the more I was certain that we weren't a fluke. This thing between us was significant and real. Like nothing I'd ever experienced. Was she starting to feel the same? "It's not that I don't want that. Things didn't work out with Wendi—thank God—but every girl after, it was the questions. How serious were we? Someone heard there would be a summer wedding. I heard I bought at least three engagement rings over a two-year span. The girls I was seeing would listen to rumors and get excited. Next thing I knew, I was in an argument about how callous I was." I didn't need those rumors getting back to Madison and muddling her thoughts about me, about us. There was an us. I was sure of it.

Her expression softened. "Sorry. I didn't know it got that bad. I'd like to go to Curly's. I haven't been out in . . ." She frowned. "Well, a long time."

She'd been scrimping her pennies. "Tomorrow. Let me know when you wake up."

"I'm also going to meet with Sal."

Another bite of hurt. She hadn't told me. "What does that asshole have to say?"

"I don't know yet." She lifted a shoulder, but a mysterious smile lifted her lips. "I figured it was time to start asking questions about the sale and any conflicts of interest that could be benefitting him."

I reclined on her makeshift bed. The comforter smelled like her fresh-linen scent. Why was it so hot that she listened to me? "I seem to recall saying something like that."

"Did you?" she asked innocently. "I don't remember."

"I'll spell the conversation out with my tongue next time."

"Promise?" She kicked a hip out, looking cute and sexy in her scrubs. I'd never had a nurse fantasy after what my ex had done, but I was developing a CNA fetish.

She grinned and grabbed the lunch she'd packed, stopping to frown inside. "Did you buy me more jelly beans?"

"Red apple."

This time, her smile was as sweet as the cookies she baked. "Thank you."

Then she was gone. I had the bar to myself, which was fine, but I couldn't walk through the place without memories of us stamped into every surface. Her open to me on the pool table. Against the back wall. Then there were the more tender moments. When I'd said the nickname she hated over and over until her pupils dilated and the pulse at the base of her throat fluttered. When I'd wanted to hold her so bad after the bricks smashed the windows.

So much of her was in the bar and it wasn't even done. Once the cabinets, booths, and bar were installed and I finished the bathrooms, she'd be ready to open. By some miracle, we hadn't had delays other than the windows, which were scheduled for installation in a couple of weeks.

I picked up my tool belt and got to work. After a couple of hours, there was rapping on the front door.

"Police! Open up!"

"Nice try, Cruz," I called back.

More than one guy laughed on the other side of the door. I unlocked it and found Lane and Cruz Foster staring back, giant grins on their faces.

"We're here to kidnap you," Lane said. His dark hair was slicked off his face and he had sunglasses on despite the sinking sun.

When I'd first met the guy, he'd worn grease-stained jeans and ratty T-shirts. His hair had been longer, and he'd probably trimmed it himself. Cruz hadn't been much different. He still wore his hair stylishly long, but their clothing had a Western flair. Gone were the heavy biker boots. They wore cowboy boots, dusty jeans if they'd been working, and T-shirts that had holes from work, not because they couldn't afford more clothing.

Cruz rubbernecked around me. "Damn. It looks the same but different. Can we see inside?"

I stepped aside. Madison probably wouldn't mind. Cruz and Lane weren't from Bourbon Canyon. When Myles had returned to win Wynter back, he'd learned he had brothers who were already young adults. Mama had taken the two brothers in, and my siblings and I had shown them the ranching ropes. In turn, Lane and Cruz worked for Bailey Beef and Lane had saved us a ton doing mechanic work for us on the side. All billable hours. Tate had made sure of it.

Lane sauntered in, hands stuffed in his jeans pockets. "Flatlanders resurrected, huh?"

"Almost." I ushered them in and locked the door behind us.

The tour only took a few minutes. I stayed away from Madison's room, and I didn't mention that she'd been staying here. "I was just going to mount a urinal before you showed up."

Cruz made a disgusted sound. "Don't need to know your personal life, Teller."

I shot him a glare, barely holding back my snicker.

Lane appraised me. "We'll give you a hand if you let me grab a bottle of Original for us for the evening." A sly smile spread across his face. "I heard you've been trying to mount something else. A pretty little bar owner."

This time, I turned serious. "Who'd you hear that from?"

"As if bringing a woman to a family gathering wouldn't make the rounds."

"It's not like that."

"Why not?" Lane crossed his arms and his biceps bulged a whole lot more than they had before he'd worked on the ranch.

"It's just not," I said, irritated. It was like they were cracking open the door to my private time with Madison. She might run out if it opened too far.

Cruz's grin told me I'd get even crankier. "It's absolutely like that. What's going on? She friend-zone you?"

A friend wouldn't have done what I had earlier. "No."

They stared at me.

I would use Madison's tactics. "It's none of your business. Either of you."

Cruz's smile only widened. "Hot damn. You're into her."

"So into her." Lane smirked. He wandered toward the boarded windows. "Tenor said the windows got busted, so she's staying with you. For safety." I didn't respond, so he continued to pace along the exposed brick, running his fingers over the cool stone. "I've seen her around. She's quiet for someone who grew up here."

I worked my jaw back and forth. "She didn't have the best childhood." I wasn't giving away her secrets. All of Bourbon Canyon had known what her parents had been like. "Things weren't easy for her. Neither were people."

Cruz grimaced, clicking his tongue. "She'd identify better with us than the loving Bailey crew?"

I nodded. "And now she's got this bar to try and earn a living from. She doesn't need people around town speculating about us."

"They already do." Cruz shrugged when Lane shot him a glare. "What? It's true."

"We stopped in at Copper Summit to see Tenor," Lane added. "Hit up a couple of girls we thought were tourists, but they were just home for a reunion. They were mourning that all the Bailey men were off the market. Tenor's getting married and you're hooking up with Scooter's sister."

"She deserves better than just hooking up," I said vehemently.

Both guys studied me.

"So it's like that," Lane said.

"The Bailey brothers are all off the market," Cruz parroted.

There was a ring of truth in what he said. I'd already been off the market for a few years, but because of Madison, I didn't ever want to go back on it.

*

Madison

Teller: Let me know when you're up and we'll go to lunch.

I stretched in bed. A few hours of sleep on this quality mattress was better than nine hours of crappy sleep on that cot in the bar. I rolled up and pushed my hair back.

We were going to Curly's, but I craved making bread

more than I did eating it. I missed the process of mixing and kneading. When I had my own place, I'd make another sourdough starter. I ought to have enough time to do it at Teller's, but we were busy all through the day.

The new bathroom partitions were supposed to arrive soon and the cabinets for the bar were due the week after. Once the windows were installed, I could do a soft open, start bringing in money, and refine how the bar would run. I could even make some goodies, like cupcakes, cookies, and my homemade caramels.

No. Flatlanders was a bar. It was known for rough edges and strong drinks. But desserts might distract patrons from noticing the mixed drinks were actually mixed.

I rolled out of bed and took a few extra minutes in the shower. The warm-water-and-high-pressure combo was still a treat. After I was done, I grabbed my jeans and a navy-blue T-shirt. I stepped into the pants but stared at the top while I zipped and buttoned the jeans. I had brought the rest of my clothing. Did I have a better shirt?

We weren't going on an official date, but I could look like I cared a little more. I'd already braided my hair. Doing anything else would be a big ol' signal that I had my hopes up for more. I wasn't ready to show him that I cared. He could do better than me, but I didn't have to make it more obvious to everyone than it was.

I found a shirt with minimal wrinkles that was cream-colored with a bright sunflower on the front. It was too short to tuck in. To anyone else, it'd be a normal top. To me, it was like wearing a dress. Bright and girly.

I shrugged into the shirt and tugged the hem down, staring at the sunflower. I'd shown it to Damien after I'd bought it. *Not really your style, is it?* That was all he'd said and I hadn't worn it. But I also hadn't given it away.

Downstairs, I found a coffee from Mountain Perks in the fridge with "Mads" written on it. Smiling, I pulled it out and tossed it in the microwave for a minute. I wouldn't need to make food. More room for Curly's buns.

How'd he get them so soft? Someday, I'd have the space and time to refine my own recipe.

I took a sip of the warm coffee. I had the house to myself. We'd been coming and going, and in between, we'd been messing around. The chance to snoop hadn't presented itself. I loved the vibe of the place and wanted to see the rest. Were all the rooms as welcoming and cozy?

Before I poked around, I shot a message off to Teller. **I'm awake. Thanks for the coffee.**

I took a drink and wandered through the living room. Hands down, this was my favorite spot. The square footage was almost as big as the house I'd grown up in, except for the garage Mom and Dad had converted into an all-seasons rec room so Dad could watch football and drink beer. No girls allowed.

I found the main-level bathroom I'd heard Teller use that first night we'd been together-ish. There were two more doors in the hallway. One must be the office Teller had mentioned.

I opened the door closest to the bathroom and laundry room and poked my head in. Yep. An office. "Nice."

It could be a bedroom, but the way he'd decorated it was a work of art. Crisp aluminum prints of Copper Summit hung on the walls over a moderate-sized streamlined desk. No large hunk of wood for Teller, which surprised me. This room was like him. Rugged but modern.

A large window took over the longest wall. Copious sunlight streamed in and there was nothing but trees and green grass for a view. So gorgeous. I closed the door and went to the next one.

It was a bedroom, very similar to the guest room I was using. The artwork was softer, canvas prints of the Bailey family ranch with the rolling hills and the tree-filled mountains in the background.

I leaned my head against the doorframe and took another sip of my coffee. Teller loved his home. He loved his job. His family was his priority. Any one of those would be special, but to have all three? I'd never met anyone like him, and if I had, they hadn't wanted anything to do with me.

The front door opened. I closed the door and beelined for the entry that connected with the mudroom.

"Hey." Teller wiped his boots off like it was a habit. There was no mud and he hadn't been working at the ranch. He wore a black polo with the copper logo of the distillery embroidered over his left pec. "I like that shirt."

Pleasure infused me, sudden but hesitant. "Thank you." I tensed, preparing for the *but*. It never came.

Instead, he crossed to me, wrapped an arm around my waist, and pressed a kiss to my lips. He didn't take it further, pulling back almost immediately. "I'm not going to be able to drink coffee without your flavor in it anymore."

"I was snooping." The confession shot out of me like

a bullet. "I know you said you'd give me a tour, but I was curious."

Humor crinkled the corners of his eyes. "Find anything incriminating?"

"Another bedroom. Why didn't you put me there?"

"I wanted you closer to me."

A lasso looped around my heart, and he was holding the end. If he kept saying things like that, the depth I was falling for him would be bottomless.

"Ready to go eat?" he asked.

"I can drive. You're already taking so much time off." I could've met him there.

"Cruz and Lane stopped in at the bar last night, and we got the urinals done, and most of the toilets. You mind?"

Alarm hovered, waiting for permission to rise. Two strange guys had been in Flatlanders? They'd been customers before, from what Scott had said. He'd grudgingly let them stay without tossing them out like he would a Bailey. Claimed their money spent the same, but it was likely that the Foster brothers also attracted more women to the bar.

I hadn't officially met Lane or Cruz Foster, but they hadn't caused trouble with my family, though surely someone had filled them in about the Townsends. "No. It's fine."

He narrowed his eyes like he was inspecting my "fine" to determine if it was very much not fine.

"Really," I stressed. "They seem like good guys."

"They are. And they're as good with porcelain as they are engines." A teasing smile lit his eyes. "If you're going to admit to snooping, I'm going to confess to bringing Copper Summit under Flatlanders' roof."

I let out a mock gasp. "Did the walls shake?"

"No, but it gave us a chance to use those urinals. Cruz and Lane practice-flushed every toilet." He spread his hands apart. "With their help, I'm done until the partitions arrive. They're helping out at the ranch while they're here until Tenor and Ruby's wedding, and tomorrow, we're running to Billings to get the light fixtures. We'll get them wired in a full day quicker than I could do alone."

An old pressure squeezed my ribs. "I can't reimburse them."

"Trust me, Mads. They're good guys, but it's best if they're not idle. They didn't have the tamest upbringing and sometimes the wild sneaks out."

Now I liked them even more. "Okay. But I'll buy the bourbon next time."

Teller swayed closer. "We don't have to buy bourbon, darlin'."

Warm tingles spread over my skin. He had access to all the bourbon he wanted, a lot of money, and . . . me. "Show-off."

He winked and cocked his elbow out. "You can finish your coffee on the way."

"I have to meet Sal in a couple hours." Sal didn't know I was stopping in. No more excuses.

"Then I'll be your getaway driver. I can wait in the pickup."

I didn't want Teller with me. Sal would be on guard, but I also needed to handle it myself. I needed to be taken seriously, but I'd like knowing he wasn't far away. "Deal. Let's get some buns."

CHAPTER FOURTEEN

Madison

In Curly's, the group of us were garnering everything from curious glances to open gawking. I didn't make eye contact with anyone, and for the first time, I'd been seated at the front of the restaurant. Curly liked to show off the founding family of Bourbon Canyon.

The server had taken our orders right away. The lunch crowd was pushed through quicker than in the evening. Good. Less time for me to be on display.

I pushed out everyone else until my world consisted of me, Tenor, Teller, and Ruby. Good thing I'd worn more than a plain T-shirt. I might feel dressed up in my simple sunflower shirt, but compared to Ruby, I was a dull stone. Her dark curls were a halo around her head, and she was too damn cute in her pleated black skirt and sunny yellow top. Even her shoes were happy, with their little buckle around the ankle.

Tenor hadn't been able to keep his hands off his

fiancée, always touching her with little strokes against the back of her hand, a drifting of his fingers over her shoulders when she'd sat in the chair he'd pulled out, and I'd caught the move of his arm as he rubbed her thigh under the table.

Envy bloomed in my chest. I hated the emotion. There was too much others had that I didn't.

I had a job, a business, a roof over my head. The roof wasn't mine, but only because Teller had been insistent that Flatlanders was not safe. My mom was getting the care she needed, and it wasn't me that had to do it. I had plenty, though I tired of wanting more.

And for however long, I had Teller.

"I love the posts you've been doing," Ruby said. "The character of the bar has really come out, and then combined with yours, I think it's a good fit."

"I learned from the best," I said and I meant it. I'd paid for a consult, but she'd given me much more time and expertise than I was owed.

"If you got some shots of this guy"—Ruby tipped her head toward Teller—"you'd definitely attract a bigger female crowd. That is, if he wants to."

"I'd hate to show Tenor that I can draw more likes than him," Teller joked.

I followed Copper Summit's social media pages, and the posts with the guys were quite popular. That wasn't why I studied their posts. I was evaluating Ruby's tactics. But he was why I caught myself mindlessly stalled on an image with a stalwart Teller pouring corn into a mash tank.

Tenor shook his head. "I'd hate for you to realize that the girls are liking the posts for the bourbon and not you."

Teller laughed and I joined in. Light. Easy. The way it should be with family and friends. The way it had been with my aunt Tilly when she'd taken me shopping for new shoes or when she'd let me pick three different treats at a bakery in Billings. I had lost that when she passed.

"What are you doing after this?" Ruby asked. "I saw you were almost done with the bathrooms."

"Not me," I answered. "Teller gets the credit for it."

I almost put my hand on Teller's leg, but I squeezed my fingers into a fist. This was casual. Not official. We weren't a couple.

Then what were we? I still didn't have an answer.

Our food arrived, and I got lost in the good conversation and excellent food. Once our plates were cleared, Teller got the tab.

"We'd better get going," he said. "She has to meet with her real estate agent."

"I hope it's to fire him." Teller shot him a glare, but Tenor just shrugged. "Sal would run over his mom to make an extra buck."

I smothered a laugh. He was right. I should've questioned Sal weeks ago.

Teller thought for a moment. "He sort of did, remember? His dad made him life insurance beneficiary so he could take care of his mom, only Sal got a new boat, a truck to haul it with, and a cabin outside of Jackson Hole."

"I must've been gone for that," I muttered. Would it have mattered? I'd have probably hired him anyway, telling myself he was my only option without trying. "Anyone have a recommendation?" I asked, not really kidding. Who else would sell the house for me that didn't hold a grudge against my parents?

Tenor's brow creased and he exchanged a look with Teller. "There's Jeff Armstrong."

Not for me. "He said the Townsends could eat shit. He'd bulldoze our property before he passed along 'bad juju.' " I threw up air quotes for the last part.

"He'd sell it and buy another boat," Teller said. "What about Kathy Wilson?"

"She called Mom a whore." I wasn't going to say the next part, but their doubtful expressions drove me to it. "She called me Baby Ho when I was a kid."

"Jesus." Teller leaned back, storm clouds raging in his expression.

"People have bought and sold property around my parents all my life," I explained. "It's enough time to insult and piss off every agent in the county, or sleep with them, in the case of my dad and Kathy."

"Ah, hell," Teller said. "That does complicate it."

"I might have an option," Ruby said hesitantly. "Don't get me wrong, she's not my favorite person. But she has a healthy ego, so she'll fight for her clients and insult anyone she doesn't like subtly, but so thoroughly they won't know what hit them."

Tenor's eyes widened. "Cara?"

Ruby nodded but didn't take her attention off me. "She moved back to Bozeman with her husband, but I've seen her signs posted in the area."

"Was she mean to you growing up?" I asked. I wouldn't trade one ass for another, and Ruby was the sweetest girl. Who the hell would insult her?

Ruby leaned forward, her expression earnest. "Yes, but she seemed to be trying to change. There was just too much history there, you know? I'm not Tenor. I can't go play tennis with her like he does with my dad."

Right. I'd been there when Tenor and his school bully, Ruby's dad, had sort of reconciled or had at least agreed to be amicable for his daughter.

"I only play tennis with Robert because he's your dad." A muscle jumped in Tenor's jaw. "And so I can kick his ass."

"You also enjoy leading him on and letting him think he has a chance." Ruby had proud hearts in her eyes.

Okay. If Ruby could semivouch for Cara, then I could give her a shot.

It sounded like I was firing my real estate agent.

Teller

I was waiting in the pickup for Madison with my window open. She had marched inside Sal's tiny office in the corner of his wife's insurance business like she was on a mission that she would not abandon until she was the only one standing.

It had to take courage. Who the ever-loving fuck called a kid names just because their parent was mean? I pulled out my phone and called Mama.

"Teller." Mama's warm greeting flowed through the line.

"Hey, Mama. You still sell eggs to Kathy Wilson?"

"Yes. Now that Cruz and Lane are back in town, I told her my supply is going to dwindle." She chuckled. "Those boys like their eggs."

They liked Mama's food. We all did. "You mind cutting her off? She called Madison a baby ho when she was younger. And Jeff Armstrong doesn't get any of our beef."

The silence was loud. "Consider it done."

"Thank you, Mama."

"How is Madison doing?"

"She's firing Sal as we speak."

"Oh, good." Her relief flowed through the line, and I knew exactly how she felt. "That man is bad business."

"Agreed."

"Do you two want to come for dinner soon? Or does she work all week?"

"No, she doesn't." I knew her hours for the next month. "I'll ask her." A shout came from inside. "I gotta go."

She must've heard the alarm in my voice. "Give him hell. He deserves it." The line went dead.

I got out of my pickup. A man's raised voice emanated from the building. Through the window, a woman sat at her desk, staring slack-jawed straight ahead of her. I was two steps down the sidewalk when the door banged open. Madison's mouth was set in a mutinous line, but triumph lit her eyes and, fuck, that was good to see.

Sal rushed out after her, stabbing his finger toward her. The first two buttons of his shirt were undone and there was a stain around the third button. "You use another agent and I will sue—" His gaze landed on me and he reared back. "Teller?"

I kept him stuck in my gaze like a bug pinned to a science project. "I've got a good lawyer, Madison. She'll be happy to talk to Sal's legal team."

The flush from the cocksucker's face drained until he was gray.

Madison stopped next to me. "I'm sure she'll also like to hear about how Sal and his friend were planning to flip the property for seven figures more than he recommended I sell it for." She snapped her fingers. "There's also that . . . what was it? Conflict of interest that wasn't disclosed?"

"The contract between you two sounds nice and severed." I kept my tone hard. I didn't bother to wait for a response. I walked around the hood of the pickup to open Madison's door.

Her lips twitched, but when I winked at her, she grinned.

"You liked doing that," she whispered.

Sal gave up and slunk inside.

"Yeah, I did." Before I closed the door, I leaned in. "Want to go to Mama's for dinner tomorrow night?"

CHAPTER FIFTEEN

Madison

I got out of the pickup and tugged at my shirt. I was used to my scrub top not being tucked in, and for some bizarre reason, I had put shorts on. They were jean shorts, so I only felt like I'd forgotten half my clothing.

It'd been worth it to see the spark of heat in Teller's eyes.

Now I was walking toward Mae's house, clutching a coconut cake to my chest. Teller had gotten up early to get in a good day's worth of work, but I had woken even earlier to make a cake. My second time at Mae's and my nerves were worse. The last time, her son hadn't seen me naked yet.

It wasn't like Mae knew what Teller and I were getting up to. What if she suspected? What if she thought I was cheap or that I wasn't good enough for her son?

I was a divorced college dropout having a meal with a

woman who had grown bourbon and beef empires. Not just one successful venture but two. She'd also raised seven kids who'd turned into stellar adults and had helped shape countless foster kids.

I had baked a cake.

"Relax," Teller murmured as he put a hand on the small of my back and steered me through the screen door at the back of the house. "She doesn't bite. Only I do."

The dropped timbre of his voice sent shivers skittering over my skin.

I shot him a disgruntled look and he returned it with an unrepentant one.

"Come on in." Mae's smile widened when she saw what I had in my arms. "Oh my gosh. I was just thinking about how it was too soon for me to start craving that cake."

I handed it over. "I'll bake you one anytime."

"You might have to." She set the tray on the counter and admired it for a moment. "When Lane and Cruz see this tomorrow, there won't even be crumbs left. They're staying with Myles and Wynter tonight. Elsa's running them ragged so Mom and Dad can have a date night." Mae waved me in. "I hope you like roast beef and veggies."

"I like anything you cook."

Teller and I helped her carry the trays of food to the table. The roast was giant, browned to perfection, and surrounded by juices that soaked into the mass of seasoned and chopped potatoes, carrots, and parsnips. That thing could feed ten people.

"Mama always makes a lot extra." Teller pulled a chair out for me to sit.

"Lots of hungry mouths looking for food around this place." Mae sat at the end of the table, so it wasn't her across from us like a one-woman firing range. She seemed to sense what made others around her the most comfortable.

My nerves stacked on top of each other as we handed platters back and forth and I filled my plate. I couldn't get lost in a crowd like at the previous gathering.

I took a bite of the most perfect hot-pink slice of beef and a moan slipped out. Teller made a small choking sound, and the corner of Mae's mouth curled up. She didn't look upset that I sounded like I hadn't eaten for a week, but I couldn't help my shame. Not after I'd been teased in school for digging into my tater tot hot dish like a dog.

"What do you season this with?" I asked to cover my embarrassment.

For the rest of the meal, we chatted about preferred spices, seasoning methods, even brining. Then we started on baking. I rarely had a chance to make a meal for more than one. Even when I'd been married, I had used restraint, feeding the two of us to minimize cost and waste. Damien had been discouraging when it had come to my sweet tooth, so I hadn't baked unless there was a reason. A coworker's birthday or a work potluck.

Mae had spent her life in the kitchen, making more meals than a Michelin-star chef. "Do you get tired of it?" I asked. "Cooking so much."

She thought for a moment. I hadn't expected her to brush off my question—that wasn't Mae. The fact that I could even ask without thinking twice said a lot about her. "Some days, truthfully. I love it, and I love food. It keeps me busy, which is getting more important these days now that the kids have taken over so many of the chores. But being in the kitchen is still my favorite. Every meal is like a work of art. An artist can make a million bowls, but they still want the next one to be something they're proud of. Food is my art, only I get to sit down after a long session and eat it." She patted the table twice. "You two stay here."

She went to the kitchen and Teller snagged another piece of roast. "I can cook," he said. "But not like this."

"It's the seasoning salt with a pinch of nutmeg," I said. "Add too much and you risk your meat tasting like a pumpkin pie."

He shuddered. "I like my pumpkin pie, but not on my beef."

I was laughing as Mae returned with three rocks glasses. "I think the Gold will go just as well with the coconut as the Original." She reached into a credenza behind her and pulled out a half-full bottle of Copper Summit. *Gold* was emblazoned across the label in bold print.

Something about this line tickled my memory. Scott had bitched about Copper Summit . . . Yes! He'd complained about how much they sold their top-shelf bourbon for. *Real gold isn't even worth that much per ounce.*

I'd never fact-checked him, but here I was, having it for free. "Can I get the cake?"

"Sure thing, dear," Mae said as she poured three glasses.

When I returned and the cake was sliced and on plates in front of us, I almost paused. Since when was this my life? I had had a delicious meal made for me.

There'd been no arguments. No one had said anything even mildly derogatory.

My nights out with my aunt hadn't been as peaceful. She'd try to build me up and, somehow, that had shone a spotlight on how awful my days could be. But tonight, my life was good company and good food.

"My gosh," Mae said after her first bite. "Heavy but light, creamy, and so much flavor. You are a wizard."

Teller took half his piece in one hunk and stuffed it in his mouth. He followed with a sip of bourbon. He smacked his lips. "You're right, Mama. The Gold is perfect."

We ate and chatted. When all our forks were set on empty plates, I continued to marvel over the evening. No wonder Riley had been willing to bid so much. If I'd known about nights like tonight, I would've bid for me instead of Flatlanders.

"What do you two have planned for the rest of the night?" Mae asked, swirling the remains of her bourbon.

I'd had a few sips. Rich and full-bodied, I could actually see why people drank it. I had stayed away from bourbon, thanks to my parents' hatred of all things Bailey, but Scott had carried the cheapest he could. No one had come to Flatlanders for bourbon. Apparently, it was like tequila. The cheap stuff would sear someone's taste buds and scorch their esophagus, but quality tequila was better than sex.

Better than the sex I'd been having at the time, anyway.

"What do you think, Mads?" Teller's attention washed over me, warming me on the outside the way the bourbon did my insides. He tilted his glass, the amber fluid flowing to the side. "Are you up for a tour of

Copper Summit? They close early tonight. I can show you around."

"Oh." A special tour of the distillery? I'd never been in there. Out of curiosity, I'd driven by a couple of times. The building was a renovated mine. Massive windows allowed a peek at the giant stills inside. Old copper pits had grown in behind the distillery, but the landscape around it was just as stunning. It was like a little jewel hidden among the foothills. "Sure."

"You won't mind me showing off?" He grinned. "I make bourbon better than I install toilets."

CHAPTER SIXTEEN

Madison

Teller and I cleaned up the table and did the dishes Mae hadn't finished before sitting down to dinner. She really was a superwoman. Once the dishwasher was going and the table was cleaned off, I got a hug. Strong and solid, her embrace was everything I'd been missing since my aunt had passed.

Heat pricked the backs of my eyes, but I slowly inhaled and gathered myself before pulling back. "Thank you so much for dinner."

"Don't thank me." She winked. "I'm keeping the left-over cake."

I was still smiling when I climbed into Teller's pickup. "That was fun."

"I might be a grown-ass man, but I'll never pass up a meal at Mama's table."

Gah. That was so damn sweet.

He glanced at me before focusing on the road. "Can I ask you something?"

The cozy feeling vanished. His tone was hesitant, and Teller was usually free with his opinions. "Okay?"

He didn't flash me an encouraging smile. "How did you turn out so . . . normal?" He winced and shook his head, aiming the pickup down the winding gravel drive. "Sorry, it's just—"

"No, I know." I let my head rest on the seat back. "I was actually just thinking of her. Aunt Tilly. She was my dad's older sister."

"Older and more stable?"

"More stable in every way. I even asked to live with her once." That was the only time I had felt both wanted and hopeless. "My mom said they'd run over her dead body ten times before she'd let anyone think she couldn't raise her own goddamn daughter."

"Her pride got in your way."

I let out a hard laugh and watched the rolling hills thicken with trees the closer we got to the distillery. "That's the tagline for my life." I ran my bottom lip through my teeth. "After Aunt Tilly's offer, I couldn't quit imagining what leaving Bourbon Canyon would be like. I dreamed of it. But Mom? She never wanted me to go anywhere. Yet, at the same time, she never wanted me around."

"What a mind fuck for a kid. How do you deal with her?" He turned down a road leading away from town. The two-lane highway curved around the foothills, twisting and turning. On one side, the land was filled with small pastures and the Baileys' cows quietly grazing.

"I grew up with it. I don't know. She is the way she is, and what she says still hurts, but she won't change. She and Logan are my only family." When push had come to shove, Mom had wanted me. No matter what she said.

"No word on Logan?"

I shook my head, a lump growing in my throat. "Mom is bitter and mean, but I can only imagine how she grew up. I had Aunt Tilly."

Teller braked in the middle of the empty road. "Madison." His brows pinched together. "You know you don't owe your mom anything. You can walk away from her and never look back."

I smiled sadly. "And where would I go? To finish school for a job I never really wanted?"

"You never wanted to be a nurse?"

I lifted a shoulder. No one had ever asked. Mom had told me I'd never finish school, and Damien had said I should quit. Neither had asked what I really wanted to do. "It's a good-paying job with openings in any part of the country. If I became a travel nurse, they'd even pay me to move around." The freedom had sounded divine.

"And you wanted to travel?" He started driving again, but his jaw was clenched, like what I'd said continued to bother him.

"Yes," I said, wistful. I had wanted to get away from home. "Starting school was such a highlight. I applied for all the scholarships I could, got grants, and lived on campus. It was divine." I let out a sigh.

"Then Cocksucker came along?"

I smiled. "Yup."

He pulled into the empty parking lot. The distillery loomed large, the sinking sun glinting across its windows. Everything was quiet, and when I emerged from the pickup, I was struck with the pleasing smell of grain.

I sniffed.

Teller noticed and grinned. "That's the old mash. We store it and then feed it to the cattle."

"The mash?"

He cocked his head toward the entrance. "Come on. I'll show you."

Inside, I gawked at everything. Timber beams cut through rock walls and soared across the tall ceiling two levels up. To my right was the tasting room. The glass door between the entrance and the tasting room let me glimpse the wooden tables and chairs. There was also another entrance inside.

Ahead of me was a store filled with displays of bourbon bottles and packages—gift sets with small, one-ounce bottles, special batches only available to purchase here, and regular bourbon sizes for sale. Then there were hats, shirts, and candy displays.

A reception desk lined the exterior wall to my left, and a flight of stairs rose behind the merch store. Offices filled the second level, but the masterpiece of the whole view was the wall of windows.

On the far side, giant copper-and-steel stills lorded over the room. Closer to the viewing windows squatted large tanks. Metal piping soared between the stills and across the ceiling.

Impressive. "Whoa."

He stood next to me as if trying to see it from my eyes. He'd been taking in this view since he'd been born. "I'll take you through there. Then we can have a drink."

Inside, the room was quieter than I'd thought it'd be.

He pointed to the short tanks. "Mash tanks. You can smell the yeast farts."

"If it's anything like bread, I'm a fan of yeast."

"It'll do its thing and become what we call distiller's beer." He pointed to a series of pipes arching from the mash tanks to larger columns. "That gets pumped to the distillation tanks."

"And it becomes bourbon?"

He shook his head. "First moonshine, then we distill it down. Even if it's got fifty-one percent corn, it's gotta be put into a barrel at a certain proof, and that barrel needs to be new oak. Then we age it for four years."

"Never shorter?"

He lifted a shoulder. "We can if we put an age statement on it, but Dad was a purist. Four years or bust. We also bottle in bond. More rules, but bourbon enthusiasts associate it with quality."

"And Copper Summit is nothing if not a quality bourbon."

"Damn right. It's more than a name; it's our legacy."

The room didn't fascinate me just for the equipment. Or how it was a thriving environment with many moving parts left alone to do their job. It was the family history in this place. The tradition. The love.

As sentimental as it sounded, love, respect, and adoration were baked into every surface of this place. It was a clean room, and it had to be, but it was well cared for. The distillery didn't have a high turnover, and not because so many of the employees were family.

What was it like to be part of this sort of legacy?

Teller scratched the back of his head. "What do you think? It's okay if you call it boring. Some of the tourists are real frank with their opinions."

They hadn't gotten a personal tour from Teller Bailey. "I always thought brewing was fascinating. And distilling is really just an additional step. I like the science behind it."

"It's a lot of chemistry with biology." He hooked his fingers through mine. "Now to go to my favorite spot."

He led me back out, passing the tall stills and weaving through the large mash tanks. Once we were in the lobby, he unlocked the tasting room.

The quiet in here was more insulated than the lobby. I ran my fingers over the smooth top of a table. For a simple bar, it had a lot of character. On one wall hung a neon Copper Summit sign, next to it, an old black-and-white image of the distillery.

"When's that from?" I asked.

"Right after my dad's grandpa first opened the place. Rhys—you know, Junie's husband? His ex is a photographer and she had some recommendations about getting the picture blown up. I was tempted to do an aluminum print, but the frame fits the vibe in here."

The bar did have a small-town, last-century vibe to it. "It's more like Flatlanders than I would've ever thought."

His brows popped up.

I poked him in the side. "That's not a bad thing."

"No, I mean . . ." He gave me a sheepish smile. "I didn't mean to have that reaction. The two places always seemed like polar opposites, but I can see what you mean. This bar is a lot smaller, but it has a lot of wood and old-downtown ambience. That's intentional, keeping it that way."

"Part of the rugged Montana brand."

"A lot of our clientele are regulars and we want them to feel comfortable." He pulled out a stool for me. "Have a seat and pick a cocktail." He went behind the bar and slid a laminated menu in front of me.

"You have a drink list. Now this is fancy."

He barked out a laugh and leaned across the bar top. "We change our lineup, but again, with the regulars, we'll always carry what they drink. We'll always offer the blackberry bourbon smash. Jason loves that."

Jason was a rancher I'd often seen Teller talking to in town before I'd beelined in another direction. I read through the list of cocktails. Now I was humbled.

Flatlanders carried spirits and soda. Most of the time, Scott hadn't bothered stocking lemons or limes. Our patrons wanted alcohol and they weren't that fussy about how it was served.

Copper Summit gave them an experience. From the bold but welcoming lobby to the tasting room that was as comforting as an old quilt. Then there were the cocktails. The descriptions alone were an adventure. "Local huckleberries?"

"Autumn's property has a ton of bushes."

"All your grains are Montana sourced?" I couldn't keep the awe out of my voice.

"Usually we don't have an issue. It's not unusual. A lot of in-state distilleries try to source their grain from a popular Montana supplier."

I read another description of a blackberry bourbon lemonade. "Hand-picked lemons from Arizona? Seriously?"

"One of my aunts lives there, so she picks them from her backyard."

I pointed to another description. A bourbon-and-grapefruit slush. "She has a grapefruit tree too?"

"And an orange tree." He slid the menu close to him

and read it upside down. "It's in our old-fashioned. Wynter candies them. She'll candy the peels with bourbon too."

"I have to try that."

"One old-fashioned coming up." He bent to grab a glass and a bottle. "I'll even make it with my line of bourbon." He splashed in the bourbon.

"I bought a bottle of Copper Summit once." I pressed my lips together, debating whether to tell him the rest. "It was yours. Spiced Summit."

He paused. "Yeah?"

"It was after you bit my head off." I waved a hand when the tortured look entered his eyes. "I was angry, and I thought what better way to get back at you than to use your line of bourbon for something other than drinking. That'd really get you back."

The glass container of candied orange slices was abandoned as he leaned both hands on the counter. "All I'm hearing is that you were obsessed with me."

I gasped and then broke down laughing. "No." I failed at denying it. Teller had that draw. Even if I wanted to hate him, I had to work really hard at it.

His grin didn't fade as he continued making my drink, shaking a dash of bitters in. "So what else would you do with bourbon other than drink it?"

"Vanilla extract."

He stopped to think, his gaze distant. "That's how Mama makes hers."

"It's really good. The bourbon adds this super subtle caramel flavor to vanilla buttercream frosting." I shook my head. "Sorry. I tend to geek out about all things baking. Anyway, when I was really upset with Mom or

Scott, I would make them something that used at least two teaspoons of that vanilla extract."

The glass was slid in front of me. "You can geek out."

"Sure." I took a sip. The caramel notes I had loved from his line played over my tongue, mellowed by the bitters, then followed by the faintest spice and sweet citrus. Bourbon flavored my mouth, as rich and bold as the man in front of me.

"You more than like baking." His hands were planted on the counter again. It was just the two of us, but the bar could be full and I'd still feel like I was the only one in the room.

"I do enjoy it."

He tilted his head. "You more than enjoy it."

I pushed the menu toward him. "This isn't therapy. You need a drink too." I had bared so much of myself already. I couldn't be the only one stripping themselves down.

He slid the menu back, keeping his fingers on it as he leaned in. "I'll make myself something you want to try."

"The lemonade." I took another drink. Dang, it was good.

"Which one?"

I set the glass down. "You have more than one?"

"It's summer, but Scarlett's hard cherry lemonade is a popular choice."

"Oh. Um . . ." I read the description of both and let out a dramatic gasp. "You don't source the Maraschino cherries locally?"

"It's our one fault." He dug out two glasses, both a highball. "I'll make both."

Since I wanted to try both, I didn't argue. He made

smaller amounts than what was shown in the pictures on the menu.

"Oh god, that blackberry one is good."

He nodded. "People who aren't a fan of bitters like the bourbon-and-fruit cocktails."

I took a long pull from the hard cherry lemonade. "That would be perfect on a hot day with shortbread cookies."

"What would go well with the blackberry one?"

I took another sip and let the flavors sit on my tongue. The sweet and sometimes tartness of the blackberries parried with the bourbon and lemonade. "Hmm . . ." Images of desserts danced through my head as I took another long pull. "Cobbler. But not one that's too sickly sweet. Raspberry maybe?"

"And the old-fashioned?"

"Pie. Because it's also old-fashioned."

He laughed, his throat working up and down. After taking a drink of my hard cherry lemonade, he ran a sink of soapy water and cleaned up the mess he'd made. Then he came around the bar and took the seat next to me. He took the old-fashioned since I was more partial to sweets, and each lemonade cocktail was its own dessert. Neither of them needed to be paired with anything.

The AC was strong in the tasting room. His heat wound around me like a cozy blanket. He had to be a furnace in bed. I used to dream of curling up with my husband during a cold winter morning.

He turned, bracketing me with his legs. "If you could go back to school for anything, what would you pick?"

I shook my head. "You first." Fuzziness crowded the corners of my brain. I was nearly naked in front of this guy. He knew all my desires—family, travel, school. My parents might've been crap, but they'd taught me self-preservation.

"I wouldn't do a single thing differently."

He said it with so much assuredness it amplified my longing tenfold. "Nothing?"

"I got to grow up ranching. You know how fun that is for a boy?" He knocked back the rest of the old-fashioned, his Adam's apple bobbing with his swallow. "Sure, it sucked to get up early when it was fucking freezing out or when I wanted another twelve hours of sleep. The tradeoff was that I got to be out on horseback all day. I'd drive tractors and trucks that other kids got for toys. Did I mention the horses?" He grinned.

"Yes," I said, laughing.

"I went to college and got to do all that, but I learned the most from Dad. The most about business, the most about distilling, and the most about life. Him and Mama."

"The house full of kids didn't bother you?"

"I was barely inside, but no. It was my normal. The girls delighted Mama and even my kid brain could see that. When they were adopted, it was almost a relief we wouldn't have to say goodbye to them." He swirled the empty glass and the ice chunk clinked from side to side. "I guess Wendi would be a do-over, as in I wouldn't have wasted my time with her. Maybe I'd start a family earlier, but there's no reason to if you're not with the right person."

My emptiness echoed his. "I thought I'd have two or three kids by now."

"I thought I'd have five."

I was in the middle of a drink when I coughed. Slapping the back of my hand in front of my mouth, I struggled for control. His deep laughter rumbled through me before he waved a napkin under my face. I took it from him.

"Five if I started early," he amended. "Now I'm an old fucker. Two or three sound just fine."

"Damien always had a reason to wait, but it was a blessing in disguise. I wouldn't want to be tied to him, and I wouldn't want a kid to have Wendi for a stepmother."

"Amen to that." He flattened his big hands on my thighs. "I answered. Your turn. No nursing school. What would you do?"

"Is money no object?" I had dreamed of what exactly I'd do so many times.

"Will it make a difference?"

"I suppose in how I'd travel." The fantasies fell fast and hard in my head, stacking into a familiar wall of dreams that was always out of my reach. "I'd love to go to pastry school."

"Pastry?" When I nodded, he thought for a moment. "I shouldn't be surprised."

"I've debated—should I go to culinary school? Get a degree or a certificate? Stick to pastries or train as a chef? If I was doing it again, I'd get a degree and get to know people. I grew up seeing how much networking benefited others." And I'd seen the opposite. Doors were slammed in my face, thanks to my family's lack of connections. "But now? I think I'd do a program. There are some fourteen-week ones in Boston, and I've looked at the pastry one. Pie in the sky? London. Then I'd travel. Like a taste-testing world tour."

"Why pastry?"

"The only thing my aunt loved more than baking was

going to bakeries, and she'd bring me. I like cooking too, but it's not as interesting. If I could sell bread, I'd make it all the time. Kneading dough is therapy."

The corners of his eyes crinkled with his smile. "You can smack it and it always bounces back."

"You know what I'm the most upset about with the divorce?" He shook his head as if he was afraid of my answer. Like I would say I missed baking for Damien. "I had to leave my sourdough starter behind."

"That bastard."

I laughed. "I wasn't living somewhere I could bake even though I could finally make bread and goodies without his comments."

A dangerous glint darkened his eyes. "And what exactly would he say?"

The dream in my head collapsed as real memories bulldozed over it. "The usual controlling stuff assholes say to their wives about sweets and hobbies they don't think will impress the partners in the firm they work for."

Teller's eyes narrowed as he chewed over my answer. Then he picked up our glasses and slid off his stool, careful not to knock me off in the process. I wanted to ask what he was doing, but I just watched the muscles in his forearms flex as he washed the glasses and put them on a rack to dry. Next, he wiped off the counter.

What are you doing? screamed through my head, but the words didn't leave my mouth.

He rounded the bar to my side and held an elbow out. "We're going back to my place, and you're going to bake whatever the hell you want, and you're going to do it naked until you don't remember a thing that asshole said."

CHAPTER SEVENTEEN

Teller

Madison refused to bake naked, but I got her down to her bra and underwear and an old apron that I had gotten as a housewarming gift from one of my sisters. The front read *My ego is as inflated as my buns*.

Madison giggled every time she looked down at the words.

She pulled a batch of sugar cookies out. Three bowls of colored frosting were lined up on the counter. The shy way she'd told me that decorating cookies was something she loved to do still gutted me.

Why had everyone in her life been so terrible?

I snagged a warm cookie and shoved the whole thing in my mouth.

"They're better cold and frosted," she said.

I lifted a shoulder, still chewing. They'd be better if I could eat them off her bare stomach.

She turned the oven off and studied her cookies. "I'll

put the frosting in the fridge. These need more time to cool, or the icing will ooze everywhere after I pipe it."

I selected a cookie and took the narrow spatula from the pink icing and spread it over the cookie. It thinned and crept close to the edge, but it didn't drip off. "Come here."

Her eyes flared. She moved to put her hands on her hips, realized she wasn't wearing much for clothing, then started to fold her arms, clocked the floury apron, and clasped her hands instead. "Why?"

"You haven't eaten one yet."

"I don't usually when I'm baking."

"You're done baking." I turned on my stool and pushed the seat next to me a few inches out so she could slide on. "Come here."

Tentatively, she crept toward me, her gaze dipping from mine to the treat in my hand. She stopped by the stool and licked her red lips. I lifted the cookie to her mouth. She took a cautious nibble as if she was afraid I'd shove the thing in her face.

"Take a goddamn bite, Mads," I growled.

Her eyes locked with mine. She opened wide and chomped half the cookie off.

I gave a grunt of approval. Her eyelids fluttered and the faintest moan left her.

"Good, aren't they?" I asked gruffly.

She delicately wiped the corner of her mouth. "I wouldn't bake them if they weren't."

A grin stretched my lips. "That's my girl. Don't hide from your talent."

A blush stained her cheeks and I offered her the rest. She chewed, her gaze darting around like she didn't trust when the focus was on her.

I framed her hips with my hands, my fingertips hitting just above her underwear on her warm, bare skin. "Tell me what you're tasting."

Her brows crunched together. "I'm chewing," she said around her mouthful.

I placed a kiss right above the top of the apron. Her plain black bra was the sexiest thing I'd ever seen, and it was hotter that it was partially covered by her apron.

I wrapped a hand around her throat. My thumb moved as she swallowed. "What are you tasting?"

"Sugar. Butter."

I brushed up to stroke the pad of my thumb over her bottom lip. "And?"

"The way they almost caramelize in the oven, but the rich creaminess of the butter shines through, not to be overpowered by the sugar."

There she was. My little baking nerd. "What else?"

"The icing almost overpowers it all," she said, her voice husky. "But the butter would be too rich without it. It's a nice balance, and why I like this recipe."

I took another cookie, spreading some icing over it. This time, it didn't thin as it spread, but I got frosting on my fingers.

I lifted one to her mouth. Her pupils dilated. She licked her lips before swirling her tongue over my fingertip. I'd been battling an erection all night, but I lost the second her tongue touched my flesh. I adjusted my position on the stool. Things were getting damn uncomfortable behind my fly.

Holding the cookie up, I let the challenge in my eyes say everything.

She took another big bite, her teeth sinking through the frosting. She pulled back and that wicked tongue licked out to catch all the crumbs. I'd never watched anything more intensely in my life.

"What do you taste?" I didn't recognize my voice. Deep and rough.

She held my attention while she chewed. Then she swallowed, the movement of her narrow throat mesmerizing me before her tongue darted out to catch the few small crumbs remaining. "It's what I feel."

I didn't think I could get harder, but goddamn, my vision was crossing from the pain. "Tell me."

"It's crunchy. Satisfying. A little rough on my tongue and then it just . . . melts."

"I like sweet treats like that." I offered her the rest of the cookie.

As soon as her lips closed around it, I rose. I reached around her and tugged on the string to the apron. When it fell loose, I lifted it over her head.

"I want to carry you upstairs, but I don't want to take you to your bedroom, Maddy. I want you in mine."

"What?" She put her fingers over her mouth and swallowed.

I kissed her, long and slow, before pulling back. "I know how sweet you taste. Now I need to know how you feel." I trailed kisses along her jaw to her ear. "I want you to melt around me."

"What happened to over and over and over again?"

"You'll always be my priority, Madison. Because you deserve to be and because I want you to be. Do you want this? Between us? If you do, I'm going to make it happen."

She didn't say yes. But her hair tickled the side of my face as she nodded.

I lifted her and she automatically wrapped her legs

around my waist. The juncture of her thighs cradled my erection. I went for the stairs and crested them like the house would collapse if I didn't get inside of her soon.

"If you're trying to show off," she said, nipping my ear as I turned into my bedroom, "I'm seriously impressed."

"I haven't gotten around to showing off just yet." I set her in the middle of my bed and drank her in. She propped herself on her elbows and looked around while I dragged my shirt over my head.

"You have such good taste. It's simple and not over-done, like the rest of the house." Her gaze landed on my chest and her eyes widened.

My pants and underwear came off next and her lips parted. "Like what you see, Mad Maddy?"

"I can't hear that name without getting turned on."

Good. No one could hurt her with it again. I took a condom out of my nightstand.

Madison looked away, but I caught the flash of disappointment in her eyes. I read her as easily as the menu she'd studied in the tasting room. I'd told her I didn't date. So why did I have condoms in my nightstand?

"Don't worry—they're not expired. Brand-new box." I tossed a packet on the pillow above her head. "Which also means I have plenty. You know why it's brand new?"

Her headshake was nearly imperceptible.

"I've never brought anyone here."

The flare of her eyes validated my wait. My resis-tance to letting someone random into the house I wanted to be mine forever.

"It's not my business." She tilted her head from side to side. "Except for how well you are stocked now."

"Maddy," I said, crawling over her, "a lot of my business is quickly becoming yours."

She didn't lie back right away. "You seem to be in a lot of my business too."

Her response lacked heat, but there was a hint of bewilderment and more than a little satisfaction. "That's because you fascinate me. And a whole lot more."

She dropped her attention to my erection. "What do you feel?"

"Like I'm going to explode and implode at the same time if I don't find out how you feel coming around my cock."

Those red lips of hers parted.

I braced myself on my knees to reach around and unhook her bra. Her perfect breasts spilled out. I might be ready to combust, but I was also a man who liked to play.

I laved open-mouthed kisses down her chest until I reached a peaked nipple. Pulling her tight flesh between my lips, I sucked. I kneaded her other breast. My dick protested being smothered against the comforter instead of her, but she was worth the wait.

However, she still wasn't fully bare to me. I released her nipple, loving how she arched into me, then slid her underwear down her legs, scooting lower as I went. My cock fucking throbbed, but still, I took my time.

When she rolled up, I stiffened, panicking. This was it. She was going to tell me this was a mistake and we couldn't mess around anymore. And I'd have to tell her that nothing about her and me was messing around.

The longer I was around Madison, the more I wanted to stay in her orbit. I wanted to be that buffer between her and the world. Her safe space.

It was humbling to think she might let me.

But instead of telling me she needed to get back to her own room, she encircled my cock with her warm hand. My hips kicked out and every muscle locked up. I could come so easily, and not just because her hands were the only ones besides mine on my dick in a long time.

"It's my turn to play," she said. "To taste."

"Christ, Mads. I'll come in your mouth as soon as your lips wrap around it."

She gave me a pump and my eyes damn near rolled back. "Later?"

"I sure as fuck won't stop you any other time."

She twisted and reached for the condom. Ripping it open, she said, "Then I get to put this on."

I stayed on my knees and let her roll the condom on, flinching and jerking the whole time. Her fingers could just as well be laced with electricity.

"Lie back," I said gruffly.

When she did, I pushed her knees open. My bedroom door hung open and the light from downstairs filtered in. Her hair was still braided, but my next goal would be to see it spread behind her.

"Take your hair out."

Her expression flickered, but she reached back. Plait by plait, she undid her braid and fanned her hair out behind her.

"Now you're completely unbound. Just for me." My caveman brain pounded against my skull. *Take her. Take her.*

Her tits were full and her nipples strained upward. Her pussy was wet and glistening, begging for my tongue.

I said I was a man who liked to play and I meant it. I stretched over her and dragged a finger through her folds. She soaked me to the knuckle. "Fuck, you're wet for me."

I circled her clit and she groaned, her hips rolling up.

My resistance broke. I'd been waiting too long, giving myself the worst case of edging ever. Goddamn torture. But worth it. So damn valuable to see her come undone over and over again. To witness her consumed with pleasure, lost to it. And the power to know it was because of me.

Because she was fucking mine.

I raked the tip of my dick through her seam, wetting the tip before pushing inside. I should've waited, teased us more, but I couldn't. I wasn't superhuman.

Her heat surrounded me, gripping me tight. "*Fuck.*"

She arched and rocked, adjusting to my size. "Oh god."

Clarity flooded back. "Did I hurt you?"

She gave me an incredulous, albeit heavy-lidded look. For an answer, she widened her legs and grabbed my ass.

Pleasure stabbed me between the eyes and I bucked my hips against her. "You're so fucking tight. It's like you're made for me."

Her eyes widened. I didn't want to ruin the night, so I went for distraction, catching her lips with mine. I pulled out and thrust back in. Her groan went right into me.

"Teller." The catch in her voice was there, the one that told me she was so damn close.

I broke the kiss to wet the tip of my finger between her lips, and as I pumped, I dragged my fingertip down her sternum, loving how her tits fucking bounced, over her belly and all the way to her clit.

Her tight little bud was begging for attention. I gritted my teeth and tried to hang on. I wasn't coming without her, but if I took too long, I wouldn't have a choice. The squeeze of her was absolute bliss. Her moans and whimpers were rapture.

"Teller," she whispered. "I'm close."

"Come for me, Mads."

She rocked with me. We were one.

The pressure inside me built to atmospheric levels and then her body fisted mine, holding tight.

I dropped to an elbow by her head, thrumming her clit while I pumped. My chest heaved and my rhythm went erratic like I'd never fucked before. "You're mine, Mads. Just for me."

Her explosion hit. She convulsed, hugging me tight, burying her face in my chest and clamping her legs around me.

Fuck, yes. My release slammed into me. I stiffened as lightning crashed through my body, sizzling and licking over my nerves, racing up and down my spine. I closed in around her as much as she embraced me.

"Fuck, fuck, fuck." I'd never come this hard before. I could barely breathe. She milked everything I had and then more. I was all too willing to give it.

After my world quit catapulting through space, I sank onto her and rolled us to the side. She had a leg pinned under me, and an arm, but we were each limp. Sated.

For now. An eternity could come and go and I'd never tire of her.

Madison

We reclined in the massive soaking tub in his equally spacious bathroom. I ran my hand over the bubbles.

After our first round, we'd gone two more.

Two. And while I was sitting on his lap with warm water and bubbles up to my nipples, he was half-erect underneath my ass.

I leveled the bubbles in front of me. "I do not understand how you're not worried about the two of us in this tub full of water. That's a lot for a floor."

He pulled my loose hair to the side and kissed my nape. "I left the details to the architect. I told him I wanted the biggest fucking tub he could find. I work hard, but I like my comfort."

I did too, but that was a face mask when they were on sale. Sitting on his lap alone was a luxury. Getting carried up the freaking stairs like I was just a bulky scarf was a once-in-a-lifetime thing. Having him steal my cookies and then feed them to me ranked as an erotic fantasy.

I could very easily get used to this.

Who was I kidding? All that and then the sex? I was a goner.

I laid my head back and the ends of my hair floated out to the sides. "I can't believe you were hiding this in your room. I bet it's the most popular part of your house."

"Like I said, no one's been in here but me."

I peeked at him, but he was focused on the bubbles. Or my nipples. I couldn't tell.

"You didn't believe me?" He sounded almost hurt.

"It's okay if you did, you know. We both have pasts. But . . . *no one?*" Maybe I hadn't truly believed him. Guys said a lot to get laid, and it wasn't like I had stopped to ask myself if he'd been sincere. I'd wanted to get laid too. "I'm sorry. I should've known you meant it."

"Don't be sorry. I'll earn your trust one day."

"No, I trust—"

"*All* of it."

Fair enough.

"No one's been in my room." He trailed his fingers through the wet strands of my hair. "I've never had a woman here."

I sat up, my butt grinding against his thighs, and half turned. "Why?"

"This is my safe space." The corner of his mouth lifted and his gaze went distant again. "I wouldn't change anything about my past because I wanted what my parents had. They loved each other. If someone doesn't believe in soulmates, then they haven't spent any time around Mae and Darin Bailey. Those two were in sync. Somehow even their arguments ended in laughter. I thought it was a one-in-a-million thing. Then Tate married his first wife and only confirmed it."

I barely recalled that Tate had been married before. Mom had complained when he'd moved back to town and made some snide comments about his marriage failing and apparently those Baileys weren't good when it counted. I'd only listened with one ear.

"But then he met Scarlett. And Wynter tracked down Myles."

I turned my head again. "Tracked him down?"

His fond, big-brother grin was everything I had wanted growing up. "He had no clue who she was when she started working for him as an assistant. Then he shows up for Dad's funeral, and bam, there she is, at the kitchen table." He went quiet for a moment. "All my siblings fell like dominos. One by one, holding out until they found their perfect match. After the way I behaved once Wendi split, I didn't want random anymore. I didn't want to fill my house with memories that weren't from me and my perfect partner."

I swallowed hard. "Then someone threw a brick through my bar's window."

"You're not random, Madison," he said quietly.

"You've had a long dry spell."

"You're very much worth it."

An exhale puffed out of me. "You're a real sweet talker."

"I'm honest." He flattened his hands on my stomach. "This thing between us isn't coincidence, and I hope I'm not the only one who wants to see where it goes."

"You want to?" I hated how scared I sounded. Being cheated on had left a gaping wound over my heart that threatened to swallow me up in the name of self-preservation.

But I could trust Teller.

He slipped his hand farther down my belly until his finger tunneled through my seam. I squirmed and my breasts lifted above the bubble line. He cupped one while making lazy circles with his other hand. Under my ass, his dick grew, prodding at my flesh.

He nipped my earlobe. "I want to."

I forgot the question.

"I also want to take you to Tenor and Ruby's wedding as my plus-one." He pumped a finger in and out of me and my eyelids fluttered shut as I succumbed to unparalleled pleasure.

"I got my own invite," I murmured.

"What'll it take to convince you to go as my girlfriend?"

Girlfriend? I rode his hand. The water lapped around us, splashing close to the edge. It would take nothing. Absolutely nothing. But it wasn't in my nature to make things easy for anyone. "A few more orgasms and I'll think about it."

His low growl vibrated right through my back. "I'll have your answer by noon."

I couldn't laugh. My climax was building, quick to wake up despite the sexfest I'd just been through. I'd gotten off three times already. This shouldn't be possible. But Teller made it seem easy. And it was—with him.

CHAPTER EIGHTEEN

Teller

Birdsong registered a moment before a shot of adrenaline charged through my vessels. I was late for work. Then a soft, warm body rolled over me. The events of the night flooded back and I didn't bother opening my eyes. No wonder I was so damn tired.

"You sleep like the dead, Bailey," Maddy murmured. "And your alarm is going off." The bed shifted as she smacked something on the nightstand. The birdsong stopped.

Her weight was gone and I missed it. Rolling to my side, I buried my face in her hair. I hadn't had a tender moment like this in a long time. Perhaps ever. There was no undercurrent of stress waking up next to Madison. No *What the hell is she going to be mad about now?* or *I've gotta get to work and she's going to be upset about it.* Or worse . . . *How can I get her to leave without being a dick?*

I didn't want Madison to leave.

"You gotta be up?" I said, my voice sandpaper rough.

Her hair moved, tickling my nose as she shook her head. "Only for the hour it's going to take to brush out the rat's nest of my hair. Otherwise, I'll go to Flatlanders and install some partitions in the bathroom."

"Before Flatlanders is done, I'm gonna see you in nothing but a tool belt."

The bed shook with her laugh. "Baking while naked. Constructing while naked. What next?"

"Technically, you weren't baking naked."

"No one wants cookies made by someone without any clothes on."

"Wrong again, Mads. I'll take five batches." I let out a long groan. "I've gotta get to work." I pressed my lips to her shoulder and left them there. "Let's go out tonight," I said against her skin.

"You mean like meet Tenor and Ruby again? Or another one of your siblings?"

"No. Just us." I tried to swallow past the tightness in my throat. We could work all day and night on Flatlanders, but people would shrug it off as a business arrangement. She and I could double with another couple and it was still a group. Eat at Mama's? No one else saw.

Then there was my home. My oasis away from everything that was now my special place with her.

"A date?" she asked.

"A real one," I confirmed.

"Curly's?"

"Anywhere. We can stay in town or go to Bozeman."

"Hmm . . . There are some nice distilleries in Bozeman. I wonder if they serve a better hard lemonade."

I nipped her shoulder and she giggled and playfully slapped me.

"I like Curly's and all, but I wouldn't mind anonymity," she said.

"Bozeman, then. I'll surprise you." Options ran through my head. There were steak houses, bistros, even bakeries, but those were likely closed in the evening.

"It's a date."

"An official one." I rolled to my side of the bed. "Let me make you breakfast."

"Cookies aren't an option?"

"Not unless you want me to explain why I have frosting all over to everyone at the distillery."

She giggled again, but it cut off when I rose and the sheets slipped away. My bare ass faced her, and when I walked to the bathroom, she saw my morning wood. I made sure of it.

When I was done cleaning up, I came out to an empty bedroom. The toilet flushed in the guest bath, so I dressed quickly and went downstairs. I wasn't a baker, but I could make mean scrambled eggs and sausage.

By the time Madison entered the kitchen, the coffeepot was almost full, the sausage was almost done, and I had the eggs beaten and ready to scramble.

"Have a seat. Food's not quite done."

She peered at the time. "Don't you have to get to work?"

I gave her a wink. "I'm the boss, baby."

She rolled her eyes, but her smile was indulgent. She tidied the cookies and frosting from the night before. "I'll pipe these later tonight. Or tomorrow since we're going on a *date*."

Her voice rang with disbelief. I'd show her. "Honestly, there might not be many cookies left by then." I'd eaten at least three since I'd started making breakfast.

"I can make more. Another night."

"I'll let these count as your cookies for the week." I'd keep her too busy to bake tonight anyway. I poured her a cup of coffee and set it on the island with the sugar. Then I got her cream from the fridge and took out the three different creamers I had.

"We both seem to have a sweet tooth," she said, pouring more than a dollop of cream into her cup, followed by the caramel-flavored creamer.

"Tate always asks if I want some coffee with my cream and sugar."

"I almost quit drinking it. Damien— Sorry."

"You can talk about him. I'm not intimidated by Cocksucker."

A small smile graced her face. "The partners at his firm also owned a coffeehouse, and they'd talk roasted beans during their social time. Damien wanted to impress them. We had so much gourmet coffee at home, I had to buy storage carts for them."

"Sounds like a waste."

"So much waste. I started making homemade marsh-mallows just to have something sweet to put into my cup. His partners loved those, so I made a double batch, and I could keep some for home. Sometimes, I think they liked me more than him."

"I bet they did."

Her expression turned shy. "I never knew it could be like this. Fun, yet relaxing. I'm not on edge."

That was a punch right to the solar plexus. I took the pan off the stove and went to her. Kneeling in front of her, I put my hands on her thighs. "I want you to have everything, Madison. I promise you, I'll never be the one holding you back or standing in your way."

Her eyes shimmered. "Oh my god." She swiped at a tear that broke free. "I don't usually go for the gushy stuff."

"Have you ever had the gushy stuff?"

Another tear slipped free and she sniffled.

Jesus, this woman. I captured the next drop rolling down her face with my thumb. "You deserve to have everything you ever wanted. If I could control the universe, I'd make sure you never heard another negative word."

Her shoulders shook. "You're unreal, you know that?" She sucked in a breath. "I think that's why I always resented you a little. You were too good to be true."

"I'm just a man. I'm going to fuck up, but I need you to trust that I'll have your best interests at heart. I'll always want what you want."

She blinked back another flood of tears and failed. "You want to go to pastry school?"

I took her hands. Emotion flooded the air around us, but I couldn't have her hiding from them. She'd probably been berated about them in the past. "You promise that if you ever get the chance, you'll go?"

"I can't—"

"Madison."

"I'm not leaving my family. Okay?" She brushed at her eyes. "Scott left me everything to take care of them. They're all I have."

"You have me now too."

"This is so new, Teller." A fear I'd never seen filled her eyes.

"One day at a time, all right? You'll get your parents' place sold, and you'll secure long-term care for your mom. You'll have enough left over to buy your own house, with a kitchen you can bake in." Or she'd move in with me permanently. But she might need her own space after the dust of the renovations settled. I'd give her that. I'd give her anything. "Then you'll go do fun things with your nephew."

Her eyes welled up again. "If I ever get to see him."

"Trust me," I said dryly, "once Wendi hears how much the property goes for, she'll be around. She'll use her son to siphon it off you."

Madison released a watery laugh. "I hate that you're right."

"Then we'll get the bar going, and you'll have regulars and new customers who'll keep you afloat so you can keep baking and having sex with me."

"Sounds pretty long term, Bailey."

"I thought you were going to think of an annoying nickname."

"Turns out I'm not so irritated by you."

I grinned. It wasn't like I hadn't been called *Bailey* before, but I had two brothers and there'd been my dad. People had to use our first names to differentiate us. Yet every time she said it, it went straight to my dick. She never called anyone else *Bailey*. "I like the sound of long term, Mad Maddy."

"I'm not feeling so mad these days."

≈

Madison

. . .

Teller pulled up in front of a bakery. Stella's Sweets. The large sign above the door featured a lineup of pastries. I checked the time. It was six. We'd left as soon as he'd gotten off work, but bakeries closed early.

"Is this place open?" But lights were on inside and people were sitting at tables.

"Sure is. They even have a café menu." He got out and jogged around the front of the pickup.

I put my hand on the handle, but I was still staring at the place. It wasn't like seeing my dream. I'd meant it when I'd told Teller that I couldn't open a bakery in Bourbon Canyon. There was too much animosity between me and too many others in that town, and even if there hadn't been, would I even get enough business to stay open? Bakeries didn't serve alcohol, and that was Flatlanders' saving grace.

The town could use more quick lunch places that weren't Curly's and the coffee shop. If someone was so inclined. Not me though.

Teller opened my door and my gaze jumped to him, taking in the man before me. My *date*. He wore a dark blue polo with no logo and a dark pair of jeans with his boots, but he still gave off boardroom CEO energy. Apparently, cowboy boss was my thing.

He waited expectantly.

"I haven't been to a bakery since I was visiting Aunt Tilly in high school," I said to cover how I'd been ogling him.

"Aren't there any in Missoula?"

"Yes, but as a broke college student, I wasn't going there. Then I was a broke newlywed. And then . . ." I chewed the inside of my cheek as I clocked the pink-striped wallpaper inside and the donut shapes hanging off the ceiling. A screen over the counter flashed from donuts to fritters to bagels to fluffy loaves of bread. Gah. It was so cute. "By then I was making everything myself, and it was treated like a waste of money. As if I'd ever been anything less than frugal."

"As if all sorts of coffee he doesn't drink wasn't a waste."

"Exactly." I slipped out and Teller slid his arm around me. So natural, like we'd done this forever.

I wore my jean shorts, but I'd paired them with another shirt I'd never worn before. A lavender blouse that was summery and frilly. My sandals weren't new, but my feet said they were. Hopefully tonight wouldn't include a lot of walking. I'd repainted my toenails to match my top and kept my hair down.

I felt like a new girl. "So I'm going to walk into a bakery with the bachelor I paid fifty grand for."

His grin flushed heat right down to my toes. "I'm considered a good business decision in bachelor auction circles."

He led me in. The sweet, doughy smell wrapped around me like sunshine on a picnic.

A young girl waved us to a table. "Have a seat anywhere. I'll be right with you."

Teller picked a spot by the window. We had a lovely view of downtown. I was almost as distracted by that as I was by the menu.

Teller leaned over the table. "We can also go get a steak after this if you want."

The menu was mostly finger food and various plat-ters of bread and dip. Teller wouldn't fill up on bread and charcuterie meats.

"There's not a lot of protein in bakeries," I said.

He leaned his elbows on the table and pressed his fingertips together. "How about we consider this an appetizer?" He thought for a moment. "And dessert. We'll eat out of order tonight."

The jokes. My excitement over something so simple. How easily was this turning into the best date I've had? "Deal."

We settled on our order, and after the server came by, he pointed to one of the many brick buildings.

"There used to be a boot shop here Dad would take us to all the time. We chewed through boots when we were younger."

So had I, but they hadn't gotten repaired or replaced that often. "Were you a Lucchese family?" I teased.

He laughed. "Dad loved a good quality boot, but it'd kill him to put a pair of Luccheses on teen boys and send them to work with cow shit." He pushed a smaller menu in front of me. "What are we getting to bring with us after we eat?"

Every time he said we, a zing raced down my spine. It was early yet. This was our first real date. I wasn't as experienced as him in the mechanics of dating, and I wanted to enjoy this. I didn't have to question it, and if I started thinking about the future, I would.

I studied the menu to hide my chaotic thoughts. I liked Teller. A lot. What I felt for him was starting to make my feelings for Damien look like a little girl's crush. That could be because Damien had been a crap husband, but that was the thing. I didn't have enough experience to know. I wasn't worldly.

Teller had done stuff that wasn't just about survival. He'd never lived paycheck to paycheck, and that had given him a lot of freedom to just be. I wasn't there yet, and I was afraid to dive in. However, I could savor the slow consumption of all things Teller. He cared for me, and I believed him. I believed him when he said he wanted what was best for me.

"What are you picking?" he asked.

"I'm a sucker for an almond croissant."

"What else?"

I floundered. How much did he think I could eat? We were having an appetizer, baked goods, and then he seemed serious about getting a full dinner.

He took the little menu from me. "We need to get a couple of donuts, obviously." There were several varieties of old-fashioned donuts still in the case. "You like bagels?"

"Is there someone who doesn't?"

He flashed a grin. "I haven't had many. Once in a while, I'll get the breakfast bagel at Mountain Perks."

"I've made them before."

"Yeah? Are they hard?"

I shook my head. "They can be a little tedious since you have to boil them first." I traced over the grains on the table. "One of Damien's partners, Lyle, approached me after I sent some bagels to work. Offered to contract with me to provide bagels a couple days a week at one of their coffee shops."

A hard glint entered Teller's eyes. "I want to drive straight to Missoula and kick your ex's ass. Damien didn't want you to?"

"Correct, but it also would've been a lot to add to my already full plate. The offer was validating though. Someone thought I did well. That partner was older and he reminded me of Aunt Tilly." I abandoned the wood grain and took up the paper clasp from around my napkin and silverware, folding and unfolding it. I've never discussed Lyle or my past with anyone, and somehow it all slipped out with Teller. "Lyle always complimented me, but instead of just telling me how talented I was, he would allude to the training. He'd ask where I learned to make the bagels or marshmallows, and at first I was embarrassed to tell him YouTube or some social media video, but he'd only nod and quiz me on how many attempts it took to nail a technique."

"Would you have taken that contract if you'd had encouragement for your ex?" he asked.

"Maybe." I had researched commercial kitchens I could rent and any certifications and licenses I might need to bake in my home. I'd more than speculated on how I would do it. "Yes. I would've. One of my jobs would've had to go. Then I could've started a cupcake or cookie side hustle."

"It wouldn't have been a side hustle."

What would it have been like? To have the unyielding support from my partner that Teller had been giving me? I couldn't wrap my mind around it, yet at the same time I could. Because of him. He'd seen me at my lowest and it didn't matter.

He made me think—he made me believe—there could be more for me. Even more, he wanted it for me. A girl could get used to that.

Our food arrived, and I grinned as Teller's gaze darted all over the charcuterie board like he was looking for the rest of the meal. Once the server left after topping off our water, I leaned forward and whispered, "Don't worry, we'll get steak after this."

Madison

"Be honest," Teller said, pushing his plate away. "How is it?"

I finished chewing my last bite of steak. I wasn't sure if I had room in my stomach for the last swallow, but I'd rally. "It's good."

The restaurant only had a few couples remaining in the dining areas. We'd eaten at Stella's Sweets, then bought a dozen different baked goods to bring back with us before going to a steak house Teller had picked out.

It was the fanciest place I'd ever been in. I might've started the night feeling like I was dressed nicely, but it turned out my style was everyone else's standard. The women in the restaurant had worn anything from leggings to power suits to slacks, paired with sheer silk shirts or some other blouse that was nicer than any I owned. The dresses had left me slack-jawed. The summer dresses had been just as pretty as the wrap and cocktail dresses.

Teller strode in with his jeans and cowboy boots like he was wearing a tux. He might literally be the richest guy in the place and no one would know. So, if he didn't care, I tried not to. When he looked at me, I glowed like a fairytale princess I'd read about as a kid.

"Just good?" he asked. "Or are you placating me?"

I stacked my plate on his and set our silverware on top. I'd adopted the habit after waiting tables in college. "Did I miss something? Are they serving Bailey beef, or did you sneak back there and grill the steaks yourself?" He'd never left the table.

"No to both, but I don't want to impress you with a

night out only to take you somewhere with mediocre food."

"Didn't you like yours?"

"I did. Did you?"

His concern was etched around his eyes, and dammit, it was endearing. My pleasure was his pleasure. "Yes. It was excellent, but I hate to admit . . ." The creases at the corners of his eyes deepened. "I'll take your mom's beef any day."

He grinned as relief passed through his eyes. "That's a given, Mads."

I chuckled and took a drink of my ice water.

A couple turned the corner from the other seating area at the back of the place and the lemon in my water turned extra sour. I didn't recognize the guy dressed in a charcoal suit with a little gray at his temples. Hanging on his arm was a redhead in a low-cut dress that would have made Beth Dutton on *Yellowstone* blush. Riley Graves.

My expression must've changed. Teller's gaze shot in the same direction. He sat back, clearing his throat.

Riley spotted me. The smile fell off her red, expertly painted lips. The corner of her mouth curled into a sneer until her gaze slid toward Teller. Then her jaw fell open and a small gasp escaped.

"Teller." She stopped, and the older man with her frowned, glancing back and forth between us. "Do you feel obligated because she paid fifty-five thousand for you?"

A jolt rammed through me. I'd forgotten that we'd actually bid higher than the fifty grand I'd had to my name. The shame of being unable to afford the full bid roared back until I was breathing through a wet rag.

"I'm having a nice night out with my girlfriend,

Riley," Teller said evenly. "If you can't be nice, you can keep walking."

Her eyes bulged. "*Girlfriend?*" She let out a bitter laugh. "Oh my god, are you and Wendi just exchanging partners?"

"You'll have to ask Wendi," I said silkily, "since you're the one who covered for her during her affair with my husband."

The man with Riley arched a brow.

Riley had the grace to show a smidgeon of guilt. "Does she know?"

"I don't care if she does," Teller answered before I could give her my standard—it was none of her business.

I wouldn't leave it at that. Teller might've shown me a nicer side of life, but I had still been raised a Townsend. "You can tell her, and I would love to know Damien's reaction to hearing how interested his girl-friend is in her ex."

Riley's nostrils flared. "Wendi's *fiancé*."

I waited for a jolt of anger or jealousy. The emotional well was quiet. "They deserve each other."

A sneer twisted her red lips. "They definitely deserved more than they had."

After talking to Teller tonight, her words clattered to the floor like dull butter knives, each one missing its mark.

"What a coincidence," Teller said. "So did we."

Her date appraised her a second before sliding a hand around her waist. "We should get going, bunny."

Her glare stayed on me. She didn't move at his first nudge.

"Tell Wendi I said hi." I was the epitome of politeness.

"Tell Damien he's a dumbass," Teller added.

I snorted and covered my mouth. I hadn't meant to make that sound, but Teller's comment had been a surprise. And really damn funny.

Riley sucked in an indignant breath, but the guy gave her a firm nudge and murmured something to her.

His words carried to us. "Don't embarrass me."

Riley stumbled away with him.

Giggles took over. The audacity. The irony. The drama. Everything I usually tried to avoid but was a magnet for. "I can't believe we drove to Bozeman to be anonymous. And I forgot I bid fifty-five grand for you."

"Worth every penny?"

"Well, you paid five of it, and you're not done with the project yet."

He chuckled and grabbed my hand over the table. "You handled that well."

"Really? People usually get upset with me when I talk back."

"You dished out what she was giving, but you kept your tone civil." He rolled a shoulder. "Mostly. But she deserved it—and dug herself a helluva hole with that guy."

"I'm sure as soon as she shows him her tits, he'll forgive her."

"You'd get away with a lot if you did that. FYI."

More laughter bubbled out of me. Before Teller, a run-in like this would have left me stewing for hours, if not days. I'd be more self-conscious the next time I ran an errand, waiting for someone to be rude or to admonish me for what I'd said. But not tonight. Teller gave me props and made jokes.

I was falling so hard for him, tumbling into an abyss

I had never thought was for me. If things didn't work out between us, I'd truly know what heartbreak felt like. The end of my marriage had been a betrayal. An exposure to the reality that life wasn't as good as I'd hoped, as I'd dared dream.

My heart. My reality. My dreams. I'd been giving them all to him and, with them, all the power.

CHAPTER NINETEEN

Teller

Madison had fallen quiet after the confrontation with Riley. I didn't blame her. I had hoped to cheer her up and distract her, but she was stuck in that brilliant mind of hers. The drive home was close to silent. She commented on the stars we could see above the shadowed outline of the mountains while holding the box of bakery goodies. In the house, she put the box on the island.

When she got to the bottom of the stairs, she stopped and blinked at the top of the stairs. Why would she look worried— Oh.

"I'd love to have you sleep with me tonight," I said softly. "We don't have to do anything. I just want you there."

Her eyes were shining as she stared up the stairs, then she blinked slowly. When her gaze shifted to me, there was nothing but determination. She yanked me closer by the fly of my jeans and rose on her toes to place a kiss on my jaw, then another, and another, until she got to my ear.

Heat kindled in my groin. Then her sharp teeth nipped my earlobe right before sucking the damn thing into her mouth. Lust coursed straight to my cock and muddled my brain. I fought for clarity. She hadn't been this bold before. I opened my mouth to say something just as her tongue swirled around the flesh of my earlobe and she started kissing her way toward my lips.

Something was off. "Madison?"

"Mm." She licked across my lips.

I should kick myself to shut up, but something was wrong. There'd been Riley, then Madison's silence, and now this. She'd never made the first move, always me, as if she had an anaphylactic reaction to rejection.

I returned her kiss but gripped her shoulders. "What's this?" I asked against her mouth.

She paused.

"What's wrong, Madison?"

She stiffened and stepped back. An embarrassed blush raged across her tanned skin. "Nothing."

"Don't get me wrong—" She looked away. I ducked my head to keep her attention on me. "Mads. I want you all over me. But something's wrong, and I'd rather we talk about it."

"I'd rather suck your dick."

My groan came as hard as I would between her sweet lips. "You are invited to blow me at your earliest convenience, but I'd rather you do it because you want to and not because you're upset about Riley."

She drew back, genuinely confused. "I've forgotten about Riley."

Oh. Then what the fuck had she been in her head about? "Her date?" Our date?

"No." She took another step back.

I could argue with her, beg her to tell me, but Madison had only ever opened up to me in her own time since we'd started this venture. Would she with this, whatever it was?

It wasn't up to me. "I'm going to bed, Mads. I still want you there, whether you're ready to talk to me or not. But the last thing I want is for you to feel used."

A crease formed between her brow. I gave her a small smile before I started for the stairs.

"Teller."

I stopped on the third stair.

"You have the network. The confidence. The money. You have all the power."

Carefully, I turned. Her fear cut straight to my heart.

"All the resources," she continued and bit her lower lip. "And when I'm around you? I don't care about any of that."

"You trust me."

She clenched her jaw.

I took a step down, and she rushed to the bottom of the stairs. I sank to my ass onto a step to keep from towering over her.

"I'm afraid to trust you," she said, her voice tight. "It's different when my subconscious is whispering this isn't right. When I'm trying not to question why I had to put up with awful behavior. It's different when I'm getting pitying looks, or 'that poor girl' stares, or even hostility. Riley was jealous tonight. *Jealous*. Of *me*." Her chest rose and fell faster. "I've never experienced that. No one is jealous of me, Teller. And now . . . there's you."

Each word shot through my heart until it turned into a hunk of Swiss cheese. "Jesus."

She'd laid it all out there. She was scared. Putting all her trust and faith in me would leave her wrecked if something happened between us. She'd known she'd never gotten what she'd deserved. She'd even said good riddance to her ex and moved on. What she'd said about me was humbling as fuck.

But what did a blow job have to do with it? "Do you think you need to pleasure me to get me to stick around?" What had I done wrong to give her that impression?

She pressed her fingertips to her temples. "No. It's . . . I thought . . ." She dropped her arms and sighed, tipping her head back. "You unravel me, Teller. So easily. You can hold all of me suspended on the tip of your tongue. I wanted to feel that power for once."

I scooted down a step. If I stood, I'd crowd her and she needed her space. She was being raw and vulnerable and open. I could do the same and I could do it sitting on my ass. "You don't see that you *do* have all the power. I don't think you realize how much you turned my world upside down." I squeezed her warm fingers. Her grip was loose, ready to break away and run. If that was what she needed, I'd let her. "Before you, I worked, Maddy. I did chores in the morning, I was at the distillery past closing, and I spent all weekend at the ranch."

"You're still only working."

"I'm enjoying myself. I get to go on dates with you."

Doubt darkened her eyes. "You could go on dates with anyone."

"I wouldn't enjoy myself. You have your own mind. Your own plans. Aspirations that aren't tied to my name.

Yes, you needed to borrow my influence to keep from getting screwed over with Flatlanders. That's bold. You donated fifty grand to a charity to get my help. That's a big fucking leap of calculated faith—in me." I rubbed my thumbs over the backs of her hands. "People put me on a pedestal and they don't like it when I don't live up to their expectations. I'm just a guy who works damn hard and wants a quiet life. You saw that. You saw *me* right through the Bailey name. I don't have to be anyone with you but a guy who thinks you're fucking amazing."

Tears gathered in her eyes, spilling over her cheeks when she blinked. "God, Teller."

The tears were my undoing. I tugged her toward me to straddle my lap. I tangled my hand in her long locks and captured a tear with my lips. Then another, the salt staining my tongue with the flavor of her trust and her vulnerability.

She opened up this way for me and me only. An experience I wouldn't take for granted.

She wrapped her arms around my shoulders and I claimed her mouth, delving inside. Electricity crackled between us as emotion zinged back and forth like we were carrying each other's burdens.

The saltiness of the tears lingered, but her sweet flavor shone through and I drank like I was dying of thirst. This woman got to me in a way I'd never expected, not from anyone.

She cupped my face, her palms scraping over my beard and her fingers tunneling through my hair. She was ferocious, biting and nibbling my tongue and my lips. She was unrestrained, no longer willing to be on standby, catching the scraps tossed to her and making do. She was taking what she wanted.

I grabbed her ass and ground her down onto my erection. The position wasn't the easiest and the edge of a stair dug into my back, but I didn't care.

She rocked over me and I groaned.

"Take what you want." I might be undoing her initial intentions. She wanted to have power in the relationship —and that was what this was. Only she didn't see that I was just as helpless when it came to her.

Madison

I rode the hard ridge behind Teller's jeans. My emotions were flayed wide open, but he was proving to be a safe spot for that to happen. It'd only occurred with him. Only Teller.

Desire built inside me. How could I go from a raw, gaping mess of feelings and tears to an inferno of arousal? It was too big for my skin and my peak was way closer than it should be for having all my clothes on.

Yet, I was on top. Teller's big hands clasped my butt cheeks and he grunted each time I ground onto him. I wanted him to feel as powerless and powerful and hungry as I did.

I broke away from our frenetic kiss and laid a path of sloppy, open-mouthed kisses down his neck, sliding off his lap as I went.

I had begun with the intention to blow him, and my motivations had changed, if only slightly. I wanted power over him, but not just that anymore. I wanted to give him the same mindless pleasure he so easily and generously gave me. The drive to have my mouth on him was for both of us, not just me.

"Are you sure?" he asked, his voice rough.

"Lean back, Bailey, and let me undo your jeans."

He slid his ass to the edge before I finished speaking and propped his elbows on the length of the stair behind him. "Fuck, Mads. Seeing you like this, on your knees in front of me, your hair a sexy mess from me? I won't ever fucking forget it."

"I'll keep reminding you," I purred and his pupils fixed, making his eyes almost black. I opened his fly and yanked his underwear down as far as it'd go with his jeans still on.

His ragged groan cut through the quiet house, growing stronger as I gave his shaft a good pump, then another. He was hot in my hand, smooth, yet rough with veins and the ridge at the crown.

I glided over him, rhythmically squeezing. He sucked in a breath, his gaze fixed on what I was doing to him. Was this how he'd felt when he was getting me off all those times before we'd had actual sex?

I was enjoying this. He was at my mercy. He was allowing it, but he was also powerless. He could carry me up the stairs to his bedroom and have his way with me, but he let me play. He wanted me to. From the tint on his cheeks, the way his mouth puffed open with each breath, and his rigid position, he needed me to.

I stroked up and down. "Are you going to taste like a strong bourbon? Rich and smooth? Bold with a nice finish?"

"Fuck, Mads." He thrust his hips up into my grip. His cock twitched against me.

Oh, I liked this. "I'm going to start by taking a little

sip." I shoved his legs wide and wedged between them, then licked across his crown, circling it with my tongue. My hair fell on each side of me.

"Fuck," he repeated.

I did it again, licking at him like a lollipop, tasting the salty precum. I'd been right. Rich and bold. When he vibrated like he needed more, I sucked him all the way in, as far as I could go. His tip hit the back of my throat and I swallowed him.

"Fuck me," he growled, rocked up, restrained, like he was afraid to choke me.

I'd choke myself on him.

I hummed and his entire body went rigid, like I had spark plugs lining my tongue.

"Christ, Maddy." He gripped the step he sat on.

I pulled up, almost releasing him, and then plunged back down.

"Fuck," he moaned, his hips jerking.

His cock spasmed along my tongue and he grunted. He was close.

I wiggled my hips, trying to relieve the throb between my thighs. Working his length, I let my eyelids flutter shut and enjoyed the feel of his strength in my mouth, his taste on my tongue.

"I like you like this," he said roughly. "On your knees in front of me." Another hard exhale, then a hiss. "*Yes*. Do you feel that? How much control you have over me? I can't fucking move, Madison."

I held him still with nothing but my mouth. He was taut, every muscle pulled tight, flinching at each swirl of my tongue. I worked him in a punishing rhythm.

"Jesus. So fucking good." The small buck of his hips punctuated every word.

I hummed again.

"Ah, fuck. I'm going to blow, Maddy." He said it like a warning. A once-and-only notice if I didn't want him exploding in my mouth.

I sucked harder and his breath whooshed out of him.

He yanked at the step. If he wasn't sitting on it, he might've ripped the boards up. So controlled. So restrained. Because of me.

The power. The trust. He could grab my hair, pump my head up and down at the speed he liked it, but he was handing it all over to me.

I hummed again.

"Mads!" He rocked his hips up and his erection pulsed, pumping hot jets into my mouth.

I swallowed it all, working him until his entire body went slack except for the aftershocks that kept his hips thrusting weakly. Then I let up, releasing him with a pop.

His shaft bobbed in front of me, wet and flushed like my mouth probably was. He lifted his head off the steps and peeled his hands away from the edge of the stair. Taking my arms, he gingerly lifted me to straddle him again.

"That was . . . *fuck*." He pushed a hand into my hair and drew me down to him. A stab of fear went through me. Any second, he'd recall where my mouth had just been and push me away. Instead, he captured my lips and kissed me like nothing would ever keep him from doing it. The tempo between my legs increased, loud and demanding.

I sank into him, returning each stroke of his tongue, trying to keep from rocking on his sensitive cock.

When he stopped the kiss, he held me close, our foreheads touching. "Did I mention that was amazing?"

"Something like that," I murmured. I didn't mean to squirm against him, but he was still hard and prodding against my demanding core.

"I don't think you're finished with me."

I lifted my head. His gaze was half-lidded, but the spark in his irises was still there. He could go again. No, I wasn't finished with him.

I would never be finished with him.

CHAPTER TWENTY

Teller

I stared out the new windows, then turned in a slow circle. The bar was almost done. I was proud as hell of the work we'd done, but I admired how dedicated Madison was. She didn't give up, and I liked being by her side, helping her fulfill her plans and dreams. I hoped this was only the beginning.

The booths had been delivered. The benches and the tables were waiting to be installed. Cruz and Lane had said they'd help install those. Tenor and Tate had offered to get in on it. Then Myles, Gideon, and Jonah learned about our plans and decided to turn it into a guys' night. I'd enjoy tonight, but I'd been having a good damn time every day.

The last couple of weeks had been domestic bliss. The bar had been installed, the security system, and the windows. I wasn't needed at Flatlanders every day, so I was back to helping with baling and stacking hay and I kept more regular hours at the office.

If Madison wasn't working, she spent some time here, cleaning and stocking. The storeroom was filled with paper towels, toilet paper, and various spirits she'd been ordering in. Sometime in the next two weeks, a plumber would install new tap lines and a soda fountain along the bar.

When she wasn't here or at the nursing home, she was at my house, baking. I still got weekly cookies even though I preferred to taste the baker. She'd made bagels for Copper Summit too. They'd been a hit, as if I'd had any doubt. Then there were the cookies and cupcakes she'd made for the nursing home. Mama said the residents looked forward to events when Madison brought baked goods.

The guys would be here shortly. We'd waited for the weekend when Madison would be working. I wished she could do something fun with my sisters, but she'd had to switch shifts to get the wedding off.

Three pickups pulled up outside the bar. My brothers, brothers-in-law, and Cruz and Lane piled out and filed inside. I locked the door behind them.

Cruz whistled and spun in a slow circle like I'd just done. "Look at it. It's a bar again."

Madison's comment about wanting to go to pastry school and open a bakery ran through my head. She didn't want to operate a bar, catering to people getting tipsy and running their mouths. How much would she become a target of bad behavior?

How caveman would I turn if someone hurt her feelings?

But it was her decision, and as far as her plans went,

it was solid. Cara, her real estate agent, hadn't gotten an offer on the house, but only because she'd been a bulldog about property lines and what was actually included in the sale. Little details Sal had worked out with verbal agreements and handshake deals but hadn't passed on to Madison, like the price she ought to sell it for. Cara was making it all official and it had added more time, but that'd be more money in Madison's pocket.

Madison had balked at the two-and-a-half-million-dollar asking price, but she had the encouragement she needed. It was my mission to show her she deserved the best, and Ruby had been right about Cara. She'd fight for her clients and insult everyone else. There'd been a few lookers since Cara had made the listing public, but no solid offers.

Tate was behind the bar, the old distillery CEO in him unable to stay away from inspecting the bar and figuring out where Copper Summit products could go.

I walked toward the bar and propped my elbows on it. "I told Madison she needed to keep excluding our spirits. It's Flatlanders' signature move."

He chuckled and nodded. "You're right. She needs to. It'll get the town talking. Enough people have witnessed you two together they'll flock here to see if it's true."

I grinned. "That's the plan. It'd make it even more gossip-worthy if the Baileys continued avoiding the place." I'd love to be here, and maybe I'd hide in the office, but the absence of Baileys would maintain what Flatlanders was known for.

Lane took his ball cap off and set it on the bar. "Cruz and I are coming. We'll be here opening night."

"Wouldn't miss it," Cruz said. "Is she going to carry Foster House?"

"There's a case already stocked," Myles said. "I dropped it off last week as a bar-warming gift."

Madison had balked at the gift, but Myles had only scoffed. Claimed they broke way more bottles than that in shipping. The cost was nothing. He was correct. The cost to people like us was nothing. To Madison, it was the difference between making her mother's rent next month and eviction.

Having the Fosters here on opening night would be good. Madison would have support, and their presence would stoke the curiosity of the townsfolk further.

Jonah tapped a stack of big boxes with his cane. "You haven't unpacked these yet?"

I had recommended Jonah's woodwork for the stools. He would've poured a bar top, but she'd figured out the hefty discount he was giving her and refused, deciding to order polished wood seats from him instead. The boxes were a delivery from him. He'd ordered the stool supports Madison had chosen, made the seats, and assembled them.

"Let's do it now." I dug a pocketknife out and crossed to the stack. "We can have something to sit on."

Tenor scratched his head and eyed the boxes dubiously. "You sure unbolted stools are the way to go? Isn't that what Scooter used to destroy the place?"

"He used pool cues too." Madison wanted to flaunt the chatter about those loose barstools. "But he's not here to ruin it again."

Tenor gave me an *I know that, dumbass* look. "It'll give other jackasses ideas though, and I hate to point out that Flatlanders will draw jackasses. Every bar does, and this place has a reputation."

I gritted my teeth. He had a point.

Tate took my pocketknife and nudged a box away from the stack with the toe of his boot. "Maybe the Baileys do turn out on opening day. Show the town we have her back."

"She shouldn't have to prove anything," I said through clenched teeth. Anger that Madison would be worrying as soon as the doors opened piped hot through my blood. "No one should fuck with her in the first place."

"You're all afraid they will," Jonah pointed out.

"Sounds like even Madison is concerned," Myles added.

"I'm too old to really have known Madison and Scooter, but I remember their parents." Gideon shuddered. "And I know all about grudges. We show up here on opening night. Pack the place with all of us. Everyone will know that if they fuck with Madison Townsend, they fuck with all of us."

All the guys were nodding.

"None of you are worried?" I didn't expect them to be, but we all had our own businesses. Even Cruz and Lane were attached to Foster House since Myles owned it. Hard feelings could spill over and affect everyone in this room.

What if Jonah's orders went down? What if a negative post went viral about Copper Summit or Foster House?

Tate cut open the box at his feet. " 'Doing the right thing is never something to worry about.' "

Murmurs of agreement sounded in the room.

"All right, then," I said. "Flatlanders is known for not carrying Copper Summit bourbon, but I now consider it under the Copper Summit and Bailey Beef umbrella of protection and support."

"Percival Farms considers it the same," Gideon added.

"And Foster House," Myles said.

"Abso-damn-lutely," Cruz said. Lane dipped his head in agreement.

Jonah lifted the first stool out of the box and tore the plastic wrap off it. He flipped it upside down. A *JD* was carved underneath the seat. "Anyone tips these over, they'll see this and think twice."

Jonah had been the recluse of Bourbon Canyon before marrying Summer. People knew his work more than they knew him. That hadn't changed.

"That's just us," Myles said. "The girls are a whole different threat."

Jonah barked out a laugh.

Gideon nodded, his expression solemn. "Don't mess with Autumn. I tried to once and I ended up with all of you assholes as in-laws."

Laughter filled the room and we started tearing open boxes. Everything was falling into place for Madison. Bourbon Canyon might not be where she wanted to settle down. She didn't get to travel. But I'd make as many of her dreams come true as possible.

Madison

. . .

I stopped in the locker room at the end of my shift and grabbed my purse. I stifled a yawn. Sun streamed through the windows and the birds in the bushes outside were chirping up a storm. A gorgeous Montana summer morning that I'd sleep through. Another night when I wasn't in Teller's bed, next to his big warm body. I would be glad when I was done with night shifts.

I'd be a business owner. Not the type of establishment I would've chosen, but it was mine. A small tool for freedom that my brother had left me. He'd been selfish growing up. In death, he'd been generous. Or perhaps vindictive. Determined to make sure Wendi didn't get a cent. But he'd chosen me to be his beneficiary, so that was something.

Raquel popped her head through the door. "Hey, Ramona called. The ambulance is coming for your mom. She fell getting out of bed. Might've broken something."

Alarm made me go cold. "Thanks for telling me." I hitched my purse and the empty tote bag I'd carried cookies in and rushed out of the locker room. I jogged down the halls and turned down Mom's wing. Staff milled around Mom's room at the end.

Ramona held her palm up toward me, silently urging me to quit running. I slowed but continued my rush.

"Hey," I said, breathless. "How is she?"

"Of course I know what goddamn year it is!" Mom yelled from inside her room. "Only one of us doesn't have a mind and it's not me."

Ramona gave me a flat look before taking a fortifying breath as she turned into the room. "Madison's here."

I entered the room, steeling myself for the view. Mom was sprawled on the floor, pillows supporting her, keeping her still and as comfortable as possible until the ambulance arrived.

"Goddamn late as always." Mom's words were tiny paper cuts over old scars. "Dammit! Don't move my leg! Fucking hurts."

"Cheryl," Ramona said calmly, "the paramedics are on their way, but please don't swear."

Mom hissed in pain. She aimed her glare at me. "Why are you here?"

I was her daughter. Wasn't that reason enough? "I can go to the hospital with you."

"And do what? You're not a damn nurse, are you?"

Shame burned up my face, but anger sparked behind it. I'd been around the Baileys so much that Mom's insults weren't hard to shrug off.

"Do you want me to pack a bag?" I asked before Ramona could make a retort that would further anger Mom. "At least one night's clothing?" The hospital in town couldn't handle a hip break. She might get transported to Bozeman.

Why couldn't she have fallen after the house and land had sold? The ambulance bills wouldn't have devastated us then. And if she had broken her hip or another bone, then the rehabilitative care would wipe out the rest.

Guilt ate its way up my throat. I was counting pennies while she was helpless on the floor.

"Might as well make yourself useful for once." Mom made a shooing motion.

Jerking into action, I went to her little dresser and withdrew her underwear and a shirt.

The paramedics arrived, wheeling the stretcher behind them. I hurried to finish grabbing a few things.

"About goddamn time," Mom snapped. "Did you walk here?"

To give them room to work on Mom, I filed out with the others.

Ramona looked me up and down, a twinge of sympathy in her expression. "You clocked out?" When I nodded, she gave me a rare sympathetic smile. "You can meet her at the hospital. It'll give you some time to . . . prepare."

To prepare for Mom's berating in the single ER room at the tiny hospital. Me, the staff, it wouldn't matter. "Thank you."

Ramona gave me a thin-lipped smile. That flash of sympathy wouldn't save me from the next round of bills and threats to toss Mom out.

The house needed to sell. Quickly. At this rate, if Mom lived twenty more years, she could go through four more nursing homes.

I rushed to my car, texting Teller as I went that I was going to the hospital with Mom. I liked knowing that he'd care. He'd also worry about me, and wasn't that thought like being wrapped in a warm, cozy blanket. I drove to the clinic before the ambulance arrived and waited in the parking lot.

When the rig pulled up and unloaded a complaining Mom, I walked in behind them. The next hour was a flurry of questions she hated to answer, an X-ray that she yelled through. The poor radiologist had been near tears when she'd wheeled Mom's bed back. Then the bad news came. Broken hip. Surgery. Hospital stay.

Then I was alone with her as the ambulance crew prepped to transport her to a bigger facility.

"I can bring you some more things tomorrow," I said.

"Why not tonight?"

I crossed one leg over the other and ran my fingers along the seam of my gray scrubs. It was going to be a long night. "I need to sleep and you'll probably be in a hospital gown."

"You need sleep?" She snorted. Her sharp eyes bore into me. "You need to quit being a Bailey whore."

I jolted, my leg sliding off my knee. My foot hit the floor with a thud. "What did you call me?"

"You know what you are."

Shock clogged my brain. The small-town gossip line had gotten to her, and I wouldn't be able to slough her off. People had seen me and Teller together. Plenty had passed me driving in the direction of the Bailey ranch. Riley had probably painted me in a poor light to everyone who'd listen. "It's not like that."

"Keep telling yourself lies. Ain't nothing you got worth what—"

"Shut up." I snapped my lips together. Had I really said that?

Mom could only turn her head, or she'd risk making the pain flare up. "Listen here, you little—"

"No. You listen." My heart ricocheted against my ribs. Anger made my throat thick and that blood pressure spike from earlier returned tenfold. My temples pounded. I fisted my hands. "I can't believe you called me that. I'm your *daughter*." I glared at her. "Mae Bailey would *never*."

Mom sucked in a righteous breath and pain puckered the corners of her eyes. Her pulse spiked on the monitor. "How dare—"

"How could I not?" Adrenaline flushed through my veins. She'd humiliated me and she'd called me names. It wasn't even noon. "All this time, I stuck around because you're all I have, and I don't get to see Logan. I wanted to take care of you because you never took care of me. To prove I'm not like you."

I blinked rapidly, reality hitting me from all sides. Maybe I'd needed to prove it to myself more than anyone else, but that had been before.

Before I'd been treated with love and respect by people who took nothing from me. "You need me, Mom. I don't need you."

Her hard facade cracked, a hairline fracture. I'd hit on the truth. Was that why she resented me so much? The kid she'd never wanted was the one she had to count on? Perhaps it was one of many reasons.

"I don't need you," she said in a rough whisper.

"Good." I yanked my purse over my shoulder. "You have a chance to prove it. I'll make sure everything's paid on time. Wait until the house sells to get kicked out, otherwise you'll have to find a shelter to take you in. Don't call me and don't expect me to stop in. I'm done, Mom."

I stomped out.

"Madison!"

I ignored her. A wide-eyed young nurse I didn't recognize stared at me from the nurses' station. She got to witness the infamous Townsends firsthand.

"If she wants to remove me from her contact information, let her," I said.

"Madison, goddammit!" Mom yelled. "Get back here."

I smiled at the nurse.

Her big eyes shifted toward Mom's room. "O-okay."

I breezed out of the hospital and nearly vaulted into

my truck. I gulped down air and blew it out hard. My hands trembled on the steering wheel. When I glanced in the rearview mirror, tears were streaking down my face.

"Damn." I swiped at my cheeks as I tore out of town.

At Teller's house, I didn't even pull into the garage. Sobs racked my body. Had I done the right thing? I'd cut off my mom. Wendi was being a manipulative hag with my nephew. I was alone.

I cried harder and rested my forehead on the steering wheel. Would Aunt Tilly be proud or horrified?

Was I proud or horrified with myself?

The door ripped open and strong arms gathered me to a hard chest. "Madison? What's wrong?"

He was there for me. Concerned like I thought he'd be. Acting like I wasn't an imposition. More tears fell. Faster and harder. I wept until my ribs hurt and my throat was raw.

Teller held me, stroking my back, rocking me as much as he could.

"She was so mean." I hiccuped. "So mean."

"Your mom?"

I nodded against his pecs. My face had to be a blotchy red mess and my hair was falling out of its braid. "She broke her hip." I sucked in a shuddering breath. "And she called me a Bailey whore."

He went rigid. "She did what?"

The obsidian edge to his voice cut through some of the rawness inside of me. It'd been so long since someone had told me her behavior was wrong.

I pulled out of his hold, but I only had the energy to stare at his chest. "I said I'd manage her care, but I'd never see her again." I tried to inhale, but it sounded like I was driving over washboard roads.

He brushed loose strands of hair off my face. "Good for you."

"I don't want to be like her," I whispered. "But I left her hurt and alone in the hospital."

He kissed the middle of my forehead. "You're a good person. The fact that you're questioning what happened tells me you're the exact opposite of her. I didn't know your aunt, but I bet she'd be proud." He smoothed his thumbs over my cheeks. "After you get some rest, you'll see the situation clearer. You'll see I'm right."

"You're not always right, Bailey."

He placed his next kiss on my lips. "There was one time I was wrong, and that was about you. I'll never make that mistake again. Right now, I just want to run you a hot bath, sit with you while you soak, and then tuck you in and hold you while you sleep."

I cupped his face. Having his strength, his care, made doing hard things easier. Before, I felt like I was locked outside of a warm house, looking at the people like the Baileys. I wasn't a part of them. But Teller had brought me inside. He'd carried me up his stairs and into his bed. He made me feel like I was worth loving. And I just might be falling in love with him.

CHAPTER TWENTY-ONE

Madison

My eyes were crusty when I woke. Teller had let me sleep for the last couple of days. My nights had been fitful. I hadn't slept well the night after my blowup with Mom. Then, like the obedient daughter I was, I'd worried about her instead of the business I had to open.

I rubbed my eyes and rolled up. My phone buzzed, but I didn't answer right away. The hospital hadn't called since Mom's accident. All I could do was sit and worry about her.

I'd focus on Flatlanders, then.

The windows were in. Same with the booths. The taps and soda fountains would be installed this week. Then I'd be ready for a soft opening. I was aiming for a couple of weeks after Tenor and Ruby's wedding. I wanted to attend and there was no way I would risk working through it.

Swinging my legs over the side of the bed, I blew out a hard breath. What could I bake?

That wasn't the question. I'd loaded Teller's kitchen up with flour, sugar, and butter. I could bake anything I wanted. I had no one to give it to, and I'd already filled the freezer of his beer fridge with sweets. If I made something, who would I give it to?

Ugh. I hated being in a perpetual pity party. I could make a sweets drop at the senior center.

My phone buzzed again. I yawned and grabbed it off the table.

Ruby: Call me when you're awake.

What would Ruby want? We didn't have a social relationship. We had a social media one.

I squinted at the time. Ten. Teller had probably been working for hours already. It hadn't mattered how much he'd worn me out last night, I'd tossed and turned. All in all, ten wasn't bad. I'd have my hours switched around by the wedding. I'd taken the weekend off. I even had a dress. One I hadn't shown anyone. I might change my mind one or three times by then.

I called Ruby.

"How are you?" she asked instead of saying hello.

"Good." I was, mostly. If I admitted I was bored, I'd feel like I wasn't doing enough at the bar. I'd also have to confess that I wanted my own space. That had been the benefit of staying at Flatlanders. It'd been mine. "I'm trying to figure out what I'm going to do all day to be productive."

"Do you have posts scheduled?"

I smiled. "Yes, ma'am. Tenor got photos of guys' night for me." Instead of getting everyone's faces, he'd gotten a lot of denim-clad ass. My likes were going to blow up.

"Nice. I can't wait to see them. So—can we come over?"

"Over where?"

"Wherever you want. Teller said we could all go to his place. We'll bring food and drinks, and we have rides if we get too tipsy."

I risked sounding dense. "Who's we?"

"The sisters and me." It was how Ruby and I had started referring to Summer, Autumn, Junie, and Wynter. We also included Scarlett, since she was so close with them all. "He said you had a crappy week, and we wanted to cheer you up."

I blinked. Confusion mingled with astonishment to rob all the words from my brain.

"But it's okay if you have other plans," she rushed on. "We don't want to bother you."

"No." Panic welled, threatening to spill over. I couldn't ruin this. But also, I didn't know what else to do. "Sorry, I'm not used to getting invited anywhere."

"Technically, we're inviting ourselves over."

"If Teller doesn't mind, it'd be fun to have you all over." Excitement simmered. The sisters—Ruby included—likely wouldn't bail or make the night miserable for me, but I would stay in a holding pattern. I'd wait and see. My caution had been trained too well.

"Great! I'll let them know. Don't worry about a thing. We've got it all handled—food and drinks."

When we disconnected, I flew out of bed. I might not want to get excited and be let down, but I also didn't want to risk greeting all the sisters with bedhead and morning breath. I tossed on a pair of jean shorts and a

loose, plain pink shirt, then zipped through the bathroom. After my hair was brushed, I sat to braid it but
my nerves got the best of me.

Instead, I secured it in a loose bun on the top of my
head and rushed downstairs. Like a kid waiting for Santa
in the middle of July, I peered out the window. The
green trees that dotted the foothills stood stark against
the blue sky and white puffy clouds.

I sent Teller a text. **I hear I'm going to get
swarmed by women.**

Teller: I'm surrounded by ass.

He sent a picture of a donkey in a pasture. A horse's
ears punctuated the bottom of the picture. He'd
mentioned that Tate had started using donkeys as cattle
guardians. They were hell on predators.

Me: It's been ages since I've ridden.

Teller: I'll take you anytime.

Me: Not sure my PTSD will make it fun.

**Teller: Any time you want to make new memo-
ries, I'm your guy.**

My heart grew three times its size. Any more of that
and the damn thing wouldn't fit in my chest.

Me: Maybe someday.

**Teller: Have fun with my sisters. Junie just
came and raided Mama's bourbon supply.**

The corner of my mouth tipped up.

**Me: I'm day drinking with a famous country
singer?**

Teller: She might come up with a new song.

I giggled. When I looked up, three pickups were
ambling up the long driveway.

Me: They're here.

Teller: Relax and have fun.

My stomach flipped. There were no kids to go play with to avoid making awkward small talk. It'd be me, quiet in a corner, while they all talked and laughed about inside jokes.

"It'll be fine," I muttered and rushed to open the garage door so they could come through the house.

"Mad-i-son!" Junie sang as she jumped out of a dusty ranch pickup. "We have croissants and bourbon!"

Did those two things go together? "Brunch and bourbon?"

Autumn climbed out the other side of the pickup. Another truck parked next to them on the cement pad. Wynter and Ruby. Summer and Scarlett were in the third pickup parking behind them.

Junie grabbed a bag out of the back seat. She paused with the back door half open. "*And in the end it was nothing but brunch and bourbon . . .*" Her lovely voice carried over the lawn. The tune sounded like love gone wrong. She tapped the toe of her strappy sandal. "What about . . . *Brunch and bourbon and a broken heart.*" She added twang and it was a party song.

"I like the one that sounds like there'll be a line dance for it." Wynter flounced past her. "But it's not your style."

Junie closed the door. "I can write it and sell it."

Had I just witnessed the magic behind June Bee's music? She made decisions that could make her millions on a random Saturday morning?

Everyone rushed toward me. Each one was carrying a bag. I stepped aside and lingered as they chatted and unloaded their goods. Fruit trays, veggie platters, charcuterie arrangements on a board with a shovel for a handle.

"Jonah started offering smaller-scale woodworking,"

Summer explained when she caught me looking at it, pride filling her expression. She feathered a lock of strawberry-blond hair behind her ear. The rest was secured in a low ponytail. "He knows he won't be able to flip tables around forever, so he's starting to make cutting boards and charcuterie boards. You won't believe what someone will pay for a cutting board."

"Does he etch his picture into the back side?" Wynter asked. "You could tack on thirty more bucks for each product."

Summer grinned. "He would give out cutting boards for free to keep from having to do that." She leaned against the island and opened a bottle of orange juice. "We also brought mimosa supplies—except we had to buy ginger ale instead of champagne for the nursing ladies. Virgin mimosa, anyone?"

"Ginger beer would've made it a virgin mule," Wynter said, "and I thought that fit this crowd. But I forgot to grab some from home before we went to the store."

"Want one?" Summer asked, holding up the OJ bottle.

I'd drink whatever they put in front of me. "Yes, please."

"Don't let me forget to add ginger beer versus ale to my content lineup." Ruby grinned and nudged me. "You and I can take ours with a splash of bourbon."

"Which would make it a Kentucky mimosa," Wynter said, then frowned. "Or an orange mule?"

Autumn pursed her lips. "Hmm . . . still no ginger beer. I'd go with Kentucky mimosa."

"Ooh, I'm tracking that discussion in my posts too," Ruby added.

Scarlett grinned. "Whatever you call it, make mine one too." She thumped a bottle of half-empty bourbon on the counter. "I brought Original."

"How much are we drinking?" My stomach rumbled. The food intrigued me more than the booze.

"Depends how much telling off your mama bothered you." Summer handed me a flute.

"How did you—" I'd been rooted in one spot and they already had a feast laid out and a drink in my hand.

Three drinks. Ruby had a line of filled glasses in front of her. "These are all virgin. Unlike every one of us."

Junie whooped and grabbed one. She held it in the air. "Load your plates up, ladies."

"Mind if we go to the deck?" Wynter asked, handing me a plate.

"I . . ." I didn't, but would Teller?

Wynter smirked as if she'd read my mind. "You could host a rager and tear the literal roof off and I think that man would just ask if you felt better."

I took a nervous drink of my mimosa. "Not so sure about that."

"Oh, we are," Autumn said. "You know how we know?"

Summer lifted her arms to encompass the whole kitchen. "We're here. He hardly has company over—not even family. I call dibs on the hammock chair." She wrestled the sliding door open.

I filled my plate and drank half my juice. Ruby topped it off before I went outside. Heat wrapped around me, along with the fresh smell of pine trees and sunshine.

The umbrella on the patio table was up and the plexiglass surface was dust-free. Same with the chairs. Teller had gotten it all ready.

That man.

My man.

I sat and stuffed a chunk of croissant in my mouth. Rich and savory, and that was just the croissant. I hadn't made these in a while.

The others found seats. One for each of us. Teller had made sure of it.

I'd been planning my future in regard to how I'd take care of myself. What about my personal life? I'd given it no thought. I was divorced and I was single. But then Teller had called me his girlfriend and it'd turned my insides warm and gooey. Still, I hadn't pondered us as a long-term thing. I'd been so focused on opening Flatlanders.

Now that hurdle was almost crossed. Almost. What would life after that look like?

"Penny for your thoughts," Wynter said softly.

I finished my mouthful. "Thinking about what happens when Flatlanders is open. I never thought I'd get here."

"You were worried?" Summer asked. "I mean, I know you had the brick incident. But before that?"

I'd been worried for an eternity. "I had no idea what I was doing or *how* I was going to do it."

Junie lifted her flute in the air. "Here's to buying our brother as a good business decision."

"Hear, hear," everyone else said.

"It was embarrassing," I muttered.

"No." Wynter's white-blond hair flew when she shook her head. "It was a delight. Let me tell you, watching him squirm all week before the auction was fun, but then the bidding war? Oh my god. Tate said Teller wanted you to win so bad."

"So bad," Summer echoed. "Now it's been fun to watch him rush away from the distillery to you."

"*Rush to you*," Junie sang, then she pulled a face. "Sorry. All this time off has made my muse go wild." She waved a hand. "Enough about me. How are you doing? Really?" She poked her fork in the air. "If you're not okay with sharing, then I can keep talking about me and the girls' riding lessons."

I had never had anyone to talk to about my parents before. I'd tried to talk to Damien, but he'd told me to cut them off if I was so unhappy. "I guess it's my fault for continuing to care about Mom when she never seemed to care about me."

Summer's eyes went wide. "Madison, no. It's never your fault for caring about someone."

Ruby shook her head. "Listen, my dad can be . . . a lot. But even if he didn't try to change himself and I had to cut him off for how he was to Tenor when they were younger, I wouldn't quit caring. And if he had a medical emergency, I'd probably be there."

But her dad had changed. He had tried for her. "It wasn't just medical emergencies. I kept checking on her and she resented me for it. I should've walked away a long time ago."

"Walked away to who?" Wynter said gently. "Would I be wrong to guess that your ex probably wasn't a sympathetic ear for you?"

"You mean the man who ran off with my brother's wife?" My mimosa could use more bourbon. It'd need a different name with the amount I wanted to add right now. "My ex didn't understand. Scott got some of it, and I could at least talk to him."

"People are complicated," Autumn said. "And families even more so. Gideon did cut off his dad, and while it was the right decision for him at the time, he regrets it."

I didn't know Gideon or his dad well, but I'd seen them around town, chatting and laughing. Hank James didn't strike me as a mean or menacing man, but I'd seen him coming out of the church that held Alcoholics Anonymous meetings.

Gideon's father and Ruby's dad had each worked on themselves, and their loved ones had likely been a big reason. "Mom never changed from when I was little to now." If anything, she was more callous.

"That has to be hard," Scarlett said. "Autumn and I see dysfunction all the time at the school, but we never fault the kids for loving their moms and dads."

I wasn't a kid anymore. "I don't know if I ever loved Mom." The OJ churned in my stomach and boiled upward. Again, I felt like I should be wearing a *Bad Daughter* label across the front of my shirt. "I felt responsible for her, and I wanted to care for her in a way she'd never cared for me."

"Just saying that means you're not like her," Junie said. "We've always seen it."

"You don't know me." Curiosity filled my response. How could they? I'd made it impossible for anyone to get close. They were the ones who'd hurt me the most.

Summer tapped her chin. "Remember that one school assembly when you told the old sheriff that if he had to actually obey the law, he'd despise his job?"

I flashed into that moment like it'd happened this

morning. "I was minding my own business when he came to give the 'say no to drugs' spiel, and then he singled me out about my dad."

Dad had liked to smoke the occasional joint, but he had otherwise steered clear of harder drugs, preferring beer and spirits—as long as they weren't Copper Summit. I'd just repeated what Dad had ranted about the sheriff at home.

My parents weren't always wrong about people. Unfortunately, they were often correct and that was another facet of the issue. "If he could've arrested me on the spot, he would've."

"I was appalled by how he acted that day." Autumn downed her mimosa like it was a shot. "How did Daddy describe him?"

Junie hummed. "He said . . . God, what was it? 'If that man ever cracked open a law book . . .' "

" 'If the sheriff has ever cracked open a law book,' " Summer said in a low voice, mimicking her dad, " 'then I'm a rocket scientist.' "

Junie nodded so enthusiastically the pink ends of her hair bounced. "Yes! 'He's like the yeast in our mash, Junie. Gassy under the right conditions.' " She'd used the same gruff tone as Summer and dissolved into giggles.

Everyone started laughing, and I joined them. For a girl who'd felt like the whole town was against her, it was nice to see that I hadn't been the only one not wearing rose-colored glasses. The main difference between me and the rest of Bourbon Canyon was that they knew when to keep their mouth shut—or they hadn't needed to open it in the first place.

A phone started to buzz and everyone looked at theirs.

"Oh, it's mine." Ruby stood, phone in hand. "It's for the wedding. I'll be right back."

She rushed into the house.

"I cannot wait for the wedding." Autumn sighed. "I'm giddy at the thought of seeing Tenor stand in front of everyone with her."

"He's so happy," Summer said. "We've wanted that for him for so long."

Ruby opened the door and stumbled out, her face pale.

"Oh my god." Wynter jumped up and crossed to her.

"It's nothing." Ruby let out a maniacal laugh. "It's so nothing." She fanned herself with her hand. The knuckles of the one clutching the phone were white. "It's just the cake. So why do I feel like I'm going to have a panic attack?"

"What happened to the cake?" Summer asked.

"Nothing. And nothing will because it's not happening." More disbelieving giggles shot out of her rapid fire. "The bakery in Bozeman double-booked and they have people out on vacation, so guess whose cake order they dropped?" Ruby's big blue eyes filled with tears. "I guess we don't need a cake. It's not, like, critical or anything." She sniffled.

"You want one though," Wynter said, "and the one you picked was gorgeous."

"How can we help?" Scarlett asked. "I can make cupcakes, but I can't decorate that well."

"I'll do it," I said, startling myself. What was I thinking? I'd made cakes for potlucks, but I'd only played around with piping bags at home, and it'd been a while since then.

Ruby turned to me and nothing but hope surged in her wide eyes. "You will?"

I sat straighter. I didn't want to let her down, but dammit. Could I do this? "Making the cake is not the issue, but I don't have a lot of experience decorating. What look were you going for? How many tiers?" *Please no more than three.* I'd made exactly one of those before.

"Three tiers and then three dozen cupcakes," Ruby said, swiping through her phone. She pointed the screen toward me. "It's a really simple design. Wildflowers twisting down the sides, and then one different type of wildflower on one dozen of the cupcakes. So they're mixed around, like the pastures."

Oh, shit. The cake Ruby showed me was an art piece. Smooth cake with off-white frosting had a hint of crumb layer, giving the cake a less formal feel. Wildflowers that were either real or fake, but definitely not frosting, twined along the side.

I squinted at the photo. "Are those pressed wildflowers? I don't know if I can do that," I confessed. "I don't want to show up at your reception with a Pinterest fail."

"I'll take anything." Ruby waved the phone around. "You don't have to do the real wildflowers. I'll take fake. I'll take anything. I don't want to be a bridezilla, but I really want cake. Isn't that a thing? To have a cake?"

"It's a thing if you want it," Wynter reassured her. She dipped into the house and came back with the bottle of Original. "I think you need to have a drink."

Wynter added a splash of bourbon to Ruby's almost empty glass.

"I don't want you working the wedding." Ruby's earnest gaze was on me. "I want you there as a friend. I don't have many." She clamped her lips shut and pink tinted her cheeks. "You guys are all I have." She clasped her hands on her lap.

The sisters surrounded her, murmuring to her, saying the kindest things.

You're one of us, Ruby.

We're more than friends. We're all sisters, and we don't need a wedding for that.

You'll always have us.

Tears singed the backs of my eyes. My nose twitched. I scrunched it up to keep the tears from spilling. The women surrounded Ruby, oozing support and affection. I'd never seen anything like it.

The emptiness I kept covering up yawned open so wide it was going to swallow me whole. My chest ached. Only four of these ladies were related by blood, yet it didn't matter. They were there for Ruby. They would be there for each other. I didn't have to witness it to know.

Autumn lifted her head from the huddle. "Madison, bring it in. You're with us now."

Was I still dreaming? Or had I just woken up to six friends? Zero to six. Just like that. And I'd be going to the wedding as Teller's plus-one even though I had an invite of my own. From my friend.

I joined them, and Scarlett and Summer yanked me into the fold. "I'm going to make your cake, Ruby. As a friend. It'll be my wedding gift to you."

I was with them now.

CHAPTER TWENTY-TWO

Teller

My island was covered with flat knives, spreading tools, piping bags, fake wildflowers, and cake stands. Last Sunday, Madison had run to Bozeman to buy supplies for Ruby and Tenor's wedding cake. Monday, Tuesday, and Wednesday, she'd been practicing her frosting spreading and piping skills. She'd baked several practice cakes.

I'd had lemon cake with raspberry filling for dessert Monday, vanilla cake with homemade lemon curd for breakfast on Tuesday, and white chocolate strawberry for Wednesday breakfast, lunch, and dinner. That flavor was my favorite.

I'd kept Madison fed—with something other than cake—and hydrated. I'd also refilled her red apple jelly bean supply, adding root beer flavor when she'd been especially harried.

Thursday had been for the real attempts, and then she'd decorated on Friday. I'd taken the day off to help my siblings get Tenor's shop ready for the reception, but I'd hung around the house in case there were any piping disasters and Madison needed a shoulder to cry on.

She'd done a wonderful job. She and Ruby hadn't wanted to copy the design the first bakery was going to do. The final result was three tiers of summery perfection. She'd lightened the color and added more yellow with a wild sunflower anchoring the twine of wildflowers.

Then there were the cupcakes. She'd made three dozen of each and frozen half. Just in case.

I was salivating over what was in my freezer.

Who knew I had such a sweet tooth?

And Madison was the perfect confection.

It was just before noon. Tate had swung by earlier to grab the cake and cupcakes. Madison and I would head to Tenor's so she could get the cake tiers assembled and fix the decorations before the ceremony started.

She was upstairs getting ready. I tugged on the cuffs of my sleeves. Tenor had wanted the day to be semicasual. I was wearing my good black jeans and a pressed white shirt, and I had polished the dust off my best pair of boots.

I might've told Madison that my dad couldn't bear expensive boots mucked up with ranch work, but that didn't mean I hadn't bought myself a pair of black Luccheses. The light gleamed off the silver tips.

Why was I nervous?

I ducked into the bathroom and checked my hair one last time. It was combed like normal. My beard was freshly trimmed. I looked like myself, yet I was double-checking my reflection like I was going on my first date in high school.

Heels tapping the hardwood above my head spurred me out of the bathroom. I rushed to the base of the stairs, and my heart stopped. "Goddamn, woman. You take my breath away."

Madison wore a loose, dusty-blue sleeveless dress with pale pink flowers etched around the hem, so light they looked like they were floating up the skirt to her hips. The skirt billowed around her legs with each step, teasing me with glimpses of the smooth flesh underneath. The brown square-toed boots with classic stitching on her feet kept the dress perfectly casual. She'd fit right in.

She hit the landing and my gaze went right to her cleavage. The V only hinted at the creamy globes underneath. Her hair was in a loose braid and wound around the crown of her head. Loose tendrils fluttered around her face.

She smoothed her hands down her front. "You really think it's okay? Not too much or too little?"

"Just right." I feathered the backs of my fingers over her face. "So damn beautiful." All I wanted was for the wedding to be over, to bring her home and flip that skirt up. But I wouldn't take one second of today from her. She would get to hang out, have fun, and be an immortal part of my brother's day.

"You look pretty good yourself, Bailey." She brushed a piece of lint off my shoulder.

I took her hands and twirled her around. She laughed and her skirt flared up as she spun.

I pulled her into me at the end of the spin and started a slow two-step. "Ready to go get that cake almost as gorgeous as you?"

"I'm so scared I'm going to fumble a tier."

"You won't. And even if you do, it'll be fine." I kept dancing with her and she followed my lead, haltingly at first, then with more confidence. She didn't dance much. I'd change that tonight. "Just make sure to drop the white chocolate strawberry tier so we'll be forced to eat the remains and save the rest of the cake for the other guests."

She grinned. "No promises."

I let go of her hands, only to wrap one around my elbow. "Promise me the first dance."

"I can do that."

A buzzing phone cut through the day. Mine was in my pocket. "You got a call?"

She released my elbow. "It's probably someone from work forgetting that I took the weekend off." She peeked at the screen and her finger paused over the disconnect button. "It's Cara." Putting the phone to her ear, she stopped, head down, the fingers of her other hand worrying at her lower lip. "Hello?"

Cara's high-pitched voice carried through the line. I couldn't make out the words, but her tone was a mix of professional excitement and no-nonsense instruction. I hadn't met the woman, but she sounded like the female version of Tenor's soon-to-be father-in-law.

"Okay. Yeah, I mean . . ." Madison paused as Cara chattered. "What do you think? No, I'm okay with it." Another major pause. "Yes, I'm sure. The first one. I just want it done more than I want another three hundred grand. Email me whatever you need, I'll take it." She hung up but kept her head tipped down. A crease slashed across her brow. Then she raised her gaze and hope simmered there, bright and uncertain. "I got an offer on the property. Two, actually."

"Hey, how 'bout that!" I clamped my hands on her arms. "That's a good thing, right? Or did they underbid?" Anything was better than the pennies Sal had listed it for, but Madison deserved every dollar that place was worth.

"One offered two hundred thousand more than the asking price and they just want to buy it. No loans, no inspection, nothing. Just a flat-out purchase. The second offered more, but it'd go through financing."

"Damn, that first one's a good deal. Both are." I ducked my head to catch her eyes. "Right?"

"It's a great deal. Cara asked if I wanted to counter with a higher offer. She thinks I could get three million." Her laugh dripped with disbelief. "Can you believe it? That three hundred K alone would probably take care of Mom for life." She shook her head. "No, two point seven is more than enough. Mom's care, a reserve for Flat-landers, a house for me, and some more to live off."

She wasn't allowing herself to be happy. I tipped her chin up. "You nailed down long-term care. The doors to Flatlanders are going to open in two weeks. You did it."

Her smile was slow. "Yeah. I guess I did okay."

There was something else she wasn't telling me. A reason she couldn't really celebrate and was treating the news like business as usual. "Then what's wrong?"

She stared at me for a moment, then blinked. "Nothing. Don't count your chickens and all that."

She was too practical to celebrate this early. I'd make sure she treated herself when the money did land in her account, but her caution wasn't the issue. "I'll count a few of your chickens for you. And when we toast at the wedding, we're going to sneak one in for this. All right?"

"I can do that."

Madison

I wasn't a photographer, yet after a week of letting my creative side loose, my fingers had itched to take a picture through the whole ceremony.

The pastor stood in front of Tenor and Ruby, with the backdrop of the tree-covered slopes surrounding Tenor's place. *Their* place. Ruby's off-the-shoulder dress stopped before her ankles and she wore white sandals with a chunky heel that wouldn't sink into the soil. A light breeze ruffled the curls around her face. Tenor towered over both her and the pastor. A gentle giant. His focus was all on his bride. No others stood with them. They'd invited only family. And me.

When the panoramic view wasn't holding my gaze, it strayed to the cake inside the shed. A plastic tent protected the food from bugs and probably from the children that would be running around later. All the food was covered, and the cords running to the buffets were concealed behind the table.

Fairy lights and white tulle dressed up the inside of the shop, converting the interior into a classy but unfussy reception hall.

My own wedding hadn't been this relaxed. I had wanted a small ceremony, but Damien had pushed for a show. We'd married in Missoula, which had been fine, and my parents had complained about how long of a drive it'd been. Everyone had been drunk.

A seamless wedding didn't guarantee a happily ever after, but the atmosphere surrounding the couple and all of the property could make a person think Ruby and Tenor were for forever. Not even the clouds building in the distance gave me pause. The vows were done. Tenor was kissing Ruby.

Whoops went up around me. Little kids cheered. Teller squeezed my hand, smiling at me. When I looked at him, at the line of his jaw and the slope of his nose, I flashed to a fantasy world. I was the one in a simple white gown, saying I do to a guy who'd promised to love and cherish me forever and meant it.

I smiled.

This dream was new and so damn vivid my lungs stalled, forgetting how to draw in air or let it out. *Breathe.*

I inhaled. Exhaled.

I liked what I saw.

I said I'd never marry again unless the guy was the opposite of Damien and had proved he was a good man. Genuine. Sincere. Truthful. Teller was all that. If I was to get stuck in Bourbon Canyon for the rest of my life, he was a nice consolation prize.

Only he was more than that.

Didn't mean I wasn't stuck in circumstances I couldn't control. I'd be a millionaire, but the money from the sale wasn't really mine. Mom needed it. I could replenish my savings, but then I'd need to invest for Flatlanders' future. And there was my nephew. He had his trust, but I needed to run the bar to make sure he had a legacy. A better one than I'd been left with.

"You're stuck in your head, Mads," Teller said as we rose and followed the group to the shed.

"Just thinking about how this summer is turning out."

"Good? Bad?"

"For being so bad, it's turned out really good." That was truthful. There would always be a little part of me that was sad for the girl who'd missed out on college, for the girl who'd wanted to travel farther than two hours away, for the woman who wouldn't get the career she desired. The rest of me knew I was lucky. I had a home and a business. I was already further ahead than my parents had gotten.

He nodded, his expression thoughtful.

Mae approached us, dabbing her eyes with a lace handkerchief, but she was smiling. "What a beautiful service." She grinned at me. "Don't you two look sharp?"

"Thank you. I love your dress."

She lifted the skirt of her taupe summer dress. "My son's wedding was a good excuse to buy a new one."

Brinley rushed to her. Mae's smile got somehow wider and she hugged her granddaughter.

The next two hours were full of laughter and chatter. Everyone raved about the food. Then came time to cut the cake. I gripped Teller's forearm, my nerves surging to life. This was it. Ruby had liked how it looked, but flavor was just as important.

Ruby and Tenor posed by the cake for pictures. The wildflowers made Ruby's eyes bluer and complemented her white country dress. If I never made another cake again, I would be happy to go out on this masterpiece.

There was a small tug on my heart. Despite the stress of the week, I'd had a blast. Teller had let me take over his kitchen, and that one week was everything I'd imagined it could be. If I continued, I wouldn't need as much practice. I could play with flavors ahead of time and cut out that step. But I was a bar owner, and what

I'd told Teller held true. I'd never start a new business in Bourbon Canyon. My parents might've been their own worst enemies, but the townsfolk hadn't helped. Scott had barely stayed afloat and had little leftover to pay himself.

The happy couple posed behind my three-tiered masterpiece and cut the first piece together. Lemon with raspberry swirl. Tenor carefully fed his bride the first bite. Not one single crumb smashed into her face, and Ruby smiled at him while chewing. Then she lifted a slice to his mouth. He licked across her fingertips as he took his piece.

"Save it for later!" Teller called. Laughter rose up.

Ruby wiped the corner of her mouth and caught my eye. "Oh my god, Madison. This is delicious." She waved her arms, beckoning everyone toward her. "Come get a slice before I eat it all."

Relief poured through me and I sank against Teller. "She likes it." Days of obsessing over the decorations and nailing the delicate flavors were over. I was elated, but disappointment followed on its heels. It was done.

"Of course she likes it," he murmured against my hair. "You're excellent at what you do."

After the others went through the cake line, I got to enjoy my creation.

Ruby stopped at our table and wrapped me in a giant hug. Her limoncello scent washed over me. "Thank you so much," she said when she pulled away. "It's even better than I imagined. I insist on paying you. That's hundreds of dollars of work, not to mention the supplies you went out and bought."

It had carved out a chunk from my last paycheck, but I'd do it all again. "Don't worry. Really."

"Just wait until Flatlanders' soft opening, then," she whispered conspiratorially.

"You just wait until I stare at your boobs like Allen would've."

She chortled. "Are you worried that customers are going to complain they don't get their tits ogled since Allen moved?"

"I'll be able to recoup any lost business by using half the alcohol he did."

She grinned and gave me another side hug. "Thank you for coming." She gave Teller a pat on the shoulder. "You too."

He stood and gave her a hug. "Keep making my brother crawl out of his hermit shell."

"Only on the days I don't want to be curled in there with him," she said.

When she was gone, Teller squeezed my hand. "You wait here."

He helped Tate and Gideon move tables. Myles and Tate fiddled with a set of speakers with Chance.

Tate clapped his hands together and the shop fell quiet. "As the oldest Bailey, I told my siblings that I get to introduce the new couple. Tenor—you might cast a shadow over me, but you'll always be my little brother. And, Ruby? I can't imagine a better employee turned sister." Everyone laughed. "Alone, you are each amazing individuals. Caring, hardworking, and smart as hell. Together, you make each other even better. An impossible task, in my humble opinion, but you do it." He lifted a tumbler with Solemn Summit, the only bourbon available tonight. "To Tenor and Ruby. May forever be too soon."

I lifted my glass with the others.

Teller tinked his glass against mine. "To the sale," he said only loud enough for me to hear.

"To the sale." Should it go through.

"Like she did for the rest of us," Tate continued, "Junie wrote a special song just for the couple."

He nodded toward Chance, the DJ for the night. A slow country melody carried through the speakers. Tenor took Ruby's hand and twirled her into him. She curled into his chest and he bent over her. Their sister's voice carried through the shop, sweet and bright and pure. The tenderness made my chest tight. Teller stroked my shoulder.

Once the song was done and another sweet but slow country tune poured through, Teller grabbed my hand. Tate was pulling Scarlett to the dance floor. All the couples were breaking. Kids were running the perimeter or spinning on the dance floor.

I was in Teller's arms, just like I'd been at his house. His movements were so easy that I forgot I could barely dance. We wove through the other couples. My world was centered on Teller, but I was also a part of this night, a part of these people. Maybe there was a place in Bourbon Canyon for me after all.

Teller

Stars scattered across the sky like one of my nieces had taken a handful of glitter and blown into it. My headlights cut through the night and bounced off trees. Before my driveway, I pulled to a stop.

Madison frowned out the window. There was a small clearing out her side leading to the gate in the fence. We didn't often need this end of the pasture, but if the cattle got out, we wouldn't have to drive them down the road and around the trees to the valley.

I killed the engine. The headlights would stay on for a few minutes. "Wait here."

I jogged around the pickup. The smell of impending rain hung in the air, but there was no lightning.

I opened her door, and I held a hand out. "My lady."

She laughed. "What are you doing?" She slid her warm fingers into my palm and got out of the pickup, smoothing her dress down.

"Taking my girl dancing under the stars." I tugged her to me just like we'd been on the dance floor. "Not sure what else to get a millionaire."

She looked away. "It's not really my money. I'm the executor of it."

"You can do more than be the executor." When the headlights lit the crease in her forehead, I placed a kiss in the middle of it. "I'm not going to pressure you. Just give you something to think about."

Her identity was being a Townsend, and that wouldn't change overnight. Her family had shrunk her world so small, she saw no way out, even when presented with millions of dollars.

I didn't bother with the radio. I did a slow side to side with no other music than what the night had to offer. Crickets and frogs sang around us, and she laid her head on my chest, her arms hooked around me.

"Today was wonderful," she said. "I keep feeling like I'm going to wake up back in Missoula, working nights and wondering if my husband has to *work late* again."

"Tomorrow, you're going to wake up in Bourbon Canyon, and you'll still be working nights, but I'll be working late with you."

"Full circle."

"But it'll be different for you."

She tipped her head back. "It already is."

But was it enough? The evening had been amazing so far, I didn't want to risk her answer. *Why, no, Teller, never getting a chance to live my dream, even in a small way, isn't enough.*

Her bad fortune was my good. She had gotten stuck in Bourbon Canyon to be around for her mom—who resented her—but I got a woman I couldn't have conjured in my fantasies. A loving, intelligent, driven person who loved with her whole soul. I woke up to her and I went to bed with her. And on a night when I'd been prepared to come home and stuff down the bitterness about my empty house, I was dancing with her under the wide-open Montana sky as a summer rain drifted across the land.

I stopped. "I love you."

The headlights timed out and she jumped.

I kept hold of her and continued to dance. Her moves were sluggish, but she let me lead. We were close to the truck and the moon gave us enough light that I didn't fear steering us both into the ditch. Unless I'd done that with my confession. "You don't have to say it back. I just had to tell you."

Her boots crunched in the dirt as she stopped. Her chest rose and fell, her breasts brushing against my chest. "Teller . . . I . . ."

The buzzing of her phone reached us from inside the

cab. She turned her head, but I couldn't make out her shadowed expression.

The vibration stopped.

"I . . ." She sucked in a breath. "I never thought I'd say this again, to be honest. I've said it to someone before and I thought I meant it then. I really did. But this? What you make me feel? Teller, it's so much more."

She couldn't see my smile.

The buzzing started again.

For fuck's sake. I was having the most heartfelt talk I'd ever had with a woman and someone had to get ahold of her now?

"Who would be calling this late?" Worry edged her voice.

"The last time it was to tell you that you were getting millions."

"Two point seven," she uttered. "What if it's a call that will take it all away?"

"Not every good thing is going to get taken from you, Maddy."

She was still looking at me as her phone went wild, vibrating against the cupholder in the console.

"Go ahead," I said. "Answer it. Find out for yourself."

She stayed where she was for a moment. Then two.

The phone went silent.

"I should see who it was," she said.

It started again.

This time, she leaped for it. Three consecutive calls. Foreboding crowded in my chest. Was something wrong?

"It's the home," she said as she punched the screen to answer it. "Hello?"

A drop of rain hit my forehead. Another plopped on my shoulder.

I couldn't hear a word, but Madison didn't move. She didn't say anything. Seconds ticked by.

"Okay," she finally said in a wooden, empty tone. "Thank you for calling. I'll be right there." She dropped her hand with the phone. The screen was dark.

The sprinkles got steadier.

"Madison?"

She rubbed her hands down her skirt. "We need to get to the house. I have to change and get my truck."

I crossed to her and blinked against the increasingly heavy rainfall. "Why? What's wrong?"

"It's Mom. She died."

CHAPTER TWENTY-THREE

Madison

I never thought about the day I'd end up burying Mom, but if I compared it to my dad and my brother, it was almost unfair that she got the nicest weather. Scott's funeral had been in the middle of winter, and the only word I'd use to describe my dad's autumn funeral was gray. Today, white wisps of clouds streaked across the cornflower-blue sky. Flowers were in full bloom at the cemetery.

The rest of my family had been cremated and interred in the columbarium at the oldest cemetery in Bourbon Canyon. Since they'd all shunned church as much as any other official establishment, we were only holding a small service at the cemetery.

I hadn't expected anyone to show. Wendi hadn't picked up her phone, so I'd had to text her the news and then the details. She'd never replied.

Ten days ago, I'd had the best night of my life. I'd

been dancing with Teller in the glow of his headlights, ready to tell him that what I felt for him was so much stronger than a simple "I love you" that I couldn't trust it. I thought I'd been in love before and it'd been a lie.

Today, I had changed out of jeans once again, into a long floral skirt and a nice blue blouse. My hair was up in a thick bun. I'd almost worn jeans, but I didn't need anyone gossiping about another redneck Townsend funeral.

I was sitting beside the columbarium with its four rows of lockers. My dad and brother were on the other side. Mom would be situated on the end, flanked by an old mayor she'd cursed at two or three times. Below her was one of the residents from the nursing home who'd had dementia. At least Mom had left him alone. Above her was the former bank president who'd bullied them until they'd paid off the mortgage.

I didn't have a mortgage. I'd never have one once the money from the house sale left escrow.

The funeral director, Stanley, checked his watch. He'd been a dick when I'd had to deal with him for Scott's death, but Teller's presence had softened his personality.

I shouldn't need Teller with me to get some respect in this goddamn town.

"You mind if we get started?" he asked Teller.

Teller tipped his head toward me. "It's not up to me, Stan."

Stan had the grace to look abashed. "Yes, apologies. Madison?"

I had expected a nonexistent gathering, but I'd hoped that Wendi would bring Logan. I didn't want to be alone. Selfish, but there it was. I'd cut Mom off and then she'd died. Probably out of spite. She'd known my soft heart and exploited it to the end.

Yet . . . her death hadn't been expected. I'd pulled my hair out trying to figure out how to care for her. I'd had a plan. I was close to having the money. Mom could've gone anywhere for long-term living. But she was gone. Leaving me torn between the dutiful daughter who should love her mom and the girl who'd been hurt more times than she could count.

Did I mind if we got started?

Yes. I didn't want to do this. I didn't want to be sad about my mom around people who only knew her as a cranky bitch.

To be fair, *I* only knew her as a cranky bitch.

I looked around. Mae Bailey was on my left, and Ruby was next to her. The others had asked about coming, but I'd wanted to keep it small. Less embarrassing that way if I ended up crying over a mean woman. Instead, I was opening the bar afterward for a small reception. It'd be a soft opening of sorts. I wouldn't take money though. I just wanted the company.

A car door shut and we all turned around.

Oh my god.

My ex-husband was frowning at me from the other side of a BMW. What had happened to his pickup? Damien slid his sunglasses down his nose and his gaze jumped to Teller, then down to where Teller's arm was wrapped behind me.

Wendi got out, and her red lips tugged down. Her blond-highlighted hair tumbled with large curls. She flipped the tresses over her shoulder and opened the back door for Logan to scramble out. He had his mom's fine features and light-brown hair.

I stood up, unsure what to do. Anxiety twisted in my stomach. All I knew was that I wanted to hug my nephew. "Logan. Hey." I was about to walk around the few empty chairs on the other side of Teller, but Logan shrank against Wendi.

Ouch. Okay. He hadn't seen me in a while and he was only four years old.

"Wendi," I said. "Damien." My tone flattened more than the road through the cemetery. "Thanks for coming."

Wendi's brows lifted at Teller and Mae. Her gaze skipped over Ruby, swinging back to Teller. The breeze fluttered the skirt of her pink summer dress.

She slid her hand over Logan's narrow shoulders. "Teller. Mae. What a surprise."

Damien nodded to Teller. What had my ex heard about his girlfriend's ex?

Teller ignored them and gave me an *Are you okay?* look.

I didn't know, but I flashed the smallest of smiles. I wasn't bothered by Damien and Wendi, but I was a stranger to my nephew. He was my only remaining family.

"We were just about to start," I said to them. "Come have a seat."

I wouldn't be like Mom. Not today.

The corner of Wendi's mouth curled up, but she nudged Logan. Damien went around the car to fall into step with her. She came to his chin with her tall wedge heels. He eventually outpaced them to be the one to sit by Teller.

For once, he'd done something that gave me comfort. On a good day, I wasn't secure enough to have

Wendi and her long, tanned legs right next to Teller. Today was not a good day.

The service was quick. I'd told Stanley I wouldn't tolerate any slander about Mom. This wasn't the day to be passive-aggressive. Whether he'd listened to me or hadn't wanted to upset the Baileys, I'd never be sure, but he was polite enough, saying the most neutral things about Mom and concentrating more on the family moving on after death.

I was the only family. And my nephew. I tried to peek at him, but he was sitting the farthest away.

Once it wrapped up, Stanley left as soon as possible.

Mae pulled me in for one of her warm, gentle hugs. "Are you sure you still want us at Flatlanders?"

"Absolutely." I'd be grateful not to sit in an empty bar all night pondering a future of running it.

Ruby crowded in after Mae. "I'm so sorry."

"Thank you. Thanks for coming."

"Okay. We'll see you at Flatlanders. Tenor's picking up some munchies, but Scarlett made a batch of lemonade." Her gaze strayed to the side. I didn't have to look to know Damien and Wendi were there.

Teller's heat seeped into me. "Cruz and Lane are bringing some sandwiches, and the others will fill in the rest."

It'd be a proper reception. The family Mom had hated most were the only ones who'd put in an effort for her.

Ruby gave me one last squeeze and I closed my eyes, soaking up the support, fortifying myself for making nice with my ex-sister-in-law.

Ruby and Mae walked toward the road. Teller slipped an arm around me.

"The reception's at Flatlanders?" Wendi asked, her tone brimming with impatience.

"Yes. You're all welcome." I twisted my hands together but leaned more into Teller's hard side. "No need to bring anything. The Baileys have it covered." I couldn't help myself.

The tic under Wendi's cheek made it worth it. So did the grinding of Damien's jaw.

I tried to catch my nephew's eye, but he was frowning at his shoes. "Wait'll you try Scarlett's cherry lemonade, Logan."

He ignored me and looked at his mom.

Was this the kid I used to give piggyback rides to?

I searched his face for my brother, but his eyes were light like his mom's, and his default expression was petulant like hers too. Damien put his hand on Logan's shoulder.

"I have a stop to make first," Wendi said with a sniff. "Riley's showing us a property she wants to rent. Then we'll be there."

"See you soon." I wound my arm around Teller's waist, and together, we walked toward his pickup.

"Jesus," he said in my ear, tickling my hair. "Was that as awkward as it felt?"

"Ten times more," I murmured back.

He chuckled as we reached his pickup. He opened the passenger door for me. When I slid into the seat, he leaned in. "Are you doing okay?"

I peeked over his shoulder. Damien and Wendi were furtively glancing at us while they walked to their car.

I stroked his beard. It wasn't for show. I craved the connection. If it had been appropriate, I would've sat on his lap during the service. "I'm really glad I decided not to wear jeans."

He gave me a quick kiss. "I mourn every time you have to put on clothes."

I was grinning when he closed the door. And I didn't miss the dirty look Wendi shot in my direction.

CHAPTER TWENTY-FOUR

Madison

I fluttered around Flatlanders. The bar was lined with sandwiches and snacks—chips, dessert bars, and light salads. Scarlett had made a few pitchers of lemonade. I wouldn't be testing our payment system or mixing drinks, but I was grateful I had a place to send off Mom.

Teller was my shadow. He'd be chatting with his siblings and in-laws one second and then at my side the next, making sure I was doing all right and getting what I needed.

My gaze continued straying to the door. Tension rode over my shoulders and down my spine, an unwelcome shawl on a stifling hot day.

Mae took post behind the bar, looking at home chatting with her daughters on the other side. She'd probably worked the tasting room at Copper Summit a time or two. Maybe I could hire her so I could get away from town.

No. That was the shock of seeing Damien and
Wendi. Of my nephew looking at me like he was going
to run. He was just a kid and this had to be a confusing
time. He'd lost his dad earlier this year and then a
grandma he hadn't known well. I was his only family on
the Townsend side. How was Damien's family treating
him? I hadn't been good enough for a daughter-in-law.
How would they handle not only another man's son but
the son of the guy Wendi had cheated on to be with
Damien?

A wicked part of me hoped they accepted Logan and
gave Wendi the same shit attitude they'd given me. If
they treated her like she was some unrefined peasant
with relatives she should be ashamed of, well, I'd sleep a
little better at night.

I brushed a tendril of hair off my face. "What can I
get you?" I asked Lane. His lemonade glass was empty. I
wasn't serving alcohol, but the soda fountains worked.

"Not a thing," Lane said. "But you can let me help
clean up."

"I have nothing else to do." The saving grace of the
last week had been my job. It'd worn me out enough to
sleep during the day after my shift.

I should've scheduled Mom's service for Thursday or
Friday, but I'd wanted it over with. I'd wanted to put it
behind me so I could figure out how to live without her.
I'd been doing everything to care for her and now my
future only included Flatlanders. The house was sold.
The money was in escrow. This place was my last tie to
my family. Except for my nephew. I peered out the
window.

A BMW was parking a few spaces down from the
entrance.

I lifted my gaze to Teller. He watched me, his jaw hard. His eyes asked me if I was ready.

I didn't know. Were you ever ready to speak to your ex and the woman he'd cheated on you with? The love I'd felt for him had evaporated like raindrops in the sun, but the betrayal was there. The reminder that I hadn't been good enough. Yet with Teller, it was all dulled. I nodded and brushed my hands down my skirt.

I was almost to the entrance when they walked in. The room didn't go silent, but the conversation around me fell to a murmur.

Wendi entered first, then Damien right behind her with his hand on her back. Logan clung to Damien's leg.

Good thing I had weeks of history with Teller, or that would've wrenched open the break in my heart. I had wanted kids, Damien had insisted we keep waiting, and here he was, with someone else's.

I pushed it all away. Damien was a different life. I'd been a different person. At the moment, I almost believed it. "Hey," I said. "Thanks for coming. It would've meant a lot to Mom."

They both gave me dubious expressions, but I shrugged it off. Wendi's brows drew together as she took in everyone, and she shrank against Damien. The bar contained more Baileys than there'd been when she and Teller had dated. The sisters were all married now, and the guys too, except for Lane and Cruz. She probably only knew of them from before she'd moved out on Scott.

Teller came up behind me and put his hand on the small of my back. Damien drew himself up straighter, but he'd never be the height or width of Teller.

"There are still plenty of places to sit," I said.

Wendi gave her head a little shake. "When is the paperwork getting taken care of? Riley's at the old salon a few doors down. I told her we'd pop in and sign whatever we needed to. Shouldn't take long, right?"

"Excuse me?"

Wendi jutted her pointy chin out as if to prompt me.

I blinked. A "fuck" escaped Teller's mouth.

"The will reading?" she said like *duh?*

My stomach churned. Of course. Why had I thought she'd come for any other reason? They weren't here to pay their respects. Their body language and tone should've warned me, but I had hoped for the best. At what point would that personality trait be stomped out of me?

"What will?" My volume was louder than I'd intended, and she and Damien stiffened. Teller's hand was a heating pad at my back. Will reading? What the hell did she think Mom had to leave behind? "Mom didn't have a will."

Wendi paled, then flushed as realization sank in. "Your mom had nothing?"

"Since you contested everything about Scott's will and trust, I'd think you'd know better than anyone else," I said tightly. Dad had left everything to Scott. What had been Scott's was now mine.

"Nothing?" Her voice went up an octave.

I wanted to ask if she regretted not staying with Scott so she could've bled him absolutely dry, but I pushed the cattiness back. I was not my mother.

"No," I said carefully. "She had her clothes in the home and an old chair. You're welcome to that."

She drew back. "And the house sale? Where is all that going to go?"

I had no clue anymore. I couldn't comprehend that much money. But I did know that I didn't owe Wendi an explanation. "That's my business."

"Just like this shithole?" she snapped.

This time, I flinched.

"That's a bad word," Logan said. Wendi pursed her lips and her gaze jumped between me and Teller.

His heat seeped into my side. "We're not doing this here. You can talk to her through her lawyer."

I soaked in his strength. He wasn't censuring me, and I reveled in the aghast expression on Wendi's face that he'd kick her out.

"Wendi, we should go," Damien said quietly. "Riley's waiting—"

"Shut this bar down." She wasn't done with her demands, and her snide tone was back. "Scott used it to drain every last cent from the family and ignore his son. I guess you're going to do that as Logan's aunt."

Her manipulation was almost tangible, and Damien had the audacity to nod.

Teller was stiff at my side. "It's time to lea—"

"Mommy." Logan tugged on his mom's hand. "You said she isn't my aunt."

Wendi jerked like his words were a whip.

My anger escaped its confines. How dirty was that? "You told him I'm not—"

"And you're my real daddy." Logan blinked his big eyes at Damien.

Damien's clean-shaven cheeks paled. "Not now, kiddo."

"Shit," Teller breathed quietly, echoing my dawning horror.

"But I look like you," Logan insisted. Now he was pulling on Damien's hand. "Right, Daddy?"

Horrible awareness crept into my brain, slowly at first, then bashing down the door of my complete ignorance to reveal *years* of betrayal. "Oh my god." I looked from the boy to my ex. Same small ears. Same narrow-set eyes. No wonder I'd never been able to see any of my brother in Logan. Outrage poured through my veins like an oil spill.

"How long?" My voice shook. Logan was *four*. How long was the affair?

Wendi sucked in a breath and exchanged a glance with my ex. It told me enough. Half my marriage? More? Did it matter?

"We should go." She spun so fast her blond hair flew up. Damien gathered Logan in his arms and rushed out the door, Wendi hot on his heels.

The bar was quiet around me. Blood rushed between my ears and my heart rate crept higher. The wound I'd thought was healed ripped right open, only this time I hurt for my brother. For his loss. For the anguish he must've been in.

Teller faced me, cupping my face with a big, warm hand. "Madison, I'm so sorry. You didn't deserve any of this."

I knew I didn't, but hearing someone else say it was more than I would've asked for before the night of the auction. "I didn't. Neither did Scott."

God, had he known. If he learned the truth, he would've lost his mind— Oh. My. God.

My mouth dropped open. "The night of the accident. He knew."

Shock filled Teller's dark gaze before fury darkened his irises. "Goddammit."

I needed answers. That was the least our shitty exes owed me. I pulled away from Teller's comforting touch and slammed out the front door. He stayed on my heels, not leaving me to handle this alone.

Riley was on the sidewalk, hovering by an empty storefront two doors down with a For Sale sign. She'd have to get her sugar daddy to foot the bill since she'd lost the bid for Teller.

Her gaze widened when she saw me, and she waved Logan over. "Come on in. I have some cookies for you."

To make my fresh wounds burn more, he went right to her and they disappeared inside the empty store. Damien and Wendi stood guard, a united front against me, like I planned to run in and tackle Riley and spirit Logan away or something.

"That's why he snapped." I marched closer. "Scott found out."

The guilt that flashed through Wendi's eyes recounted the whole story. I could see it playing out. The stools smashed into the mirror. The pool cue shards. The hammer against the booths. The shattered light fixtures. Scott had been angry, and he'd been so damn hurt.

Damien propped his hands on his hips. "Madison. You need to c—"

"If you tell her to calm down," Teller growled, menace dripping from each word, "you're going to find out what I'm like when I'm very much not calm."

Damien snapped his mouth shut.

Teller stabbed his finger at them. "You two have

been lying and using Maddy and her brother for years. You can answer a simple question."

Damien's gaze turned hostile. "You know nothing about—"

"You coerced her to quit school to support you." People were stopping to listen to Teller's voice carry across the sidewalk. "You manipulated her into working three jobs to pay for your law degree and then left her with half your debt in the divorce like a goddamn weasel." His livid gaze bounced back and forth between then. "You each cheated on us. You both financially screwed Madison over, and you still had the audacity to keep the lie going to try and cheat her out of more money. You both are pathetic."

When we'd been married, I'd have never talked to him that way. Turned out I didn't have to now. Teller had my back.

"We're not the pathetic ones," Wendi sneered, her flinty gaze pinning me "Look at you. Charging out on the street acting like your mom."

I laughed, bold and obnoxious. "My mom never lied about how she felt about people. You let Scott think he was Logan's dad as long as it suited you." Wendi's eyes went wide and her gaze jumped around. There were plenty of onlookers. Maybe someone was even recording. I had zero fucks to give. "When did you tell him that Logan wasn't his? When you got mad he was using the bar's money to care for our mother? Would you have rather he put an old woman out on the street so you could, what? Take another trip to Cancun? Fund Damien's golf trips?" I lifted my gaze to Damien. "Nice tan, asshole."

"You're nothing but Mad Maddy and you always will be," Wendi shot back.

Tingles spread over my body, bringing warmth where cold rage touched.

Teller slid his arm around my waist. "She's my Mad Maddy, and she's fucking perfect."

I liked that nickname now, dammit.

"I can't believe this," Wendi spat out. She crossed her arms. "You two? Tell me, Madison. Are you ready to work your entire life and career around him? Around his family that will always be more important than you?" She stabbed a finger in my direction. "You'll never be his priority. People wondered why I left him for Scott. For all his faults, at least Scott had ambition. Until he moved me back to this godforsaken town to run that dive bar. I wasn't going to get dragged back to Bourbon Canyon to . . ." She lifted her dainty chin. "To become just another bitter Townsend."

I sucked in a breath. I didn't feel like a bitter Townsend. I felt like I deserved retribution. After finding out how long I was manipulated, how narrow my life had been because of them, I wanted to explode out of my skin and float away. Teller was anchoring me, his strong arm banded around me, but her words burrowed under my skin.

How much would I have to tailor my life if I stayed with Teller? He showed me how much I deserved. He defended me. But how far did it stretch outside the borders of a town I had never wanted to return to?

Regardless, I had too much Townsend in me to let her get the last word. "At least I can walk around town with my head held high knowing exactly who I am. Everyone will look at both of you and wonder who you're trying to lie, cheat, and steal from. You won't even be able to look at each other and wonder just how far that trust is gonna go. I bet there's already question."

Damien's jaw went tight. I hit a nerve. "Come on, Wendi. We're done here."

"That's the only thing we can agree on," Teller said, his voice hard. "Don't ever come to Flatlanders again."

Damien tugged on Wendi's arm and they disappeared into the building Riley and Logan had gone into. The block was quiet. People had stepped out of the surrounding businesses to watch us. I was in public, but inside, I was empty.

That was it. I had no family. None. It was me and this damn bar.

I had Teller. But Wendi and her cutting words had hit the mark. Was she right? Were his feelings for me constrained to this small town? Was I restricted to a place that had never wanted me?

Tires squealed around the corner and a pickup roared down the street. Guys' laughter spewed out an open window. Two teen boys leaned out the passenger windows, and a third popped out the rear window on the other side.

"Get fucked, Flatlanders!" They all tossed something.

Teller's strong arms cinched around me, spinning us around, and he curled over me. Splats hit the front of the bar and the ground in front of me. Drops of red, blue, and yellow littered the sidewalk. Paint?

"Are you all right?" Teller asked, his worried voice in my ear.

"Yes." No. I wasn't fucking all right.

I had no family left. My marriage had been a sham

longer than I'd ever known. And the town hated this bar. It did not want me to succeed.

I straightened just as the front door banged open. Cruz and Lane sprinted down the block, their boots striking the cement. Tate and Tenor were behind him. Tate had his phone to his ear.

"Red pickup. Dent in the rear fender," Teller told him. "Four kids. I think the Blake kid was driving."

Tate repeated the description into his phone.

I took in Flatlanders. The paint was already drying under the hot sun, staining the window and the brick around it. The sign above the door, the one I'd just had redone, dripped with garish red paint.

A choking sound left me. I tried to swallow my sob, but I hiccuped instead.

"Hey." Teller tugged me into his embrace. "We'll find who did this, and they'll pay. We'll get it cleaned."

"It won't matter." I sounded hollow to my own ears. "Nothing matters." My vision got blurry, then cleared when tears streaked down my cheeks. Teller tried to catch them, but they were falling too fast.

I broke out of his hold.

"It'll be all right, Maddy."

"No. It never is." My chest was so heavy I could barely draw in a breath. "Don't you see? It never is. It's always fucked way before I ever realize."

Teller was a great guy, but then what? Would my relationship be done way before I knew it? Would his family and the whole town know before me? Or worse, there was no other way to be with him without continuing to sacrifice the life I wanted for myself?

I shouldn't let Wendi's words taint what I'd built for

myself, but she'd always had a way to hit where it hurt the most. And there was something or someone at the ready to cause pain.

"I'm done here." Not just with the reception. I was done with trying. I was done with waiting for the next bad thing to happen. I was done with Bourbon Canyon and the shitstorms it had given me. I was done worrying about what happened next. "I'm done."

Teller's brows drew together and concern infused rough, handsome features. He'd sensed what I meant too.

Fear seized my heart. I couldn't be done. This couldn't be done. But what was I supposed to do? My skin felt too tight. A cyclone spun inside of me and I couldn't outrun it, but I was surrounded by reminders of everything I lost. Teller could be my tether, but I didn't...

I didn't have it in me.

Tate approached us. "We'll get who did this, Madison. It'll be all cleaned up before you open."

"I'm not opening Flatlanders." I was going to burst. Into tears, into a cloud of nothingness, I didn't know. I wanted so badly to cling to Teller, to everything he'd given me. To all his kind words and his big, sweet heart. Terror clogged my throat. What if I lost him too?

I backed up a step, out of Teller's shadow. Out of his ring of protection. Because I shouldn't need it. I hated that I did. I didn't want to hang around wondering when it'd all get yanked away. "I'm selling it."

My mouth was working before my brain could catch up. I hadn't planned to sell. Ever. Until now. Because I didn't need this place. I didn't need to keep it going for some attempt at filial duty or a feeble legacy. I didn't need to stay here. I could go anywhere.

I was a millionaire, after all.

Teller

I tracked Madison through the bar. My family watched us. Even the kids stayed quiet. She charged right to the hallway, strands of her dark hair fluttering behind her.

"Selling?" I asked as anxiety stacked high in my chest. She'd closed herself off from me. I saw it happen.

She pushed out the back door. In the quiet alley, she inhaled, long and deep, and tipped her head back. A flurry of voices and car engines were audible from the street on the other side. Sirens from the police. But Madison ignored it, like she was stealing a morsel of peace where she could.

"I'm not staying in Bourbon Canyon," she said barely above a whisper.

"What does that mean?" My heart stuttered. The meaning couldn't be clearer. I was in Bourbon Canyon. She'd just announced she wasn't staying.

"I have nothing," she said hoarsely. "No one."

"What about me?" I loved her. I'd told her she didn't have to say the words, but had I been wrong? Didn't she feel what I did?

Her expression crumpled. "Would you still love me if I wasn't convenient?"

"How are you convenient?"

"What if I wasn't stuck in Bourbon Canyon? What if I was able to go live my dreams and travel? Then what?" She lifted her arms and dropped them. "Because I can. For once in my life, I don't have to be tied to anyone or anything. The sale of the house is nearly complete. Cara will make sure I get a good deal on Flatlanders. I can go *anywhere*. Do *anything*."

She said it like a challenge. I was in a competition I didn't know how to finish.

"You want a family to go with that perfect house." Her eyes shimmered. "You want a quiet life where you get lost in work and then go home to your perfect wife."

"Don't you want the same?" My question wasn't helping. It made her sound like the convenient partner she feared she was. Just more obligations for her.

"I never wanted to run a bar. To get sworn at because I won't let someone drink and drive. To clean piss off the bathroom walls. You know those boys in the pickup? They hated Scott for turning them into the cops for trying to use fake IDs. Scott's been gone for *months*. How long am I going to pay for what people thought about my family?"

"You don't have to open Flatlanders. You can still sell and be with me."

Indecision flickered through her gaze, but she lifted her chin. "I never had the choices you did, Teller. I never had options. Someone's wants and needs always came before mine, and with us . . . You would come before me." She blew out a hard breath. "I promised myself I would never be like my mother. I thought I meant how she acted, but it's also her circumstances. She got mean trying to put herself first. You've treated me well. So good. But for how long? When push comes to shove, what are you going to choose? Your family's legacy, a family that cares for so many others? Or the girl who has no one else?"

I'd always choose her. "I'm sorry. About them. About Logan. You didn't deserve any of it." I wanted to go to her, to hold her, but she wrapped her arms around herself.

"I know," she whispered. "I can't stay here. I want more, Teller."

Yet she didn't think I could give it to her. The fear was scrawled into the lines of her beautiful face. "You can still have more. We can figure this out."

"What if I want to move? What if I want to travel for years? Would you give up your part of Copper Summit and follow me? Would you leave Bailey Beef?"

I clamped my teeth together, hating the gut punch of my initial response. No. I'd never leave. The work I loved was here. My family was here. They were my foundation. They were what made me *me*. I had been born and raised in Bourbon Canyon and I'd die here. But my happily would be her prison.

"That's what I thought," she said quietly.

"I love you, Madison."

"Do you love me, or do you love the idea of me?"

"The idea of you was a girl who told off anyone who pissed her off." I had fallen for that girl too. "Someone from the wrong side of the tracks who acted just like everyone expected her to because that's all they looked for. Then I got to know *you* and I fell hard. So goddamn hard, Madison."

"Oh, Teller." Hopelessness was heavy in her eyes. "I don't know who I am."

I flinched. Goddammit. I had no response. I couldn't make her stay. If she had to mold herself into the partner she thought I wanted, she'd never convince herself that I loved her for her. I loved her fire. Her drive. The way she'd told off our exes was hot. The joy on her face when she baked could sustain me for life. But it didn't matter what I thought or how I felt. In the end, if she wasn't happy, I wasn't happy. "What are you going to do?"

She hugged herself harder. "I'm leaving."

Nothing about her forlorn expression said she wanted to go, but the idea of staying here bothered her more. "Where?"

"Anywhere. Everywhere."

"Okay."

Hurt shone in her eyes and she swallowed. I wanted to take it all back. I didn't want her to fucking leave. I wanted her by my side forever. I wanted to see her soar.

"Okay." She took a step back, then another.

I squeezed my hands into fists, or I'd reach for her, but I'd become just another person holding her back.

She bit her lower lip, and her gaze stroked over the back of the bar. "Can you, uh, lock up here?"

Shock gut punched me. "You're leaving *now*?"

Distress rippled over her features. "I can't go back in there." She crept closer to her pickup. "I'll call Cara. She'll take care of the rest and get it up for sale."

"Madison. Right now?" An invisible band constricted around my chest. What about her things? What about me? I wanted more time with her. A few more minutes. The selfish part of me hoped she'd change her mind if she stayed. I wanted forever, but if I loved her, then goddammit—I had to help her make what she wanted a priority.

She opened the pickup door. "I have to."

"What about your stuff?"

"Do whatever with it." She paused before she climbed in. "Thank you. For everything. I mean it. I'll never forget you."

Then she jumped in and tore off. Out of my life.

CHAPTER TWENTY-FIVE

Teller

I sat on the cot in the back room of the bar, my elbows propped on my thighs. I pressed my fingertips together, alternating the pressure. My phone was going wild in my pocket, but I ignored it.

She was gone.

Just like that.

I had woken up this morning wanting to be there for her on a tough day. I was ending the day without her. A single man.

I'd thought I'd spend my life with her. I hadn't told her, and maybe that should've been a clue. I'd seen how she'd been caged in, doing what was right by people she should owe nothing to. Deep down, maybe I'd known that if she had a chance to leave, she'd be gone.

Why had I never thought about going with her? Had I been just another asshole who thought she wouldn't have a choice?

I heard the footfalls before Tate leaned against the doorframe. "How's she doing?"

I'd come right in here after she'd driven off, and my family had given me a wide berth. Tate had taken care of the police report, and the others had cleaned up the food, swept, and wiped down the bar. The paint would be dealt with another day. If I got my way, those little fuckers who did it would be scrubbing it off—with their faces. "She's, uh, gone."

"Yeah." He shoved his hands in his pockets. "I can imagine that she needed space."

"She wants all the space, Tate. She's *gone*."

He scratched his beard. "Sorry?"

"She left Bourbon Canyon. She left me."

He stepped back and peered down the hallway. He held a hand up. I didn't know who was still here. Then he crossed to me and sat on the cot. "Will she be back?"

I shook my head and tapped my fingertips together. "She was going to use all the money on her mom and nephew. This bar and a house. Now the world is wide open to her."

"Shit."

Relieved I didn't have to explain how epically hurtful today had been for her, I nodded. "She's never had the chance to do what she wants. I asked her once, you know. If she could go back and do anything, what would she do? Her answer didn't include Bourbon Canyon."

"She doesn't have the same relationship with the town that we do." He stated the obvious, but he wasn't lecturing. I kept my smart-ass retort to myself. "Why did she leave you though?"

I gave him a disbelieving look. "She doesn't want to be in Bourbon Canyon."

He studied me until I wanted to squirm, just like our dad used to do. "Is staying here worth giving her up?"

I could tell him she hadn't given me a choice, but she'd asked a rhetorical question that meant the same. My answer had been instinctive. Instant. I was an important part of two different enterprises.

Was I a critical part? Why hadn't I asked myself those questions? I was forty. My life was here. "What would I do?"

"Live off her?" he joked, but I scowled at him. "I don't know. You have a lot of skills. What'd she talk about doing?"

"Pastry school. In Boston. Or London."

Tate grimaced. Neither of us was a city guy.

"She's selling Flatlanders," I said. When she'd said that, a part of me had died inside. I'd put a lot into these walls. Flatlanders had character now. It was a trendy dive bar, and Madison would've run it well. A new owner might change everything. Cover up the history we'd made.

"Shit," Tate said again. "Kind of hate to see this place go. You never know what kind of owner the next one will be."

"Yep." I gripped the edge of the cot. Memories flashed through my head. How she'd shut the door in my face when I'd first stopped by. Her coming out of the bathroom in a bra and underwear. The way she'd opened for me on this very cot.

We hadn't even been dating for two months, but I couldn't imagine my life without her. Even now, when I thought of waking up to an empty house tomorrow, there was nothing. Did I just get up and go to work? An ordinary Thursday?

Was there time off for heartbreak? I was the boss, there could be.

Then I'd be wandering the house like a ghost, lost and confused as to why I was haunting the place by myself.

I sank my head in my hands. I sensed someone at the door, but I didn't look. The cot lifted as Tate got up. It dipped again and the smell of wildflowers surrounded me. Mama.

"You know," she said, "when you and Wendi broke up, I was so relieved you didn't try to win her back."

My laugh was bitter. There'd been nothing to win back. Our relationship had been floundering, worse than I had thought apparently, and it'd been severed as soon as Wendi had touched another man. "The bullet I dodged hit Madison."

"Mm."

A minute ticked by. Then two. A cord of tension coiled tighter inside me. It wasn't like Mama to be quiet during times like this.

"What are you still doing here, Teller?"

I lifted my head. "My life is here." My answer was weak. How important did I think I was?

"You don't think I saw how you felt at Tate and Scarlett's wedding? Wynter and Myles's? Summer and Jonah's?"

"Mama."

"Autumn and Gideon's—their renewal, since I know you're going to point out how none of us were there for the Vegas wedding." She rested a hand on my shoulder. "You were especially melancholy at Junie and Rhys's wedding. I think you started to write off any of that happiness for yourself. You've isolated yourself for so long. I worried about you when Tenor and Ruby got together."

"There was nothing to worry about."

"There always is when you have kids." She patted me on the shoulder and ruffled a hand in my hair. "You got all the stubbornness from your father."

"He said it came from you."

She smiled, and the loss I often glimpsed in her eyes flared up before dying back down to a smolder. "You got his fierce love and loyalty. All you boys did." She dropped her hand. "It's biting you in the ass now. Go get her, Teller."

"And what? Bring her back to the town that feels like a prison?"

"I don't know," she said simply. "But you can't figure it out on your own."

"What if she never wants to return?"

"She might not," Mama said calmly. She rose and stood over me. I was back to being that five-year-old, getting a talking-to. "That girl rearranged her life for the people she loved. Even when they didn't deserve it. I hope she finds someone someday who's willing to do the same for her."

Mama walked out, leaving me alone and feeling like an absolutely selfish dick.

Madison did deserve someone who was willing to sacrifice as much for her as she'd done for others. She deserved to have those millions and live out her dream. She didn't deserve to do it alone.

But I had a life here. I had a home. I had two jobs that fit me to a *T*. Madison could go anywhere and do anything. Be with anyone. How much was I willing to sacrifice for her?

Madison

The airport was emptying out. Only one gate was open. The last flight leaving for the day.

I'd been here for hours, and I was on my third ticket. If I didn't leave on this flight, I'd have to find somewhere to stay for the night. I stared at the destination on my boarding pass. I had three airline apps on my phone. When I'd woken up this morning, I hadn't even had one.

Couples of all ages filled the seats around me. Older couples relaxed in their chairs and chatted with each other about cattle prices and crop rotations. If they weren't discussing that, they were talking about the various trips they'd taken over their lifetime.

Then there were families with tired but excited little kids. My heart wrung like a dishcloth just when I'd thought there wasn't more sadness to squeeze out of me. Growing up, I'd thought I'd be the parent who offered their kid everything I hadn't had.

I clicked my screen off.

"Attention all passengers . . ."

I barely heard the announcement. I'd never flown before, but the last few hours had given me a whirlwind education in booking flights. All I had to do was get up and walk through the door.

The seats around me were empty as I slumped. My face was still red and blotchy, and at least once an hour, I spontaneously started crying. No wonder I was an oasis. Security hadn't approached me yet, but if I cried one more time, the ticket agent might actually do more than side-eye me.

I massaged my temples. Fatigue hung on my shoulders and coaxed my eyelids to shut. I obeyed. At least I'd have a valid reason for missing the flight if I snoozed.

What was I doing? Where would I go? More importantly, was it worth leaving behind someone who'd become very important to me. Someone who was everything.

Teller Bailey had made me happy and wasn't that ultimately what I wanted?

The answer kept me planted in this damn seat, watching travelers launch their adventures.

I loved him and he loved me. Could it be that simple? Would I really be giving up my dreams when kind, strong, handsome, bearded Teller Bailey was my own personal fantasy come to life?

What had leaving cost me? Could I even go back after fleeing Bourbon Canyon and him like they were death sentences?

What if I returned and he'd already moved on?

My brain tried telling me that was ridiculous. It'd been a half a day. But I couldn't look at him, at those dark eyes that brought me so much comfort, and see that I had killed that affection that used to be there.

Or was I just being a coward?

Airline ticket number three said possibly.

Someone sat next to me and I was wrapped in a woodsy, citrusy scent. What torture was this? I dropped my hands and opened my eyes.

Teller.

He was sitting on the edge of the seat next to me, his elbows propped on his thighs, looking at me like I hadn't just told him that the life he wanted sounded awful. Like I hadn't left him and Bourbon Canyon with nothing but the clothes on my back, my ID, my phone, and a debit card.

"Phoenix, huh?" he asked.

I glanced around. No one was giving us the time of day. That wasn't true. Some women were stripping Teller down with their eyes, no doubt making bets with each other about how many abs he had underneath that tight tee.

At the toe of his boots were two suitcases. One was mine from his house. The other was a simple black carry-on.

My confusion grew. "What are you doing here?"

He ran his thumb and forefinger over his lower lip. "Leaving with you."

Hope leaped into my chest, beating back the fear that had invaded every cell until it'd been hard to breathe. I'd sat in this damn airport for hours, beautiful view and all, and ignored the planes coming and going. Indecision had rebounded through my head like a Ping-Pong ball that had no place to go, no hole to roll into because I'd closed off the only route I wanted. A path back to Bourbon Canyon. A way back to Teller.

Yet he was here. Right next to me. With his eyes shining just for me.

My gaze vacillated between him and the suitcases. Was that really mine? He'd packed for me and himself? Which was more shocking? "How can you leave with me? You're needed back home."

"Turns out I'm not as important as I thought." He flashed a quick smile and the resulting shock of heat flushed away the cold from the last few hours. "I have a

big family, and all of them are involved in both businesses in some way. They can cover for me." His expression turned serious. "I should've left with you. I'll regret
it forever that I didn't."

"I wouldn't have left." Everyone might've blamed me
for Teller giving up everything he knew, but I would've
blamed myself more. He'd chased me down on his own.
Sure, he hadn't had to go far, but it turned out, I couldn't
go far either. "For how long?"

His gaze dipped to my lips, then lifted back up. "Forever, if needed."

He was delusional. He couldn't mean it. "You can't
leave Bourbon Canyon forever."

"If I'm with you, I can."

I put a hand on his strong forearm and the muscles
twitched. "Your family loves you. They'll miss you."

"We can go back and visit. Or they'll fly out where
we are." He pivoted toward me. "I love you, Madison. I
said I wanted what my parents had, and guess what? I
found it. It's not the house, the jobs, or a cozy little town
in the foothills of the mountains. It's you and me.
Together."

This wasn't true. None of it. I was dreaming. Made
sense because all my dreams now included him. "How
did you know I'd still be here?" I whispered.

"I didn't." He traced a thumb over my lips. "This was
the last flight out for the day, so I'd take another one
from Phoenix. I figured you'd either gone to Salt Lake
City or Vegas."

"I bought a ticket for each of them," I whispered. "I
couldn't get on. I couldn't quit thinking about you."

His lazy grin made the anxiety of sitting through
boarding calls and last warnings worth it. "Yeah?"

"I'm worried I'm on some watch list. I keep buying tickets and not boarding." I hadn't had anyone to talk to. I didn't know Mae well, yet her face had flashed through my mind a million times. She'd know what to do. Same with Ruby. But Teller was theirs. I wasn't. I'd had no one to call. I could go anywhere, but the few connections I'd made, the ones I treasured more than I thought, were in Bourbon Canyon.

Turned out I didn't have nothing. Everything was in Bourbon Canyon.

The speakers crackled to life. *"Attention all passengers. It's my pleasure to announce the boarding of flight . . ."*

My heart slammed against my ribs. I had to leave. I couldn't return to the emptiness. But I hadn't been able to leave Teller. Yet he had my luggage, and he'd said he was coming with me. Confusion swirled in my head.

He studied me, concern in his face. "I hear Phoenix is hot this time of year, but we can fly somewhere cooler from there."

"What if I don't want to leave?" What if I stayed? What if I betrayed everything I had wanted as a kid? What if Bourbon Canyon made me miserable?

What if the last two months in Bourbon Canyon were the happiest I'd ever be? I couldn't imagine it getting better. Cooking in Teller's kitchen. Going to bed and waking up to him. Being a part of his big and loving family dinners.

"Then we'll come back." He grabbed my hand. "We'll travel and we'll go home. You'll do your pastry training, and I'll live in whatever town you're in or commute. You want to go to France and have a real croissant, I'll get a passport."

"I don't have a passport."

"We'll both get one."

"I love you, Teller." More announcements crackled over the line, but neither of us listened. His focus was only on me, and my terrified attention was on him. "I love you so much."

His smile grew wide. "Glad to hear it, Mads." He cupped my face and kissed me, long and slow. Neither of us moved. He didn't take it further. We were in the middle of an airport. The kiss was the punctuation to my declaration. I loved him. I couldn't imagine not loving him. He showed me what I deserved, and I deserved him.

He gently broke the kiss and rested his forehead on mine. "I love you so goddamn much I would've scoured this country looking for you."

"I'm right here." I'd been waiting for him and hadn't known it.

He rose and held a hand out. "Ready to board?"

No. But I was ready to go anywhere with him. "We don't have to leave."

"Maddy, you want to travel. We're going to travel." He winked. "And I'm not saying that because Mama and the others would kick my ass if I brought you straight back home."

"They aren't upset with me?"

"No, they were a little salty I let you leave alone." He sobered. "My first priority was you and what you wanted. I only let you go because I want what's best for you."

The anxiety that he was doing something completely against his wishes died down. "You figured out you're what's best for me?"

"I'll make sure I am. I'm selfish when it comes to you."

I slipped my fingers into his warm palm. He pulled me up and into his chest.

People around us were gathering their luggage and forming a line, but he held me and I hugged him back. He was real. Solid and strong, he didn't let go until it was time for us to board.

"What do we do in Phoenix?" I asked. I was so far out of my realm of experience, but the fear was gone. Only excitement remained, growing stronger the closer we got to boarding.

"Anything you want." He bent to put his mouth close to my ear. "After we spend one full day absolutely naked in the hotel room getting room service."

Desire hit hard, flooding my body and making me achy. How long was this damn flight? "That's when you can do anything you want to me."

He groaned, and I grinned the whole way to Arizona.

CHAPTER TWENTY SIX

Two years later . . .

Madison

I clung to Teller's shoulders. My legs were wrapped around his waist and my ass was planted on the desk in my office. A few paper clips had fallen to the floor, but that was normal. So was getting consumed by my husband before the place opened.

"Oh my god," I groaned, my climax building fast, like I hadn't been in this same position last night.

"You're going to come good and hard," Teller growled against my neck. He grunted, the strength of his thrusts increasing. "Then you're going to go out there like a good girl and wait on customers with a smile on your face and my cum inside you."

"Yes," I hissed. It wouldn't be the first time I packed

a half dozen gourmet cupcakes for someone who'd been awful to me as a kid and was now one of my regulars.

Turned out that old bullies waiting in line and paying me money for my creations was a decent balm for old hurts. And since I was the boss, if they pissed me off, they were told to leave. If they complained around town, no one believed I was in the wrong. Because I was a Bailey.

I tightened around him, tipping my head back. Also wouldn't be the first time I waited on customers with beard burn on my neck or between my thighs. I had no shame when it came to Teller. He was the same, wearing my bakery's, Scooter's Confections, swag as jackets, sweaters, T-shirts, and winter hats.

He was wearing a ball cap now, but he'd turned it backward. When he kissed a path up my neck, his whiskers tickling my sensitive flesh, I slammed into my peak.

"God! Teller."

"Fuck, yes. That's it," he said roughly against my lips. "You're squeezing me so damn tight." He kicked his hips once, twice, a third time.

I shuddered around him, clinging to him, as his hot release filled me. "I love you so much."

"Madison Bailey, I'm so goddamn in love with you that I've been late for work all week."

"Well, you missed work the whole last year and they didn't mind, so . . ."

He grinned, pulled out of me, and gave me a quick kiss. "Worth it."

After he helped me off the desk, I scurried to the bathroom. The old Flatlanders still had the same setup that Teller had worked so hard on, but instead of neon signs of alcohol brands, there were pictures of my creations over the last year. The bar was still a bar and the stools Jonah had made were in use, but those were for the lunch crowd. Cupcake displays and jars of home-made caramels lined the counter, and behind the bar, against the wall where bottles used to be stacked, were my various bread offerings. Those were my steadiest sellers. I used only Montana grains, some of them from Gideon and Autumn's farm.

Next to the bar, the old storeroom had been cleaned out and opened up to the rest of the place while being cordoned off with plexiglass. The open kitchen was where I worked my magic. I baked bread and cupcakes, croissants and muffins, and anything I damn well wanted. It helped that I didn't need this place. It was my joy. My passion. But if I had to shut down, I'd be just fine. Me and my sourdough starter would bake in my home and I'd give away my goods.

The room I used to stay in because I had nowhere else to go was now the storeroom. Every time I walked in, I pictured that little cot I used to sleep on, and then I imagined all the times Teller had had me on my back with his face between my legs.

Lots of good memories were tied to this building, and I was making new memories all over town these days.

Once I was done cleaning myself up and straightening my clothing, I opened the bakery. It'd been easier than I thought to give up the idea of running Flatlanders as a bar. It had functioned as one for a year and a half. The boys who'd vandalized the place had cleaned the paint, and their families had covered the expense of the windows. Once the sidewalk drama from the day I'd left town had burned through the grapevine, I'd become an underdog story. People rooted for me after they caught wind of the Damien-and-Wendi-and-Logan situation. Even Scott had been somewhat vindicated in the hearts of the people.

Still, I got a sense of justice any time someone who'd been hard on my family paid me for my work. I also enjoyed that they entered under a sign with my brother's name. He hadn't been a pillar of the community, but he'd been a part of it. He'd been a business owner, and because of him, I was one too. And each time someone walked in off the street, they had to acknowledge that. They had to accept that I'd gotten where I was because of a Townsend and not just the Baileys.

I was arranging a new batch of German chocolate cupcakes in the display case when the front door opened. The bell tinkled. "Welcome to Scooter's Confections." The greeting was automatic—in case they missed the sign. My brother's legacy carried on in a different way.

"Hey, Madison." Cassie sauntered in, taking in the booths, each with an aluminum print of a specialty cupcake. Junie's stepdaughters had taken the photos for me. "Oh, that looks so delicious." Her gaze was on a red cupcake with pink frosting. The top was decorated with red apple jelly beans.

"Thanks. I actually have a few available. How are you and Deacon?"

She grinned and affection shone from her eyes. Teller had told me that she used to be after him and Tenor, but the person who'd bought my place happened to be a bachelor who'd hit it big in the tech industry. He'd wanted to get away from living in big cities and work from home. While coming in and out of town, he'd met Cassie. Now their home was being built, and he and Cassie were still going strong.

I'd been talking with her since Teller and I had returned from my pastry and confectionery training. I could count her as another friend, along with the ones I'd made while at school.

She wiggled her ring finger. "I'm here to order a wedding cake."

I let out a cheer and gawked at her sparkly diamond. "It's gorgeous! Congrats." Old anxiety started to creep in. I wished I was cured of it, and eventually I would be. "I don't have a lot of wedding cake experience."

She waved off my words. "Ruby showed me hers. We're having a fall wedding, and I wanted the same with sunflowers and mums."

"Perfect."

"Having a party out here?" Teller came around the bar to stand with me. "Hey, Cassie. Tell Deacon I said hi."

Deacon was also a bourbon aficionado. He'd met Cassie in the tasting room at Copper Summit.

"Will do." She admired her ring.

I knew the feeling. Mine was safe in a jewelry box while I worked. I'd told Teller I probably wouldn't wear it much, but he'd bought a huge diamond anyway. I loved it.

"It's perfect timing," she said, studying the cupcakes, "with you two returning and the bakery opening." She tapped the plexiglass by the jelly bean one. "I'll take two, please. I have to hear more about London. We're trying to decide where to go for our honeymoon."

"London was great," I said as I retrieved two red

apple cupcakes from the display. "I've got a million pictures." Most of them were of my cowboy at London Tower. My cowboy at the top of the Eiffel Tower. My cowboy holding up the Leaning Tower of Pisa. We'd been unrepentant tourists.

I had gone to pastry school for nine months. Teller had lived with me, and during my time off, we'd traveled all of Europe. The year before that, we'd traveled the US, Canada, and Mexico. I'd gone to bakeries, and I'd even done some training in Boston, but my heart had said there was more to learn. While I could do distance learning and practice in his kitchen, being on location had been worth it.

I'd loved every minute, but I was glad to be home. In Bourbon Canyon. With my family. My large, loud, happy family.

Didn't mean we weren't going to keep traveling. We had a trip to Japan planned this fall, a quick one, before I settled in to keep this place running. It'd been a bar until five months ago when I'd closed it to prepare for Scooter's Confections. Cruz and Lane had managed the place, hiring and training staff for me.

Now they were on to their own adventures, building their own empire, and I'd forever be grateful to two guys who had become like brothers to me.

I packed Cassie's cupcakes, took her wedding cake order, and chatted some more before she left. I'd come so far since that day when she'd been talking to Teller and he'd been blocking my emotional support jelly beans. He still bought me packages all the time. I had a container on my desk. We made sure to never knock that one down when we had sex.

He was in the kitchen, emptying the garbage for me so he could toss it in the outside bin on the way out.

"Hey," I called to him, "could you turn on the ovens for me? Just check inside and make sure I didn't forget any dough rising." I smoothed my suddenly sweaty hands down my apron.

He opened one oven before clicking it on. Then the other. He paused, frowning. "There's a bun in this one."

My stomach fluttered. This was the reason I had insisted our trip to Japan be sooner rather than later. "Really? A *bun*? In the *oven*?"

He straightened and the door smacked closed. "Do you mean what I think you mean?"

I bit my cheek and nodded. We'd talked about starting a family, whether we wanted to and how it'd work. If we'd keep traveling. The answers were all yes, and we'd make it work. But it was all happening sooner than expected. Probably from jet lag and getting used to being in Montana again. And mornings like this when he hadn't used a condom.

"Fuck me, Mad Maddy." His long strides carried him out of the kitchen as he charged for me. Then he picked me up and swung me around. "You make me the happiest goddamn man in the world."

"What a coincidence. You make me the happiest woman. The happiest baker. The most pregnant baker."

"I will always make you happy, and remind you that you're mine."

"I'm all yours, Bailey. And you're all mine."

He grinned. "Bought and paid for. I do almost wish this had happened later."

My mood dipped. "Too soon?"

"Nah, but you're going to have to wait until you can drink again to try the special batch I named after you."

"You did not!" I didn't have to wait for Christmas. This man surprised me with sweet gifts and gestures all the time. "From that hopscotch bet? That I lost, by the way."

He shrugged. "I'll save two bottles."

"What'd you name it?" I already had an idea.

"Mad Summit, and it's the sweetest batch I've ever tasted."

EPILOGUE

Five years later . . .

Mae

I don't agree that a woman's worth should be measured by who she is to others. Somebody's daughter. Somebody's mother. Somebody's sister. Somebody's wife. Each woman is her own person. Has her own identity. Her own worth. Full stop.

Yet, as I watch my kids and the loves of their lives mingle and my grandchildren run around, I'm immensely proud to be their mother. Their foster mother. Their mother-in-law. Their grandmother. Their step-grandmother.

They're all here because I was somebody's wife. Darin's partner. He's been gone for years, but I'm still his. Always will be. I love these moments twice as hard for him.

I rock in a fancy camp chair Tate and Scarlett got me for Christmas a couple of years ago. The shop is open and my kids stand in groups, often changing members, roaming from pod to pod. They're closer than ever, and even better, they're all in Bourbon Canyon.

Teller and Madison returned from Brazil last week. I watched their twins while they were on a working vacation. The way Madison has opened up Teller's world is more than a mama could ask for. Next year, they're taking their four-year-olds, London and Phoenix, to Peru. Madison blushes and Teller grins at her every time someone asks where they got the names. Teller says it's the two places most important in their journey together.

Gideon's dad, Hank, rocks in his chair next to me. He's become a good friend, someone to commiserate with when the kids are going through a rough time, and a buddy who knows what it's like to want to stay single. Darin isn't here anymore, but my heart is his. Hank's been without his soulmate longer than me, but he knows.

"We throw parties all the time, but I can't believe it," he says. His chair creaks while he's rocking. "They're growing up on us."

"If I ever forget, Chance just needs to come home from college again." I have a grandkid who's a legal adult, and in case I doubt it, his size and deep voice will change my mind. With shoulders as wide as his dad's and a mop of dark hair on his head to match, he made me a grandma, but now he can pick me up and walk a couple of miles if he wants to.

Chance chases after his sister, Brinley, and she darts away, screeching, a giant smile on her face. Darin's a year younger than Brinley, but he tries to interfere with his sister, giggling. The nine-year-old is no competition for Chance. He gets tickled for his efforts.

Scarlett beams at him, and Tate wraps his arm around her while they watch their kids play.

Sawyer skids to a stop in front of Hank, her auburn hair in two rows of Dutch braids. "Grandpa?"

Hank stops rocking. "Yes, my girl?"

While she bargains with her grandpa to lead her around on a horse, his little namesake runs to them. Hank Jr. skids to a stop next to his sister and waits for an answer. Killian, Autumn and Gideon's foster son, hangs in the back, trying not to look excited about riding a horse. The fourteen-year-old has been with them for four years, and he's really opened up. The adoption is nearly complete. We'll have another party then.

Their grandpa gives them the most indulgent chuckle and looks back at me. "Mind if I saddle Tenpin and take these kids for a spin?"

"Knock yourself out." If he thinks he's going to get away with only leading his grandkids around, he's mistaken. But knowing Hank, he's planning to lead kids around for the next two hours.

Summer and Jonah's oldest, Eliott, watches them. He scowls just like his dad, but he lights up like Summer when he's excited about something. And he's the best older brother to his little sister, Mae.

Eliott looks around for his parents. Summer's already watching and she nods. Eliott grins and darts away.

"Three, two, one," I say to myself.

"Dad!" Elsa shouts to Myles, who's already following Hank with his youngest, Devon.

There it is. I smile.

Wynter walks past me. "It's going to be a horse parade, Mama."

I chuckle. "Often turns into one." Now that the grandkids are older, we can do more than hopscotch.

Junie puts her hands to her mouth. "Horse parade!"

Junie's stepdaughters are both home from their latest photography trip with their mom. In the fall, they'll both be out of the nest. Bethany will return to college, and Hannah will head into her freshman year.

Emma is going to have a hard time seeing her big sisters leave, but her little brother, Jonathon, will keep her busy.

Emma and Jonathon run to follow the group. Gideon and Autumn break away from chatting with Rhys to go with them. Rhys's gaze goes right to Junie. That guy has the same look he's always had when it comes to Junie. The first day she brought him home, I knew they would be forever. They made me worry for years first.

"Wanna ride?" Teller asks Madison. He's gotten her on horseback again and they've ridden enough over the years that she's finally able to enjoy herself. I didn't have to ask if her parents had ruined the activity for her. They were tough people, and Madison's a tough girl, but she didn't turn out hard like them.

Madison grabs the twins and they follow the group.

Gabriel sprints to his dad. Tenor pushes up his glasses and swoops Gabriel onto his shoulders. Gabriel already has glasses. He's on his third pair, taking after his rambunctious uncles more than his mellow parents.

"You coming today?" Ruby asks.

I watch the rest of the group walk to the barn. Hank's already inside, passing out saddles, blankets, and lead ropes. Myles has the oats bucket. London and Phoenix fall in line behind Teller and Madison.

I can see most of the pasture from here. The horses hear the commotion. A few are already coming for their treats. The others are putting distance between them, but they'll fall for the bribes. Eventually.

I smile at Ruby. "I'm going to enjoy the show. The best money can buy."

She laughs and starts after Tenor, who's stopped to wait for her.

"Come on, Mama!" Gabriel shouts and Ruby starts jogging.

I rock in my chair. Two shadows tower over me.

Cruz squats down. "You aren't out riding, Mae?"

I don't get on a horse too much these days. "Maybe later. How's Huckleberry Springs?"

Myles has finally pinpointed the area where he wants to start his second distillery. Now he has to secure it. And when he does, Lane and Cruz will run it.

"I don't know." Cruz puts a knee on the cement. "Myles is tracking down the oldest Hennessy."

I recall the three Hennessy boys. They weren't under my roof for long, but they left an impression. They were close and it broke my heart when I heard about the environment they'd had to live in after their dad died.

"Myles will find him," I say.

"Doesn't mean Iverson Hennessy will deal," Lane says as he sprawls in Hank's chair.

"He'll deal. Those boys know what's good for them. Just like you two did."

Almost ten years ago, I was introduced to Lane and Cruz Foster. Spitting images of Myles, but eighteen years younger. Now Lane is just over thirty and Cruz is just under. The boys have grown into hardworking men.

I'll miss them when they move to Huckleberry Springs permanently. They won't be coming and going like they did when they worked at Foster House in Denver. Huckleberry Springs is a little over two hours southeast. My boys chose to make a home in Montana.

"We'll need more employees," Lane says. "Know any of your foster kids who want a good job?"

"I've got some names," I reply.

Myles already asked. But first, he needs to find the Hennessys. Then Cruz and Lane can make their own mark in the spirits world. And maybe I'll get to see them find the type of love their brother did.

I can't wait. Until then, I'll sit back and enjoy the bourbon sunset.

————

There's a new distillery in a new town that Lane and Cruz will run with the help of more guys who also fostered at the Baileys, like the Hennessys.

Iverson Hennessy, the oldest of the Hennessy brothers, finds out the woman he took home from the bar last night is his boss's very much off limits daughter in Whiskey Cowboy.

Want to be there when Teller proposes to Madison? You're welcome to join them in their bonus epilogue.

You can get it when you signup for my newsletter at walkerrosebooks.com

ABOUT THE AUTHOR

I live the dream in my own slice of paradise where I get to enjoy colorful sunsets from my rocking chair while I'm working. I have my very own romance hero with Mr. Rose and there's more than a few little rose buds running around. A couple aren't so little anymore! We keep things interesting with cats and a dog and the critters that roam though the yard (fingers crossed the mountain lions stay away).

walkerrosebooks.com

ALSO BY WALKER ROSE

Foster House Series

Whiskey Cowboy

Whiskey Siren

Bourbon Canyon Series

Bourbon Bachelor

Bourbon Lullaby

Bourbon Runaway

Bourbon Promises

Bourbon Harmony

Bourbon Summer

Bourbon Sunset